the stolen identity

BOOK SEVEN OF THE
SYDNEY HARBOUR
HOSPITAL SERIES

CHRIS TAYLOR

BOOKS BY CHRIS TAYLOR

THE MUNRO FAMILY SERIES
(In order)

The Profiler
The Investigator
The Predator
The Betrayal
The Deception
The Negotiator
The Christmas Vigil
The Ransom
The Defendant
The Shooting
The Maker
(Available in Audio)

THE SYDNEY HARBOUR HOSPITAL SERIES
(in order)

The Perfect Husband
The Body Thief
The Baby Snatchers
The Final Bullet
The Debt Collector
The Lab Test
The Stolen Identity
The Cliff Top Killer
The Likeable Fraudster

THE SYDNEY LEGAL SERIES
(In order)

An Accidental Murderer
At the Hand of her Father
A Woman Scorned
Lies and Deception
Ordinary Evil
The Perfect Crime
Malicious Love
Toxic Inheritance

THE BARRINGTON FAMILY SERIES
(in order)

Broken Lives
Broken Promises
Broken Bonds
Broken Spirits
Broken Vows
Broken Minds
Broken Dreams
Broken Hearts
Broken Homes

THE CRAIGDON FAMILY SERIES
(in order)

Callum
Joel
Isabella
Nicholas
Sophia
Flynn
Noah
Logan
Elizabeth

Get a FREE book when you sign up for Chris Taylor's
newsletter at: www.christaylorauthor.com.au

Love Audiobooks? Check out Chris Taylor Books on audio
on Audible.com, Amazon.com and the iBooks store.

Join Chris Taylor's Facebook reader group/fan page and be
among the first to receive news of book releases, read and
review books prior to release and other amazing offers. Join
Now at: www.facebook.com/groups/1758023621144744/

Find out more about all of Chris Taylor's books, by visiting her
website at: www.christaylorauthor.com.au/about/books

DEDICATION

This book is dedicated to my children: Angus, Imogen, Rory, Millie & Madeleine for understanding why their mother spends so much time on her computer.

And as always, to my rock: my husband, Linden. I love you.

Acknowledgments

As usual, no book comes into being without a lot of help and support by my friends and family. A world of thanks must go to my wonderful editor, Pat Thomas. Thank you for everything that you do to make my stories even more amazing than I could ever dare to dream. To Detective Superintendent Michael Kilfoyle, thank you for lending my story credibility. Any mistakes are wholly my own.

To Alisha and all of the staff at damonza.com, thank you for yet another fantastic cover. To my sister, Nicole Guihot and to my friend, Ally Thomson, thank you for your excellent editorial comments, proof reading skills and suggestions. I hope you like the final result.

To Amy Atwell and her dedicated staff at Author EMS who are so much more than book formatters. Amy, once again, thank you for your magic.

To the fantastic writer organizations such as Romance Writers of Australia, Romance Writers of

America and Romance Writers of New Zealand for all the help, support and encouragement they offer new and aspiring writers, including me.

To my readers, thank you for your support and love for my stories. Your encouragement and enjoyment make this journey all worthwhile.

And lastly, to my friends and family, especially my husband and children. Thank you for putting up with late dinners and even later conversations as I've emerged day after day from the sometimes scary but always enthralling world I've created on my computer.

PROLOGUE

Dear Diary,

It was easier than I expected... Once the initial shock wore off, he was delighted. I arrived on his doorstep with nothing. He shared everything he had. It should have been enough to satisfy me, but it wasn't.
Alas, he never saw the devil deep inside...

CHAPTER 1

The woman's scream was low and guttural and vibrated with pain. Sweat dampened her forehead and plastered her hair to her face. Morgan O'Brien called on all her professional skills as an experienced midwife to remain calm. The baby's shoulders were stuck in the birth canal. If they didn't move quickly, both the lives of the mother and the unborn infant would be in jeopardy.

With one eye on the laboring mother, Morgan picked up the phone on the far side of the room and called for the doctor. A voice on the other end of the line assured her he was on his way. Relief rushed through her and she hastened to the side of the mother.

"It's all right, Vanessa. Big breaths now. The contraction's over. Slow down your breathing and rest. Your baby's slightly larger than we expected. She's having a little difficulty coming out. I've sent for the doctor. He'll decide what's best from here."

The young mother stared up at her with eyes that were wide and confused. "What do you mean? Is my baby stuck? Is she stuck inside? Is that why I can't push her out?"

Morgan nodded briefly. "Yes. It happens sometimes. But there's no need to worry. The doctor will be here shortly. He'll assess the situation. We have a few options."

"What kind of options?" demanded the woman's partner, who had identified himself earlier as Trevor.

Morgan held his gaze steadily, projecting a calm she didn't quite feel. "We can try and manually extract the baby with forceps or vacuum suction. If that doesn't work, we'll prepare for a C-section."

As she listened to the exchange, fear filled the young woman's eyes. "A C-section? I don't want a C-section! Please, nurse! I'm scared of needles!"

Trevor took hold of Morgan's arm in a tight grip, his gaze fierce. "Are you sure that's necessary? We agreed on minimal medical intervention."

Morgan extricated her arm as gently as possible. "I understand, Trevor and no, I'm not sure that we'll have to resort to surgery. We'll wait to hear what the doctor says."

The door to the birthing suite swung open and Morgan swallowed a sigh of relief. Doctor Samuel Munro strode into the room. Taking the doctor aside, Morgan quietly brought him up to speed. With the air of competence and efficiency he was known for, Samuel approached the woman on the bed and shot her a reassuring smile.

"Hi, Vanessa, I'm Doctor Munro. I'm an obstetrician at the Sydney Harbour Hospital. Do you mind if I take a little look at what's happening?"

The woman's nod turned into a grimace as she was once again gripped by a contraction. Morgan stepped closer, talking in quiet tones to her patient, urging her to breathe through the pain. Out of the corner of her eye, she saw Samuel place his hands on Vanessa's swollen stomach.

The contraction finally subsided and Vanessa collapsed against the pillows with a gasp. Perspiration beaded her lip. She looked up at Samuel with tears in her eyes.

"Please, Doctor, tell me what's happening. I don't know how much longer I can stand the pain."

Samuel finished his examination and came to stand beside Morgan. "Your baby has broad shoulders," he said, his light tone belying the seriousness of the situation. "She's getting stuck inside the birth canal. I need to try and manipulate her body a little and see if we can get her out."

Fear shadowed Vanessa's eyes. "Will it hurt?"

"No more than the pain you're in now. We can get you something for that. There's no need to do it the hard way."

"No!" Trevor cried. "We agreed, no drugs." He turned to the woman on the bed. "Didn't we, Ness?"

"Y-yes." Vanessa sounded a whole lot less certain than her baby's father.

Samuel studiously ignored him. His gaze remained steady on the patient's. "It's your decision, Vanessa. No one else's."

"I... I understand, Doctor. I... I think I'm fine."

Samuel nodded in acceptance and glanced at the monitor beside Morgan. "All right, well, it looks like you're about to be hit with another contraction. Take hold of someone's hand and squeeze the hell out of it. I'll try to be as gentle as I can."

With that, Samuel placed his hands once again around Vanessa's swollen stomach. As the woman cried out and gasped in pain, Samuel manipulated the baby. Morgan stood at the foot of the bed and kept a close watch on her patient.

A moment later, Morgan spied the baby's head. "She's crowning!" she exclaimed. The relief in the air was almost palpable. Morgan smiled at the doctor. "Well done, Samuel! You did it."

He smiled back at her, his even white teeth brilliant against his olive skin. A sense of mutual pride and satisfaction flowed between them. Not for the first time, Morgan wondered why the good-looking doctor didn't stir her like he should. With all that they had in common, there should be some form of attraction. They were both single and about the same age. Both shared a sense of caring for their fellow man. They were both in the health profession – delivering babies, no less. Plenty of other females swooned when he walked by...

Yet, she regarded him like a brother, or a good friend. She supposed that same lack of feeling was the reason so many Internet relationships failed when the people got to meet face to face. No matter how compatible they looked on paper, a computer screen could never convey that indefinable feeling – that *zing* of awareness – that could only happen when two people met, in person. Without that face-to-face awareness, any relationship was destined to fail. Physical attraction was something nobody could force, no matter how hard they tried. At least, that's the way she saw it.

"Is it over?" Trevor demanded, looking from one health professional to another.

"Almost," Morgan replied cheerfully, squeezing her patient's hand. "Doctor Munro has managed to turn your baby enough so that she can slide through the birth canal. A couple more pushes and your daughter should be here."

Vanessa stared up at her with eyes that were wide with excitement and hope. "Really?"

Morgan smiled. "Really. Now, when the next contraction starts to build, I want you to bend your knees and pull your legs up toward your chest. Keep your chin down and push with all your might. Do you think you can manage that?"

The woman nodded and it wasn't long before her breath quickened on another contraction. Groaning and straining, she pushed while Morgan did a slow count.

"That's it, Vanessa! You're doing great!" Morgan encouraged. "One more push, and your baby will be here."

The woman scraped back a piece of sweat-dampened hair, her expression once again filled with hope. "You promise?"

"I promise." Morgan grinned and tugged on a fresh pair of gloves in anticipation.

A few minutes later, a slippery, squalling mass of humanity took her first breath and a cheer went up around the room. Working quickly, Morgan and Samuel cleared the baby's airway and checked the vitals. The newborn's cries were loud and strong and pink color flooded her skin. Swaddling the infant in a soft blanket, Morgan handed her to her mother.

"Congratulations, Vanessa. Meet your new daughter."

Trevor reached out an unsteady hand and stroked the velvety soft cheek. Tears fell freely down his cheeks. He leaned down and kissed Vanessa, his eyes filled with tenderness and love.

Morgan swallowed the lump in her throat and concentrated on delivering the placenta. In the back of her mind, she couldn't help but wonder if she'd ever get to experience the feeling of such unadulterated love that came with the joy of giving birth.

You could have been a mother already, a voice inside her head insinuated. *You chose not to, remember?* As if she could ever forget.

———

It was at least an hour later before mother and baby were settled on the ward and Morgan found time to take a break. Her friend and colleague, Georgie Whitely was already seated in the tea room. The two girls were close in age and had hit it off the moment Morgan started working there.

While Georgie had been born and bred in Sydney, Morgan hailed from the country. She'd gone to college in her hometown of Armidale, but had left for the city straight after graduation. She loved what Sydney had to offer – the vibrancy, the noise; the crowds. It made her feel young and energetic and grateful to be alive. Too bad she hadn't managed to find someone to share all that with.

"Good work with Vanessa," Georgie murmured after Morgan filled her in on her morning.

"Thanks. We were lucky Samuel was on call. He's always so calm in a crisis. He's a good man to have around."

Georgie's eyes twinkled mischievously. "Throw in the fact that he's single and drop dead gorgeous. I don't know what you're waiting for."

Morgan pulled a face. "Yeah, I've asked myself the same question. He's the total package. Every unattached female in Sydney Harbour Hospital is dying to date him. I should be one of them. I even have an advantage. His cousin is a doctor here. Chanel Munro. She's a friend of mine. She could put in a good word for me."

"So what's holding you back?" Georgie asked curiously, taking a bite of an apple.

Morgan picked up her coffee cup and took a sip. Setting it back on the table, she sighed. "There's no spark. It's stupid, right? He's the hottest man for miles around and I'm not interested. Me, the thirty-year-old woman who can barely remember the last time she had sex. You'd think I'd be knocking him over in the corridors and dragging him to the nearest bed."

Georgie laughed. "You're so funny."

Morgan pouted. "It's all right for you, Georgina Whitely – or should I say, Georgina Dawson. You're married to the man of your dreams and your son is the cutest baby I've ever seen! You have everything you could ever want. Me, on the other hand, will probably end up like Bridget Jones – perpetually single, sad and alone, left with nothing more to do but wallow in self-pity and watch sappy old movies from my couch."

"In your pajamas," Georgie added with a grin. "Don't forget those."

Morgan poked out her tongue and Georgie's grin widened. "I guess I'd better not tell you then, how the latest Bridget Jones movie has her marrying and having a baby. Oh, and speaking of babies, Cameron and I are trying for another."

Morgan stared at Georgie in surprise and delight. "Already? James is barely six months old!"

Georgie shrugged, unabashed. "Hey, Cameron's aiming for half a football team. He only has one sister and he's eleven years older than her. He doesn't want James to grow up alone. Besides, I'm already on the wrong side of thirty. I don't have time to waste."

Morgan forced a smile. "I know how you feel," she muttered.

She was genuinely happy for her friend, despite

the stab of envy that made itself known in the region of her heart. Morgan would give anything to be in Georgie's position. It was made even harder by the fact she was surrounded by deliriously happy new mothers and their undeniably gorgeous babies.

"Do you have any brothers and sisters, Morgan?"

Morgan pushed her depressing thoughts aside and focused on her friend. "No, I'm an only child. I understand exactly why Cameron doesn't want James growing up alone."

Georgie nodded. "I'm lucky. I have three sisters." She took another bite of her apple. "Are your parents still alive?"

"Dad is. Mom died a week after my nineteenth birthday. Breast cancer."

Georgie compressed her lips. "That's tough."

"No tougher than what you've had to deal with." Morgan hadn't been working with Georgie during the time Georgie's parents had been arrested for baby trafficking, but she'd heard all the stories and had seen enough news reports to know it couldn't have been easy.

Georgie brushed off her comment with a shrug. "Are you close to your dad?" she asked.

"Yes. Even more so, since Mom died. We speak on the phone most weeks and we email all the time."

Georgie smiled. "Your dad knows how to email?"

"Of course! He was a lawyer before he retired. He used to run a busy practice in the country. For a member of the older generation, he's quite computer literate."

"That's great. It must make it so much easier to stay in contact."

"It does," Morgan agreed, "although ever since he retired, he's ditched his cell phone. He says he's had enough of being on call twenty-four seven." She smiled fondly at the thought of her father. She hadn't heard from him in over a week and that had only been by email. It had been more than a fortnight since they'd spoken. But today was Morgan's birthday. He'd call her that night, for sure.

Glancing at the clock on the wall above the fridge, Morgan finished the last of her coffee and pushed away from the table. "Two hours until we're out of here. I guess we'd better get back to it."

Georgie sighed, but offered a smile. "Yes. I guess we should."

———

Morgan climbed beneath the cool cotton sheets and sighed with contentment. She loved her job, but there was no doubt about it: Delivering babies was tiring work. Her feet ached after being on them for the better part of her shift and she was relieved to finally be able to kick back and relax in bed.

A cool breeze swept in from the ocean, fluttering the gauzy white curtains that covered the open window. The sound of a bus climbing the hill soothed her with its familiarity. It was barely nine in the evening, but she was more than ready for sleep.

Closing her eyes, she snuggled under the covers and thought fleetingly of how nice it would be to have someone there beside her, keeping her warm and safe, holding her close, especially tonight. Her birthday had passed uneventfully. She hadn't told anyone at work. She didn't want anyone to make a big deal of it and preferred to slide into thirty, unseen.

It wasn't that she had an issue with her age or wanted to remain in her twenties, and neither of her parents had seen fit to celebrate milestones like that in a big way. A quiet family dinner with the three of them had sufficed for many years. And now that it was just her and her dad and she lived six-hours' drive away...

She thought of her father and frowned. He hadn't called like she thought he would. Though they kept celebrations low-key, a phone call was always made. *Perhaps he'd forgotten?* He was getting older, after all.

The thought saddened her and all of a sudden, she was filled with dread at the knowledge there would come a day when he wouldn't be there for her. It was bound to happen, sooner or later. Nobody lived forever. And then she'd have no one.

Chapter 2

Detective Sergeant Colt Barrington propped his feet up on his desk and stacked his hands behind his head. He'd attended court earlier in the morning and had given evidence for the prosecution during a couple of hearings, neither of which were serious.

The first defendant was up on assault charges. No weapon was involved. It was nothing more than a bar brawl between two friends who'd let a disagreement over a girl get a little out of hand. It was only after the defendant claimed self-defense that the matter had ended up in court. His lawyer would have to perform a miracle to convince the judge that was the case after the man had knocked his opponent out cold.

The second matter had been over almost as soon as it started. When the police prosecutor approached Colt that morning, and advised him he'd be giving evidence on the Manning case, Colt hadn't concealed his surprise.

Michael Manning had been caught by the

police red-handed in a jewelry store, still carrying a bag containing stolen property. He'd set off an alarm upon his entry and was still filling his sack when Colt and his partner arrived on the scene.

Colt could only surmise the man's decision to plead not guilty was a last desperate attempt to delay his inevitable trip to jail. Manning had a record of more than a dozen similar offenses. Colt had been in the witness box less than five minutes before the defendant's lawyer had sought a short adjournment. Ten minutes later, Manning changed his plea.

Now, barring an unforeseen emergency, the rest of the afternoon was Colt's. He'd almost caught up on his paperwork and his reading was up to date. He'd answered emails, returned phone calls from concerned members of the public and given a quote to the local newspaper. All in all, the day was going well.

The phone at his elbow pealed, interrupting his thoughts. Dropping his boots to the floor, he leaned over and picked up the receiver.

"Armidale Police Station. This is Detective Colt Barrington."

"How are you doing, little brother?"

Colt grinned at the familiar voice of his identical twin. It was a standing joke between them that Colt was the younger one – born four minutes after Beau.

"Not bad, buddy. How are things in the big smoke?"

"Busy. You know how it is. Saving lives is a hectic business. There's always someone needing help."

"Thank God for Doctor Beau Barrington. Have they honored you with a fellowship, yet? A doctor held in such high esteem must surely be first in line?"

"You're too funny, little bro," Beau replied dryly.

Colt laughed. "I'll take that as a compliment."

"Take it any way you like. Hey, Mom left me a voice mail message. Something about a family get together on the Australia Day long weekend. Do you know anything about it?"

Colt sighed with exaggeration. "Oh, no! Don't remind me! It's their thirty-fifth wedding anniversary. Mom wants us all home to celebrate."

"Don't tell me she expects us to battle the Tamworth Country Music Festival goers? Doesn't she know the place is impossible that time of year?"

"Oh, yeah, that's all part of the fun as far as Mom's concerned," Colt replied. "Have you forgotten what it was like when we were kids?"

Beau groaned. "How could I forget? One year Mom even forced us to busk along Peel Street! You and Ryan had those old guitars and I was on the drums. I think Wade had a clarinet and Ashleigh and Emily were on the flute. Christian was on the keyboard and Darcy... What did she play?"

"Was she even born then? I can't remember."

"You're right," Beau replied. "We couldn't have been more than nine or ten. Darcy wasn't even a twinkle in Dad's eye."

"Lucky her," Colt added.

Beau chuckled and Colt couldn't help but join in his mirth. They complained about their childhood, but the truth was, the two of them felt incredibly lucky to have grown up in such a large, supportive family, where every member was loved and appreciated and encouraged in their endeavors. There were a lot of kids who weren't so fortunate.

"You're going to have to take the time off and come up here," Colt murmured. "Mom won't have it any other way."

Beau sighed on the other end of the phone. "Yeah. Thirty-five years. Wow."

"Yeah, and even after all those years, they still seem to get on. I wonder how they do it?"

"I guess they work harder at it than some," Beau quipped.

Colt compressed his lips. Talk about marriage and lifelong commitment made him antsy. He cleared his throat.

"Luck or not, Mom and Dad will never forgive you if you don't show your ugly mug at their party. Mom's beyond excited at the thought of having all eight of her children together again."

"So all the others can make it?" Beau sounded surprised.

"As far as I know. I was speaking to Mom yesterday. The only person she hadn't heard from was you."

"Great." Beau heaved another sigh. "I guess that means I'll have to put in for some time off. Australia Day is only a couple of weeks away. I hope it's not going to be a problem."

"For your sake, I hope so, too," Colt said. "I wouldn't want to be in your shoes if you have to explain to Mom why you won't be there for her party. She still hasn't forgotten how Christian preferred to spend last Christmas sailing the Whitsundays with his girlfriend rather than in Tamworth with his family. I think even Chase and Josie are going to make it."

Beau made a sound of horror. "Are they bringing their son?"

Colt chuckled. "Of course. He's two, Beau. Hardly old enough to be left home alone. What's your problem? I thought you loved kids."

"I do, but Clancy Munro is one kid I haven't taken to. The last time they visited he cried every time I looked at him. People were beginning to wonder if I was doing something to him. It was beyond embarrassing."

Colt laughed outright. "Strange. He doesn't react to me that way. All you have to do is explain to any guests that you're a brain surgeon, not a baby doctor. That will be sure to impress them enough that they won't care that you've upset an innocent child."

"Yeah, well, the last time was almost a year ago. Hopefully the kid's grown a bit more tolerant of strangers since then. I can't believe it's been that long since I saw Chase. It will be good to catch up with him again."

Colt murmured his agreement. Chase Barrington was a first cousin on their father's side. As an only child, Chase had spent a fair amount of his school holiday vacations with his extended family. Colt and his brothers and sisters regarded Chase as one of them. When Chase had married the girl he'd been in love with since high school, Colt couldn't have been happier for him. It was only when Colt thought of marriage and how it related to *him* that he got panicky.

He'd made it to the ripe old age of thirty-one, footloose and fancy free, and hadn't even come close to falling in love. It was an achievement he was proud of though he had nothing against women. In fact, he loved women.

He'd been raised to treat the fairer sex with courtesy and respect and he made sure he did so. He opened car doors, pulled out chairs and always paid the bill. He had a reputation in Armidale for being able to show women a good time. It didn't mean he wanted to tie himself down to any particular one of them.

He liked playing the field. In fact, the high divorce rate frightened the life out of him. He had no intention of settling down and heading down a path that was sure to end in failure. He didn't want to become just another sad statistic. He might be the oldest child in the Barrington family, and with that status came a certain expectation, but he had plenty of brothers and sisters who could carry on the family line.

"I wonder if Christian will bring Brianna?" Beau mused, interrupting Colt's thoughts. "They've been dating at least six months. It's probably about time she met the rest of the family."

"Do you think it's that serious?"

"Like I said, it's been six months."

"So?"

"I can see you've never been in love," Beau teased.

"Hey!" Colt protested. "Just because I don't fall for every girl who smiles at me doesn't mean I can't develop tender feelings."

Beau laughed. "It's not my fault I fall in love so easily or that I fall out just as fast."

"You're a slut, Beau Barrington. You ought to be a little choosier."

"As if you can talk, little brother. I don't need to spend much time in Armidale to get word of *your* reputation."

Colt chuckled and changed the subject. "So, who are you in love with at the moment? Last time I checked, it was Monica."

"Yeah, that was more than a month ago. Monica and I are over. I was never around when she needed me. At least, that's what she said. What can I say? I'm busy saving lives. It's not easy being a renowned neurosurgeon at Sydney's most prestigious hospital."

"Yeah, yeah, yeah. We can't all wear a red cape," Colt chided good naturedly.

"How's life treating you in Armidale, anyway?" Beau asked, changing the subject.

"It's good," Colt replied and realized he meant it. "I enjoy the slower pace of country life. It must have something to do with growing up in Tamworth. It might be large enough to be called a city, but to me it's still a big country town."

"Better you than me," Beau replied. "I'm not sure I could ever live in the country again. There's something about the pace and excitement of the city. It gets in your blood."

"Yeah, well, just make sure you drag yourself home for the long weekend. Mom's counting on it."

CHAPTER 3

———————

Morgan slid the key into her post box and reached inside for the mail. The usual collection of junk mail, advertising anything from cell phones to pizzas, filled her hands. Flipping through the flyers, she just as quickly tossed them into the recycling bin that stood near the bank of post boxes. Only two letters remained. One was a bill from her electrical company. The other was a birthday card.

At least, she assumed it was a birthday card.

The envelope was a pale lilac color and oversized, in the way of greeting cards. It had to be from her dad. No one else would be sending her a card.

She turned it over and frowned. The handwriting curled and flowed like her father's, but something about it didn't look right. Perhaps he'd injured his hand in the days preceding? Or maybe he'd been overdoing the gardening and his arthritis was acting up? She'd have to ask him next time they spoke.

Slipping her fingernail under the flap, she tore open the envelope and pulled out the card. It was pretty and pink and had a standard, sweet Hallmark message printed in the center. The handwritten message from her dad was succinct:

Happy Birthday Morgan!

Love Dad

It had been four days since her birthday and she still hadn't spoken to him. A fresh pang went through her at the knowledge he'd forgotten to call her. She re-read the contents of the card and frowned. The handwriting matched that on the envelope and though it was close, it didn't quite look like her dad's.

She'd told Georgie she usually spoke with her father at least once most weeks and that was true. Occasionally she'd get busy and forget, or her father would be traveling with friends for an overnight golf trip, but they never went more than a week or two without calling. Still, he'd remembered to send her a birthday card, even if it was a little late.

Tossing the mail into her handbag, she closed

the post box and headed toward her car. Sliding behind the wheel of her little blue Honda, she checked her mirrors and pulled out into the traffic.

The day had been largely uneventful. A couple of planned induced labors had gone smoothly and by the end of her shift both mothers and their newborns were resting comfortably. She'd been a midwife for nearly six years and she still got a buzz out of being present in the birthing suite. The miracle of watching a new life come into the world never failed to move her.

She thought of the baby she could have had and was filled with a familiar sadness and regret. He or she would have been ten by now. She couldn't imagine being mother to a ten-year-old. Driving her son or daughter to Little League and soccer practice, ballet lessons, piano... The list went on. That life would be so different, so...fulfilling.

Instead, there was just her, alone in her one-bedroom condominium, with nothing to show for her thirty years on the planet except for a degree in nursing and a second-hand car. She didn't even own a cat.

Her savings account was dismal. She rarely put anything aside for emergencies. The truth was, living in the city was expensive and making her modest wage stretch was a challenge she faced every fortnight. More often than not, she relied on her credit cards to get her through to the next pay check.

Her father hated the idea she was short of money and had insisted on buying her the condo she lived in near Bondi Beach. Though she'd been overwhelmed by his generosity, she worried that he hadn't left enough money for himself.

He was only in his mid-fifties, and apart from the odd aches and pains caused by his arthritis, he was still in excellent health. He managed to walk a brisk three miles a day and swam twenty or more laps in the university pool. His blood pressure was stable, his cholesterol was low and he didn't have diabetes.

All in all, he'd aged well and though she occasionally worried about what it would be like to lose him, she was confident he still had many years to live – and living was expensive. She knew that better than most.

Pulling into the driveway of her condominium complex, she parked in her reserved spot and collected her things. She pushed open her front door and was greeted with a silence that was all too familiar. Dropping her handbag on the hall table, she moved further inside, switching on lights as she went. The place was cool and inviting after the heat of the summer day.

The light on her answering machine was blinking and she was immediately filled with a rush of disappointment at the thought she might have missed a call from her dad. Pressing the button, she listened to her hairdresser remind her of her appointment later that week. With a sigh, she headed into the kitchen.

After tossing together a quick meal of tinned tuna and leftover salad, she sat at her small kitchen table and ate while scrolling through her

Facebook newsfeed. After swallowing the last mouthful, she took her plate to the sink.

Pulling out a half-empty bottle of Sauvignon Blanc from the fridge, she poured herself a glass and took it into the small living room – about the size of a shoe box and barely able to accommodate her loveseat and TV. Still, it boasted the most magnificent view of the Pacific Ocean a girl could ask for.

The view was the main reason she and her father had gone ahead with the purchase. She loved being near the water and although she didn't get anywhere near enough time to enjoy it, she liked knowing it was close by.

Toeing off her shoes, she curled up on her imitation leather sofa and tucked her feet underneath her. She took a sip of her wine, relishing the cool, tart taste and stared out the window at the oncoming night.

A bus changed gears as it labored up the hill less than two hundred yards from her building and she caught a glimpse of the commuters filling its seats. People heading home from work after a busy day. Heading home to their loved ones, their families, their friends and their roommates.

A wave of loneliness washed over her and she took another sip of wine. It was useless to wallow in self-pity. She was doing plenty to find *the one*. She attended parties and hung out in bars and nightclubs whenever her friends got the urge to go out. But she'd just turned thirty. She was getting too old for that kind of thing and if she were honest, she was tired of it.

She was ready to fall in love and settle down and make a life with someone else. She was tired of living alone, of coming home to an empty house. Her hand drifted across her stomach and she thought of the microscopic being that had dwelled inside her for such a brief time. She'd made a decision to terminate and it had seemed like the right thing to do at the time. It was too bad she hadn't realized then that the opportunity to be a mother might never again come her way.

She stirred restlessly on the couch, disgruntled with the direction of her thoughts. It was only because she hadn't spoken to her father for so long that she was out of sorts. That and the fact she'd just begun another decade. Nobody wanted to face the prospect of growing old. The idea of growing old alone was even more frightening.

Her thoughts turned to her mother and her shoulders slumped on a sad sigh. The eleventh anniversary of Judith O'Brien's death was a mere three days away. Cancer had claimed her, cutting her life short by far too many years. Morgan dreaded the arrival of the actual anniversary day. It only served to remind her of how much she'd lost, how much her father had lost.

He was supposed to be enjoying his retirement with the love of his life by his side. Instead, he was forced to go solo, taking comfort from his friends. Morgan knew firsthand how much friends could fall short. No matter how close and how loyal, nothing could replace family, and in particular, a beloved spouse.

A fresh wave of sadness went through her. She

needed to talk to her dad, reconnect with him; reassure herself he was all right. Pushing off the couch, she padded across the living room and into the corridor. Though the phone was cordless, the base and answering machine were all in one and stood on the table in the hall. Picking up the handset, she dialed her father's number.

The last couple of times she'd tried, the call had gone through to his answering machine and this time was no different. Listening to him apologize for missing the call and asking the caller to leave a message, she blinked back a sudden rush of tears.

It had been far too long since she'd seen him. More than three months, at least. She'd gone home for the long weekend in October, but at Christmas she'd been busy at work and hadn't made it back. It was time to request some days off and make it a priority to visit.

After leaving another message requesting that he call her, and finishing with a murmured hope that he was all right, Morgan ended the call and returned the handset to the base. Her only comfort was that he'd most definitely make contact with her on the anniversary of her mother's death. He might have forgotten to call her on her birthday, but there was no way he'd forget that date. She was sure of it.

———————

He stared at the calendar on the wall near the fridge and frowned at the asterisk marked on the date that was three days away. He'd noticed it the first time he'd turned his attention to the calendar, but even then, it hadn't made sense. The date held no significance to him and yet it had been marked so it stood out among the other thirty-one days in the month. It had to mean something. It concerned him that he didn't know what it was.

He'd been lucky with Morgan's birthday. It had been clearly marked on the tenth. He hadn't risked a phone call, but he'd made sure to send her a card. He'd taken it down to the post office and then discovered it would take three or four days to arrive. He'd forgotten how long mail took in the country. She would receive it late, but at least she'd be satisfied he'd remembered. That was all that mattered.

Morgan's phone buzzed, indicating she'd received a new email. She pulled the cell out of her uniform pocket. She'd been waiting all day for her dad to call. It was the anniversary of her mother's death. He always called her on the seventeenth of January. It didn't matter where she was.

But Morgan was halfway through her shift and she still hadn't heard from him and he hadn't returned her calls, despite her messages. All she'd received was a brief email apologizing for the fact he'd missed her the last few times she'd called.

There had been no other explanation, only an assurance that he was fine.

Sliding open her phone, she quickly went to her mail account and clicked on the new message from her dad.

Hi Morgan, thinking of you. Love Dad.

She stared at the brief message in consternation and read the words again. Okay, so the tone was somewhat somber and respectful, but he hadn't made any mention of her mom. They'd both agreed years ago to accept the tragedy for what it was and forever keep Judith O'Brien in their thoughts and in their hearts. They wanted to be able to speak of her freely, to acknowledge the impact she'd had on their lives. It was the anniversary of her mother's death and her dad hadn't even mentioned her by name.

That was really odd. He couldn't be well. Either that, or he wasn't thinking right. Perhaps he'd fallen and knocked his head and hadn't told her about it. Knowing her father, he would have brushed himself off and continued on his way. He wouldn't have gone to a doctor. He could have concussion, or a delayed reaction, a bleed upon the brain...

With an impatient sound in the back of her throat, she forced a halt to her increasingly frantic thoughts. *Her dad was fine*. He'd even told her so. Still, something was definitely off. First the card that hadn't been written in his usual handwriting, now this weird email. Coupled with the fact she'd been unable to make phone contact with him for weeks had her feeling more than a bit concerned.

She was glad she'd followed through on her earlier plan to take some annual leave. Tomorrow morning she'd catch the train to Armidale and hopefully put her mind at ease. On an impulse, she decided not to tell her father. It would be a nice surprise. They could spend a couple of weeks together, catching up, reconnecting – sharing memories of the past. It would be pleasant and relaxing and the weather would be great. Summer in the beautiful New England area wasn't difficult to take.

Feeling better, she dropped the phone back into her pocket. She'd call her dad tonight and make sure he was doing okay and then she'd pack her bags. Pushing open the door to the birthing suite, she flashed a smile at her colleague.

"You can take a break, Georgie. I'll take it from here."

For the second time, he listened to the message on the answering machine and all of a sudden the asterisk on the calendar made sense. Morgan had called, talking about her mother and the anniversary of the woman'sdeath. Like she had the previous times, she asked if he was okay.

Damn! He'd sent her an email earlier that day, but had it said enough? He didn't know. Her voice on the answering machine held plenty of concern. He needed to alleviate her worries. It was time to tell her about the trip he'd been planning...

Chapter 4

There was only one train daily from Sydney to Armidale and it was just after six in the evening when it finally eased into the station. Morgan gathered her things and stepped out onto the platform. She breathed in the fresh country air and looked around her.

The quiet station building had been erected in 1883 and was constructed of rendered brick with a pavilion at each end. The entrance was flanked by a wide porch with cast iron columns decorated with filigree detailing.

The building reminded Morgan of an earlier time, a time in history when grand structures were built to last. The train station was a prime example of that and was a source of pride for the university town.

Though it was early evening, with the shift to daylight savings time, the sun wouldn't set for another hour. Plenty of time to make her way to 29 Butler Street. Anticipation rushed through her. She couldn't wait to see her father.

After collecting her luggage from the end of the platform, she made her way from the station to the taxi rank. One disadvantage of keeping her visit a surprise was that there was no one waiting to meet her. Still, it was only a short cab ride from there to her childhood home. Not much of an inconvenience.

Looking up, she noticed storm clouds gathering in the east. She couldn't remember from which direction Armidale got most of its rain, but she hoped the cool breeze that blew around her bare legs would blow the storm away. She hated storms, especially at night.

There were two cabs waiting at the taxi rank and both were already filling with passengers. Morgan came to a halt and looked from one cab to the other in growing dismay.

"Are there only two of you available?" she asked the nearest driver who was helping an elderly lady into the back seat.

"Yes, and I'm afraid we don't have anyone else to call. Bob Tremaine's broken his leg and is out of action for six weeks and Dorothy Windsor is down with bronchitis. In the middle of summer. Unbelievable, but that's the truth." The driver shook his head slowly back and forth, his longish gray hair lifting with the movement.

Morgan kept calm. There was no need for panic. She could wait for the cabs to deliver their passengers and return. She suggested as much to the driver.

"That's fine, but you could be waiting quite awhile." He nodded toward his elderly passenger.

"Elsie's going all the way across town. It'll probably take me an hour to get there and back." He indicated the other driver with his chin. "Pete's heading downtown and then he's off on a break. He'll probably be back before me, but I wouldn't count on it."

Morgan looked from one man to the other. Pete was loading heavy suitcases into his trunk.

"An hour? Do you really think it will take that long?" she asked, her voice tinged with desperation.

"Give or take," the driver replied. "Pete might make it back within forty-five minutes, but then again, he might not."

"And there's no one else you can call?" she asked, thinking of the queue of taxis at Central Station that often extended as far as the eye could see.

"No, I'm sorry. It's only Pete and I on until midnight."

Morgan heaved a quiet sigh and set her bags down at her feet. She supposed she could call her father. He'd be more than happy to come and collect her. But she wanted to surprise him. To knock on his door and have him open it and stammer and sputter in surprise. He'd envelop her in a bear hug and drag her inside, all the time demanding to know where she'd come from and why she hadn't let him know ahead of time.

She loved to surprise him like that and it had been far too long since she'd done it. She didn't want to spoil things by calling him. No, she could simply walk to Butler Street. She'd done it in the past. It wasn't *that* far. Not really.

Besides, the night was soft and balmy and the air smelled heavenly of orange blossom. She couldn't see where it was coming from and there were only two lone pencil pines outside the station, but there had to be a Murraya bush, or something like it, nearby.

"What did you decide to do? Do you want one of us to come back for you?"

Morgan focused her attention on the driver. She still had the best part of an hour before sunset and if she hurried, she'd make it home well before dark. She flashed the driver a smile.

"Thank you for your offer, but I think I'll walk. I don't have too far to go and it's a lovely evening. I might as well enjoy the country air."

"Are you from the city, then?" the driver asked, obvious curiosity on his face.

"Yes. No. Well, kind of. I've lived in Sydney for the past nine years, but I was born and bred in Armidale and I went to college here. My dad still lives here." She indicated her luggage. "That's why I'm here. I'm paying him a surprise visit."

The driver smiled. "Ah, now I understand why there's nobody here to meet you. I wish I could help you out."

"That's all right," Morgan replied. "I don't mind the walk." With that, she turned away and started down the road.

"Hey, what's your dad's name?"

Morgan paused and turned back to face the driver. "Rex O'Brien. He lives on Butler Street. Do you know him?"

"Rex? Of course I know him! He was my lawyer

for many years. How is he? I haven't seen him around lately."

"He's fine. Busy gardening and golfing and all the other things he's filled his life with since his retirement."

"Good. I'm glad. He's a good bloke. Tell him Burt Mitchell says hello."

Morgan nodded. "Thanks, Burt. I will."

And with that, she continued in the direction of home.

———————

Detective Sergeant Colt Barrington turned into the street that led away from the railway station, his thoughts focused on what he might have for dinner. Though he came from a large family and had done his fair share of preparing the evening meal, cooking wasn't something he necessarily enjoyed and he avoided it as much as he could.

But the simple truth was, he was all out of pasta and his salad things consisted of half a head of wilted lettuce and a handful of cherry tomatoes that had seen the inside of his fridge for far too long. Perhaps he could rustle up some leftover ham and he was sure there was still a bag of grated cheese in the dairy drawer of his fridge. He'd settle for toasted sandwiches. Short of stopping by the supermarket and replenishing his supplies, that was the best he could do.

A woman was walking ahead of him on the sidewalk, dragging two suitcases. She must have been a passenger on the train that just arrived from Sydney. He wondered why she hadn't caught a cab. *Perhaps she lived nearby?*

Despite the warm evening, she wore jeans. The denim hugged a curvy butt that ended in a pair of long, slim legs. Black dress boots sporting three-inch heels added to her above-average height.

His gaze drifted upwards, past the white T-shirt that was tucked neatly into her waistband. Wavy, honey-blond hair lifted and danced across her shoulders in the gentle summer breeze. He wondered who she was. Pressing his foot down on the accelerator, he decided to find out.

A late model Ford sedan pulled up alongside Morgan. After giving it a cursory glance, she ignored it and continued on her way. Already, her feet were killing her and she cursed the idiocy of wearing high-heeled boots. She hadn't given any thought to transport from the station. She'd just assumed she'd be able to catch a cab. Most of the other times she'd visited, her father had been there to meet her and the few times she'd surprised him, she hadn't had any difficulty finding a taxi.

The driver of the car beside her suddenly beeped his horn. Morgan jumped. The sound was alarming in the quiet street. She looked up and down, but saw no sign of anyone else. She was alone with the stranger who, even now was putting the passenger side window down and leaning over the gear stick to speak to her.

She'd lived in the city long enough to be wary of confrontations with unfamiliar men on an empty street and she kept her distance. She couldn't see his face clearly through the shadows in the car, but his voice was deep and gentle – nothing like what she always imagined a serial killer's voice might be. It floated over her, rich and mellow, like good red wine.

"It looks like you're struggling a little. Can I offer you a lift?"

There was a genuine friendliness in his tone and what she could see of his features were warm and open. Something stirred in her memory and she wondered if she'd seen him before. She came home reasonably often to visit her father. Perhaps she'd seen the stranger downtown...

Then again, she'd grown up and had gone to college here. She could have met him anywhere. He smiled again and she walked closer, bending down a little, so she could get a better look.

Her heart pounded and she gasped in shock. Almost at the same time, an identical expression of surprise and recognition filled his handsome face.

"M-Morgan O'Brien? Is that you?"

"Colt Barrington! I-I didn't expect to see you!" Heat flooded her face.

"Likewise," he replied with a grin. "I haven't seen you since..." He shook his head slowly back and forth and then added. "It must be at least nine or ten years."

Her chest constricted and her throat went dry. "Ten years next month, in fact," she managed.

"What are you doing here?" he asked, in the same casual, velvety voice, as if her reference to their last meeting meant nothing.

"I... I'm visiting my father. He doesn't know that I'm coming. He still lives here."

He nodded. "I remember."

Decade-old memories bombarded her and she wondered just what it was he remembered. Every second of those infinitesimal, magical moments in time had been seared into her brain. She'd graduated from college and moved to the city, but she'd never forgotten the dashingly sexy Colt Barrington and his oh-so-charming smile. How could she? He was the father of her aborted child.

Colt eyed the beautiful woman outside his unmarked squad car and tried his best to hold back the flood of memories. A decade was a long time. She'd done some growing up. At twenty, she'd been a stunner, tall and slender and with the body of an athlete. Now she was softer, curvier, fuller – incredibly feminine.

Her large blue eyes dominated a face that had perfect proportions. Her tanned skin glowed with health and vitality and a sprinkling of freckles dotted her nose. Whatever she'd done over the past ten years had agreed with her. She looked even more beautiful than she had when they'd first met.

"Get in. I'll give you a lift," he said, wanting to prolong their time together.

Over the years, he'd forced her out of his mind. What they'd had once was over. But right here, in the gathering evening, with the smell of flowers in the air, he couldn't help but wonder what might have happened if they'd tried harder, made different choices all those years ago.

Had she thought of him over the years? Of the baby they'd made together?

He made an impatient sound in the back of his throat. *What the hell was he doing?* No good would come of dredging up things best buried in the past. So what if his heart had been racing from the moment he recognized her? So what if a part of him wondered what might have been...

"Okay. Th-thanks."

She sounded hesitant, but slowly leaned forward and opened the door. He came around her side and helped her into the car, before hefting her suitcases into the trunk.

"Thanks," she murmured a second time as he climbed back behind the wheel. She threw him the briefest of smiles.

His breath caught. She was even more beautiful up close. The faintest smell of her perfume wafted toward him on the air. Steadfastly ignoring the way his pulse leaped at her nearness, he put the car into gear.

Perhaps his offer of a lift wasn't such a good idea? It was unsettling being so close to her again and having the chasm of a decade and a dead baby between them. All of a sudden he was grateful her father lived nearby and this would soon be over.

"Is your dad still in Butler Street?"

"Yes. You have a good memory."

She said it without inflection, but he wondered if she was thinking the same thing as he was. Reliving the gloriousness of their past and remembering the sad and sober way it ended. Not brave enough to broach the subject, he said instead, "I'm a detective. I'm paid to remember details like that."

She turned slightly toward him, her mouth open in surprise. "A detective? You've done well for yourself over the years."

She said it pensively and he wondered what she'd done with herself after graduation. As he checked his mirrors and pulled out onto the road, he found himself asking the question.

"So, what about you? I assume you graduated from nursing?"

"Yes. I left for Sydney straight afterwards."

He eyed her curiously. "Is that where you live?"

"Yes. I come back as often as I can for visits, especially since Dad's on his own, but my life's in the city, now. I like it."

"You don't miss the country? The fact that there are only a handful of cabs in service at any given time?" he teased. "I take it that's why you're walking?"

She blushed a little under his regard and it pleased him to know he could still affect her. It shouldn't have mattered to him how she felt, but he was relieved she didn't seem to carry a grudge against him.

Not that he'd given her any reason to hate him. It had been a mutual decision to end the pregnancy. He hadn't forced her into it and he'd made it clear he'd support her if she decided to keep the child.

Still, he couldn't deny he'd been relieved when she'd agreed to the termination. The pair of them had been way too young to be parents. Besides, they'd known each other less than a month. The circumstances weren't exactly conducive to a long and happy relationship.

As if aware of the nature of his thoughts, she threw him a sad look and folded her hands in her lap on a quiet sigh. She turned to gaze out of the window.

"There's a lot about living in the country I still miss," she said after a while. "The peacefulness, for one. The city never sleeps. It doesn't matter what time of day or night, you can always hear something. It doesn't help that my front window is two hundred yards away from a major road."

She chuckled derisively and he found himself smiling back. He liked to listen to her speak. Her voice was soft and soothing, pleasant after his long day at work.

"Are you still a nurse?" he asked, wondering if she'd put her education to good use.

"Yes. I was lucky to get a job at the Sydney Harbour Hospital straight out of college. I've been there ever since. I started in orthopedics, but I found dealing with broken bones and traction didn't really suit." She flicked him a wry glance. "I worked in a trauma unit where patients would come in with several serious fractures, mostly from car or motorbike accidents. They'd be in there for weeks, often bedridden, waiting for their bodies to heal. It wasn't the kind of nursing that appealed to me."

"So what did you do?" he asked, filled with curiosity.

Back when they'd been dating, her entire world had consisted of college and her parents. At that point, she hadn't experienced the big wide world. He was fascinated to know more.

"I trained as a midwife and I love it. The excitement and joy is contagious. Assisting a newborn into the world... Witnessing the miracle of life every day... It's...amazing."

He stared at her in surprise. She'd willingly had an abortion the week of her twentieth birthday and now she was a midwife? *What the hell was she doing? Punishing herself?* He could feel her eyes on him in the dimness and he squirmed uncomfortably in his seat.

"I know what you're thinking," she said quietly.

He glanced at her before turning his attention back to the road. "Do you?"

"Yes. It sounds weird, me being a midwife, after...what happened. But I don't think of it like that. Yes, I had an abortion, but that doesn't mean I can't appreciate and enjoy the miracle of a new life. Every now and then I feel a little sad at the thought of what I did, but I accept it was necessary at the time and I get on with it."

"What *we* did," he said softly.

"Excuse me?"

He looked at her. "What *we* did, Morgan. We both made the decision. It wasn't yours alone. I hope you don't look back and feel like you didn't have a choice."

She shook her head and looked away. "Of course not. We did what we thought was best at the time. I still think it was the right thing to do. It's only that... Sometimes I can't help but wonder if that was my only chance to be a mom. I mean, I turned thirty a week ago. *Thirty!* My time to be a mother is fast winding down. I think about the possibility that I might never hold a baby of my own and... It saddens me."

Her quiet admission rocked him. He was both surprised and flooded with guilt. Whenever he thought of their baby, it was mostly followed quickly by relief. He'd still been at the Police Academy. Morgan had another year before she finished college. A baby would have been an unnecessary complication that they didn't need.

Deciding now wasn't the time to remind her of all the reasons they'd agreed to terminate the pregnancy, he kept his mouth shut and was grateful when they turned into her father's street. There were lights on in the front windows of his house, showing through the curtains. An early model Toyota HiLux pickup was parked in the driveway.

"At least he's home."

She tossed him a wry smile. "Yes, that's another one of the problems with a surprise visit. There's a chance the person you're surprising won't be home. But I don't recognize that truck. I wonder who owns it."

"Are you sure it's not your father's?"

"Yes."

She seemed so certain of it, Colt frowned. "How long has it been since you've seen him?"

"It's been awhile," she admitted. "I was rostered to work over Christmas, so I didn't get home then. I guess it was the Labour Day weekend in October when I was here last."

"Perhaps he bought another car?"

"No." "Dad's a Ford man. There's no way he'd buy a Toyota, even an old beater like this one."

"Maybe it belongs to someone else? Maybe he's borrowed it?" Colt suggested.

"*Mm*, maybe." She didn't sound convinced.

Popping the trunk, he climbed out of the squad car and went around to the back. He lifted out her suitcases and put them down in front of the car. He moved to the passenger side and opened her door. With a murmur of thanks, she got out and reached for her luggage.

"It's all right," he said. "I've got it." Without waiting for her to answer, he started up the paved driveway, a suitcase in either hand.

CHAPTER 5

A security light attached to the corner of the house came on at their approach and Morgan blinked. She followed Colt up the front steps. He stood aside for her to knock. Though she wanted to tell him it wasn't necessary for him to wait, something told her she'd be wasting her breath. He had an air about him, like he wanted to make sure she was safe.

She was sure it had nothing to do with their past. It was just the way he was. In the short time they'd been together, so long ago, he'd often shown that protective streak. She supposed it was one of the reasons he'd been attracted to the police force. It was their duty to serve and protect. Besides, she didn't really mind.

She knocked again and called out. She couldn't imagine what was keeping her dad. Evening had fallen, but it wasn't late. He'd always been a night owl.

At last, the front door opened, startling her from her thoughts. An unfamiliar man stood on the other side of the screen door, looking enough like her father to snatch her breath. Her heart pounded.

"W-who are you?" she stammered, blinking hard.

The man's eyes widened, like a deer caught in the headlights, but a moment later, he smiled.

"You must be Morgan. You look just like your pictures. Your father never stops talking about you."

She frowned in bewilderment. Apart from his striking resemblance to her father, she'd never seen the man in her life. "Excuse me? Do I know you?"

The man pushed open the screen door and stepped closer. Morgan stepped back, her mind still spinning.

"You should," the man said. "But it's no surprise that you don't." He put out his hand. "I'm your uncle. Leslie O'Brien. I'm your dad's identical twin brother."

Morgan gasped and her mind went blank. Did he say he was her father's twin? *How could that be?* Her father had never mentioned a brother. In fact, as far as she knew, he was an only child. And yet, the man looked just like her dad. A bit more weathered and rougher around the edges, but the main features were very much the same.

"Are... Are you sure?" she stammered, shaking her head from side to side in an effort to come to terms with what was in front of her eyes.

"Of course I'm sure. Take a look at me. Can't you see the resemblance?" Leslie replied with a lop-sided smile.

Morgan continued to stare at him, confused. "How.... How come my dad didn't say anything? Where is he, by the way?"

Leslie frowned. "You mean, you don't know?"

Foreboding curled its icy veins around Morgan's heart. She hardly dared ask the question. From the corner of her eye, she saw Colt move closer and was grateful for his presence.

"Kn-know what?"

Leslie cursed under his breath and then looked at her again. With his hands on his hips, he heaved a heavy sigh. Morgan's dread increased.

"Rex told me he'd email you. I guess he didn't."

"About you?" she asked, her voice unsteady.

"Yes, and to tell you about his trip."

"Trip?" she repeated, feeling like her words were pushing through a fog.

"Yes. He packed up his pickup and threw in a few supplies. Said he was heading out west, for the Red Centre."

She frowned, once again confused. "You mean, he's gone to Alice Springs?"

"Alice Springs, Uluru, Kakadu, Darwin. He wanted to explore Australia, while he still could. I think my arrival on his doorstep last month skedaddled his senses. He said he needed to get away for awhile to think. He left a few days after I got here. He asked me to take care of the place."

Morgan stared at the man who purported to be her uncle and tried to think through her confusion. First, her father had never once mentioned a brother – an identical twin, no less – and secondly, he'd gone away on some voyage of discovery and hadn't said a word. It was so out of character. She could barely fathom his state of mind. Then something else her uncle said snagged her attention.

"You arrived here without his knowledge, surprised him... Is that what you're saying?" she asked.

Leslie compressed his lips and nodded. "He never said anything about me because until nearly a month ago, he didn't know I existed. Our parents never said anything to him about me. I was put up for adoption at birth."

Morgan was taken aback by the flash of venom in his eyes. It made her wonder what horrors he'd endured as an adopted son. She still couldn't believe the story that her father was a twin. The very thought blew her mind. She could understand why her dad felt the need to get away. She just wished he'd told her before she'd boarded the train. After all, she'd received emails from him since then.

Still, it wasn't his fault she was in this situation. He had no idea she was on her way. It served her right for wanting to surprise him. It also explained why he hadn't returned any of her calls. And then she remembered something else. She looked at her uncle.

"Are you sure he left nearly a month ago? Dad sent me a birthday card less than a week ago. It was postmarked in Armidale. I'm sure of it."

Leslie acknowledged the question with a nod. "He gave it to me before he left. He told me your birthday was on the tenth and asked me to mail it when it was time. He wasn't sure if he'd come across a post office in the outback."

Morgan absorbed his explanation, still feeling dazed and confused. "If he left a month ago, maybe he's on his way back? Do you know how long he's going to be gone?" She couldn't keep the hope from her voice.

"No, I'm sorry, honey." Leslie scratched at the whiskers on his cheek. "He didn't say."

Though she didn't want to judge him, she couldn't help but notice the scars that crisscrossed his hands and his general air of neglect. She didn't know what kind of life he'd lived, but it hadn't been sitting at a desk. She was sure of that.

It was so unlike her father's upbringing. Ivy and Alan O'Brien might have started out young and poor, but by the time her father was in kindergarten, times had definitely looked up. Her grandfather studied to become a doctor and had run a very successful practice in Armidale. Her dad had grown up with his every need seen to, both physical and emotional. And not once had his parents mentioned the existence of another son. She found it hard to believe.

"Where's Rusty?" she asked quietly, referring to her dad's faithful golden retriever.

"Who's Rusty?" Leslie asked.

"My dad's dog. A golden retriever. You must have seen him."

Leslie shook his head. "Can't say that I have."

Morgan frowned. "You mean, you haven't seen him once since you arrived? That can't be right. Dad and Rusty are inseparable. He sleeps on the back porch, right outside the door. They go for a walk every morning. They—"

"I don't know what you want me to tell you, honey," her uncle interrupted. "I don't recall seeing any dog."

Morgan's confusion increased. Leslie had arrived at least two or three days before her dad left on his trip. How come her uncle hadn't seen Rusty? It didn't make sense. Unless the dog had been at the vet's for some reason. But that didn't explain why Leslie hadn't seen him since.

Perhaps Leslie was mistaken or perhaps Rusty had stayed out of the way. He wasn't all that good with strangers. Her dad might have tied him down by the shed, out of the way and then taken him along on the trip. It was the only explanation that made sense.

She glanced back at Leslie and was filled with a fresh surge of disbelief. When she looked past the disappointments and hardship life had etched into the leather of his face, it was uncanny how much he resembled her father.

She still had a million questions, but it wasn't fair to pepper him with them all at once. Besides, she needed time to come to terms with all she'd discovered, including the fact her father was no longer in town. She suddenly realized she'd have to find somewhere else to stay. Despite the fact Leslie was her uncle, she didn't know him from a stranger on the street. She wasn't comfortable enough with him to ask him if she could stay the night.

She glanced at Colt who stood off to one side.

She wasn't sure how much he'd heard. He'd remained silent throughout the exchange. But now, as if reading her mind, he spoke.

"We'd better get going." He stepped forward and offered Leslie his hand. "I'm Detective Sergeant Colt Barrington. I'm a friend of Morgan's." He glanced at her. "It's getting late and you're probably hungry." He looked back to Leslie. "Both of you."

Leslie chuckled in agreement. "Matter of fact, I have dinner waiting for me on the table. I'm sorry I only made enough for one. I hope you don't mind."

Morgan nodded and turned away, still caught up in her thoughts. She heard Colt thanking Leslie for his time and reassuring him she'd be fine. With all the craziness of the past moments, she couldn't help but wonder if Colt were wrong. She was so far from feeling fine, it was almost laughable.

Colt strode down the driveway toward the squad car with Morgan's suitcases in his hands. She was already waiting for him. She hadn't had to tell him she wouldn't be staying the night. The whole situation was like something out of a movie. Even to him, it felt surreal. He could only imagine how weirded-out Morgan felt.

A surge of protectiveness went through him and he was immediately irritated. Morgan O'Brien was his past. It was best she stay that way. His attitude toward marriage and lifelong commitment hadn't changed in the years since they'd parted and it was clear she longed for a child. They were wrong for each other on so many levels and he refused to break her heart a second time. Still, he wouldn't see her spend the night on the streets and he was afraid she might not have another choice. He unlocked the car and opened her door and as she slid into the passenger seat, he broke the bad news.

"I'm afraid it's the Guyra Lamb and Potato Festival this week. We also have the overflow from the Tamworth Country Music Festival and others are here for summer vacation. Every hotel, motel, bed-and-breakfast, and everything in between, is booked. Do you have anywhere else to stay? A college friend, perhaps?"

She stared at him for a moment with a glazed expression on her face. A moment later, comprehension dawned. Her eyes widened and her mouth opened in surprise and then she shook her head back and forth.

"No, I haven't kept in contact with anyone. I left Armidale right after graduation. Apart from coming home to see Dad, I haven't really kept in touch. Do you mean, there won't be a single room available? Are you *sure*?"

"I hate to be the bearer of bad news, but yes, I'm sure. People book out these places months in advance."

Her shoulders slumped on a heavy sigh. She looked defeated. She'd suffered one shock after another and to just discover she had no place to spend the night... He could well understand her dejection.

Knowing he'd probably regret it, he opened his mouth. "I have a spare room at my place. You're welcome to stay. It isn't much, but it's better than the last place I had. I could probably even drop by the supermarket and pick up a couple of steaks if you don't feel like eating out. I do a mean barbeque."

She stared at him for a long moment and he wondered what she was thinking. Ten years ago, he'd shared a cramped apartment with his brother. It had been furnished with an assortment of cheap items sourced largely from thrift shops, and pieces borrowed from their mom. It had looked like the student digs it was.

At the time, Beau had been in his third year of med school and Colt was only halfway through the Police Academy. Over the few weeks he and Morgan had dated, she'd slept over almost every night.

Her eyes remained shadowed. Was she thinking, like he was, about their past? The wonder of those magical weeks, before fate slapped them in the face and then later, the sadness, the distance, until the final, awful days, when it had actually been a relief to bring things to an end.

A moment later, she nodded hesitantly, uncertainty plain on her face. "Okay, but just for the night. I... I don't want to impose."

"I hate to break it to you, but the Potato Festival runs for a week and it only started yesterday. You won't get a room until it's over. Besides, you're not imposing, Morgan. I have plenty of room. Beau moved out years ago," he teased.

A tiny smile tugged at the corners of her lips, softening her perfect features. His gut clenched, but he resolutely ignored her effect on him. She was still a beautiful woman and he was a normal, hot-blooded man. His physical reaction to her nearness was natural. He couldn't imagine any man not being affected by her presence. It didn't mean anything. It was purely a physical response to a beautiful woman. It happened to guys all the time.

"Did he finish med school?" she asked quietly, her expression now filled with curiosity.

"Yes. In fact, he lives in the big smoke, too. I'm surprised you haven't run into him. He works at the Sydney Harbour Hospital."

Surprise lit up her features. "Wow! What a coincidence! What does he specialize in?"

"Neurology. He's a brain surgeon." Colt rolled his eyes but at the same time, he gave Morgan a grin. He might joke about his brother's occupation, but the truth was, he was immensely proud of his twin.

Morgan nodded in understanding. "That's probably why I haven't seen him. The birthing suites are a whole world away from the neurosurgeons, figuratively and literally. We're not even in the same building."

"I'll have to let him know you're there next time I speak with him. I'm sure he'll remember you." *Of course he would.* Beau had been sharing the house with him way back when Morgan was a frequent visitor.

With an impatient sound in the back of his throat, he pushed the thought from his mind.

Dwelling on their past was a waste of time. They'd never go there again. After loading her suitcases back into the trunk, he climbed in beside her. Switching on the ignition, he checked his mirrors and then pulled out onto the road. He'd offered Morgan a room because she was a friend and she had nowhere to stay. There was nothing more to it.

Yeah, right, a voice in the back of his head jeered. He resolutely ignored it and headed in the direction of the supermarket.

———————

Leslie O'Brien scrolled through the sent items of his brother's email account and cursed aloud. He'd forgotten to send Morgan a message to the effect that her father was going away. He'd meant to do it right away, but somehow it had slipped his mind. After all his meticulous preparations, he'd forgotten the simplest of things. It was stupid and only time would tell how much it would cost him.

Now she'd turned up on his doorstep – or at least, her father's doorstep. She'd left in shock and confusion tonight, but no doubt she'd be back and then the questions would start. All he knew was that he'd better have the right answers, starting with where the hell her dad was.

And then there was the added complication of the cop who'd brought her home. The last thing he needed was to arouse the suspicion of the police. He'd worked so hard at his plan. He couldn't risk having it unravel now. He *wouldn't* allow it to unravel now. It was as simple as that.

Dragging the laptop toward him, he composed a message he hoped would satisfy her curiosity – and the cop's. Ten minutes later, he leaned back in his chair and allowed himself a slow, satisfied smile.

There. That ought to do it.

Chapter 6

Morgan wandered around the modest condominium Colt Barrington now called home. Though small, Colt's space was twice the size of his previous digs and the furniture not only matched, it was tasteful and stylish. The dominant color scheme was masculine browns and grays, apart from a large Ken Done painting that brightened one wall and a generous woollen rug woven in red, cream and orange hues that covered a good portion of the living room floor.

The condominium complex was perched on the side of a hill. Surrounded by bushland, it looked down on the valley where thousands of lights twinkled in the darkness, including the lights of her father's house. She still couldn't believe her father had left without telling her and, if her uncle could be believed, he'd been gone nearly a month. Their last conversation must have occurred right before he left. That would explain why he hadn't mentioned his long-lost brother – a twin, no less – or that he was planning to take off for a while.

Still, the more she thought about it, the more bizarre she found the whole situation, starting with her uncle who was now living at her father's home. *Where had he been the past fifty-five years? Why hadn't her father known about him? How did identical twins get separated at birth? Was it really as simple as her uncle had explained?* The questions kept coming and it was frustrating to know that she didn't have any answers. At least, not yet.

First thing the next morning, she planned to visit her uncle and see what else he had to say. Before that, she'd send her father an email and find out what the hell was going on in his head.

The sound of the shower running reminded her that Colt would be caught up for several more minutes and the steaks hadn't yet been put on the grill. She had time to send a message to her father and hopefully, when he found the next Internet service, he'd respond.

Opening her handbag, she drew out her iPad and took a seat on the couch. She opened up her mail. Several new messages popped up and she scanned the headings. Her gaze past over one from Rex O'Brien and then, as if suddenly realizing that the email was from her father, she hurriedly went back to it and clicked.

I'm sorry, Morgan. I should have told you. Leslie emailed me this evening. I can't believe you're in Armidale! I'm sorry I wasn't the one to tell you. I'm still not sure what to say. Leslie arrived on my doorstep a month ago and I couldn't have been more shocked. I had no idea he existed, let alone that I had a twin. I'm still in shock, still coming to terms with it. I had no choice but to get away. The very idea that my parents kept this from me. They didn't say a word and now their explanations have gone with them to the grave... I still haven't heard the whole story from Leslie, but I guess he'll share it with me in time.

For now, I hope you understand. I never meant for you to find out this way. I didn't intend to be away so long, but I'm finding it hard to return. To come back is to acknowledge what happened and to accept a terrible wrong was done – to me and to Leslie. Wherever the truth lies about our past, I can't think of any reason why parents would choose between their sons. We were both babies! How did I get to be the lucky one? I'm overwhelmed with confusion and grief and underlying guilt.

And another one read:

Dear Morgan,

Please don't worry about me. I'm fine. I have Rusty. He's good company and he doesn't mind the dust. It's hot out here, but the countryside is beautiful – red and rugged and like nothing I've ever seen, but beautiful, just the same.

I can drive hours and hours at a time and never pass another vehicle. It sounds strange and lonely, but I don't mind the silence. It gives me time to think... And there's plenty to think about.

I don't know when I'll be back, Morgan, but

stay in touch and take care. I'll be in Tennant Creek tonight. After that, who knows? Phone service is pretty ordinary – public phones are few and far between and I don't have a cell, as you know. I'll email whenever I can, but know that I am fine. We'll get through this – you and me and Leslie...

A brother! I have a brother! And not just a brother, but an identical twin! Amazing! We've spent more than half a century apart. I'm looking forward to spending the next fifty years with him in my life. I hope you're getting to know him. He's had a few tough knocks, but I can tell he's a good guy.

Much love,
Dad

Morgan blinked away the tears that had gathered behind her eyes and reread the message. Uncle Leslie must have emailed her father not long after she and Colt had left. It was lucky her dad had access to a Wi-Fi signal right when Leslie needed him to, but then again, it was evening. No doubt her dad had pulled into the nearest town and was even now, settling in for another night.

She thought of him alone in the outback and hoped he was finding the comfort he sought. He must have been even more shocked than she'd been at the discovery of his twin. She'd never been further west than some distant relatives her mother had in Moree, and even that town was several hours drive from what Australians considered the outback. Still, she'd love to experience it herself one day.

She'd been told the silence out there was absolute and the vast night sky was so clear and bright, it felt like you could reach out and touch the stars. There was something alluring about the thought of being surrounded by nothing but nature and she could understand why her father had been drawn to it after receiving such a shock. The discovery of a twin brother was life changing and he'd need time to come to terms with it, like she did. At least she knew he was all right.

With a deep, restorative breath, she sent off a reply, thanking him for contacting her and reassuring him everything was all right. She ended it with a gentle plea that he come home soon and she told him she missed him.

"So, what do you think?"

Colt's question startled her from her thoughts. She hurriedly closed her iPad and stood. He was dressed in a pair of denim cut-offs and a white T-shirt with a faded, red-and-blue Nike emblem splashed across the front. His black hair was wet from the shower and curled around his ears. His cologne smelled fresh and spicy, but dark stubble remained on his chin. She wondered if he were growing a beard.

Realizing she hadn't responded to his question, she blinked and shook her head. "Um, what do I think about what?"

"About my condo? It's a little fancier than the place I shared with Beau."

Morgan made a show of inspecting the room. Her impression was the same as the first time she'd looked around.

"Yes, it's lovely. You were both struggling students back then. I remember the feeling all too well, although at least I was able to keep living with my parents. I felt sorry for guys like you and your brother who had to leave home to get a college education."

He smiled and Morgan's heart skipped a beat. He was every bit as good looking as he'd been a decade earlier. If anything, time had matured and enhanced his good looks, etching character lines into his face. She wondered about the things he'd seen and done as a detective. If the TV shows were anything to go by, it hadn't always been good.

"Have you always worked as a police officer in Armidale?" she asked, curious.

"Yes. After living here with Beau during the summer break the year you and I met – well after graduation, I asked to be stationed here as a probationary constable. Beau was still in med school here and needed someone to help pay the rent." He shrugged. "I was happy to help him out. I wasn't earning enough to get a place on my own and living in Armidale was convenient. Mom and Dad and my younger brothers and sisters are only an hour's drive away. Besides," he added, "I have fond memories of this town."

His gaze held hers and her breath caught in her throat. Her heart thumped so loud she was sure he could hear it. And then, he looked away and a moment later, headed toward the modest kitchen. The spell was broken.

Morgan drew in a couple of calming breaths and slowly followed him. She stood by while he rinsed lettuce leaves under running water and dumped them into a bowl. Next he sliced tomatoes, peppers, red onion, carrot and mushrooms. A handful of snow peas also made it in. She was impressed. There was no doubt about it, the man knew how to put together a salad.

"Do you need any help?" she offered.

"No, but thanks. I think I have it under control. I resist cooking at every turn, but I'm actually quite good at it."

He flashed her a grin and her knees went weak. "Who taught you to cook?" she managed.

"Mom. She made sure all eight of us knew our way around the kitchen. I can't say I particularly enjoy it – not like Beau, anyway. He's in a league of his own. But I guess I know enough to throw together a meal when I have to."

Morgan smiled. "Your mom did you all a favor. I went to college with plenty of kids who barely knew how to boil water. Most of the time, they lived on two-minute noodles. Every now and then they'd mix it up by tossing in a tin of baked beans. I shudder to think how they're coping now, with families of their own."

Colt laughed and the husky sound of it tingled along Morgan's nerves.

"Hey, there's nothing wrong with two-minute noodles," he teased. "There have been plenty of nights I've come home late from work too tired and uninterested to cook. If it weren't for those noodles, I'd have starved to death!"

She laughed along with him and her tension eased. For the first time since she'd arrived in town and discovered her father gone, she felt calmer.

He'd emailed her. He'd assured her he was all right. He was working through the discovery he had a brother. It would take some time. She could only hope and pray it wouldn't take too long. She'd taken a fortnight's leave from work. Next time her dad contacted her, she'd let him know. Perhaps the knowledge she was only there for two weeks would hasten his return. She hoped so.

"How do you like your steak?"

Once again, Colt's question broke into her thoughts. He'd finished with the salad and now held a plate containing two T-bones. "Medium rare, thanks. Are you sure I can't do something to help?"

"Well, if you really want to feel useful, you could always open that bottle of Sauvignon Blanc you chose at the liquor store. A glass of wine would go down well right about now."

"Of course," she replied and picked up the bottle from the kitchen counter. She unscrewed the lid and the crisp, fruity aroma wafted toward her nose. She drew in an appreciative breath. "*Mm*, that smells fantastic."

"Good choice," he responded, deftly setting a skillet on top of the hotplate and adding a splash of oil. "I didn't know you drank white wine."

She chuckled. "Hey, back when you knew me I was a poor student. I drank the cheapest alcohol I could find. Now that I've managed to work my way up into a reasonably well-paying job, my tastes have become somewhat more refined. Nothing beats a good white and Australia produces some of the best."

He smiled. "You won't get any argument from me."

Once again, her belly did a somersault. *What the hell was she doing? Why had she agreed to stay with Colt Barrington, of all people? She would have been better off taking her chances with overbooked hotels... Wouldn't she?*

She suppressed a sigh. The truth was, so far she was enjoying his company. It reminded her of the early days of their relationship, before the words "pregnancy," "baby" and "termination" became part of their vocabulary. The thought sobered her. Did she really want to rekindle something with the man she was once head over heels in love with? Did *he*?

She had no idea, but all of a sudden, the possibility was both exhilarating and terrifying...

———————

The steaks were cooked to perfection and even the salad was good. The plates had been cleared away and the bottle of wine was nearly empty. Colt leaned back against his seat and gazed across at Morgan.

Throughout the meal, they'd maintained pleasant conversation and had caught up on each other's lives and careers. He was surprised to discover she was single and she appeared to be just as surprised that he was, too. He wanted to question her further on the topic, but he didn't want to give her an opportunity to delve into his reasons for avoiding marriage. It was an issue he refused to dwell on. Even Beau couldn't draw him into it for long. Colt cleared his throat and changed the subject.

"Tell me about your uncle."

Morgan's face filled with a fresh wave of surprise. "I learned of Leslie O'Brien's existence the same moment you did. My dad's never spoken of him. I've never seen him before."

"From what I gathered," Colt said, "your father didn't know about him, either. It seems amazing that such a thing could be kept a secret all these years. I mean, imagine if it had happened to Beau and me? Being twins, I can't imagine what it would be like if we lived the first fifty or sixty years of our lives not knowing the other existed." He shook his head at the thought. "It seems inconceivable."

"Yes," Morgan agreed, "and yet, it's true."

Colt lifted an eyebrow in surprise. "You're happy to take your uncle's word for it?"

Morgan shrugged. "What reason would he have to lie? Besides, I received a couple of emails from my father while you were in the shower. Uncle Leslie must have contacted him right after we left. Dad confirmed that Leslie is his twin and that they've been separated since birth. Dad was as shocked and confused as I am. It's the reason he took off in such a hurry without saying anything. He needed to get away, to have some time to think. I can't help but feel a little resentful toward my uncle because if not for him, Dad would still be here."

Colt nodded. He understood how she felt and was relieved to hear Morgan's father had made contact. "Wow, I can't even begin to imagine how he must feel...and how many questions he must have. Are his parents still alive?"

Morgan shook her head. "No. They've both passed."

"Any brothers and sisters?"

"No, until now, we believed Dad was an only child. No one ever thought to ask them if they'd had any other children – like a twin they just happened to give away..."

"It still seems incredible," Colt murmured, trying to get his head around the whole thing. "To give birth to two babies and leave one behind..."

"I can't imagine the circumstances that must have led to such a decision," Morgan said quietly. "It was hard enough to terminate a pregnancy that was only a few weeks in, but to carry two babies to term and then offer one of them up to someone else..."

Colt stared at her. Her eyes remained downcast, fixed on her hands which lay twisted in her lap. Her cheeks were flushed – from anger or sadness or something else, he couldn't tell. Scraping up his courage, he voiced a question he'd contemplated every now and then over the years.

"Do you regret the decision not to keep our baby?"

Her head snapped up. Her eyes blazed into his. He didn't need to guess about the emotion that was now driving her.

"Of course I do! What did you expect? That I'd terminate the pregnancy and go on my merry way? I think about our baby so many times, I'm sure it's not healthy, but I can't seem to help it."

Her voice caught and he stared, horrified, as her eyes welled up with tears. The few times over the past decade when he'd thought about the child that wasn't to be, it was with sadness and sometimes even a little nostalgia, that he could have already been a dad. He looked to his father and to some of his buddies and occasionally wondered if he were missing out.

But then he'd see other friends who'd parted ways with their spouses in less than amicable circumstances and the kids were caught in the middle of the fray. At those times, he was glad he was still single and that he hadn't risked marrying, only to see it all fall apart. That kind of thing happened way too often and nobody seemed immune. He was better off as he was, alone and childless, but also not being responsible for bringing abject unhappiness down on someone else's head.

Tears rolled silently down Morgan's cheeks and his gut clenched. Despite his better judgement, he reached over and took her hand in his. It was soft and warm and felt way too good. He squeezed it reassuringly and then set it back down.

"I'm sorry, Morgan. Please don't cry. We made the right decision. We were both so young, on the cusp of our lives. Both of us had big plans. A baby would have made our lives so difficult. Not only in ways we considered, but in other ways as well. We weren't mature enough to be parents... You would have dropped out of college, at least for a while, and you might never have gone back. I would have struggled to support us on my meagre probationary constable's wage. There would never have been enough money and that would have led to fights and besides, we barely knew each other. We'd been dating a total of four weeks."

He shook his head, trying hard to make her see. "You got pregnant the very first night we met and that wasn't anyone's fault. How could we have known the condom had a hole in it? But the fact was, when you found out you were pregnant a few weeks later, it scared the hell out of me...and you. We made the decision to terminate together," he added quietly. "It was the best thing for both of us at the time. I don't regret it and neither should you."

"But now I'm thirty!" she cried and fresh tears rolled down her cheeks. "I'm not married, I don't have any children and there isn't the likelihood of either in my near future. What if that baby was my only chance to be a mother? What if God's punishing me for having the abortion? For putting my wants and needs above the baby's?"

A fresh wave of sobs took hold of her and he couldn't bear to sit by helplessly a moment longer. Pushing back his chair, he stood and tugged her slowly upright. He put his arms around her and pulled her close. She fit right under his chin, as neat as could be.

Her arms came around his waist and she rested her head against his chest. She cried softly and her torment clutched at his heart. He wanted to stay distant and removed, but the feel of her in his arms, distressed and sad beyond measure, did him in.

Tightening his arms about her, he bent his head and pressed a kiss against the softness of her hair. It was loose around her shoulders and hung in waves around her face. She lifted her head and stared at him, her eyes dark and watery with distress. Without thinking, he kissed her tenderly on the mouth.

He tasted wine on her lips. The familiar scent of her perfume, spicy and delicious, tantalized him. When her lips moved tentatively beneath his, he groaned under his breath, bombarded with memories.

In an instant, the past ten years were swept away. He burned with need, desperate to kiss her again, but he held himself back. She felt so good in his arms, but this wasn't what he was about. He wasn't looking for a relationship. He didn't do commitment. It wasn't fair to let her think anything different.

The thought sobered him. Releasing his hold on her, he put some distance between them. She stared at him, breathing fast, looking dazed and confused. Flooded with guilt, he lowered his gaze and turned away.

"I-I'm sorry, Morgan. I shouldn't have done that."

Twin spots of color reddened her cheeks. Her eyes narrowed. Despite her anger, when she spoke, her voice was surprisingly calm.

"Why are you apologizing? I participated as willingly as you."

He grimaced and ran a hand through his hair. *Shit, this was not going to end well.*

"Thank you; that's kind of you, but I still shouldn't have done it. What we had was over with years ago. I didn't mean to give you the idea that we... That is, I'm not in the market for a wife, or anything else. I don't do commitment."

He held up his hands and pointed at his naked ring finger and shook his head, feeling helpless. Nothing he said was going to improve things. He ought to shut his mouth and get the hell out of there while he still could. Taking a step in the direction of the hallway that led to the bedrooms, he was pulled up short by the sternness in Morgan's voice.

"Stop right there, Colt Barrington!"

Slowly, he turned to face her, bracing himself for what was surely to come. And whatever it was, he deserved it.

"You kissed me and I kissed you back. Just because we got a little excited, doesn't mean I expect you to get down on one knee. Sure, I want to get married and have a family, but I'm not singling you out for the job. As you said, what we had is over. There's no going back."

Colt stared at her. Despite himself, he couldn't

help but feel a little disgruntled by the defiance in her tone. He expected her to be way more upset. He could have sworn he felt passion in her kiss. Had it all been a purely physical reaction to the situation they'd been in? She'd been upset, he'd offered her comfort, and they'd kissed. *Is that all it was?* Apparently so.

A surge of relief went through him. It was a kiss and now it was over. They could go back to being friends.

CHAPTER 7

Dear Diary,

Well, what's done is done and there's no going back. All I can hope is that the emails have done the trick. The girl is way too smart for my liking and then there's the cop. I'll have to keep my wits about me if I'm to keep them off the scent.

The best thing is, she's an only child. Rex told me before he departed. So it's really only Morgan O'Brien I need to convince. If I manage to do that, everything else will fall into place. She'll return to her home in the city and no one will be any the wiser. I can go on as planned. Life doesn't get any sweeter.

Morgan stared at Colt and did her best not to let her hurt and disappointment show. She hadn't consciously agreed to stay at his condo with the intention of picking up where they'd left off a decade ago, but when he drew her close and kissed her, she couldn't help the way her heart leaped with hope. Though it embarrassed her to admit it, their unborn baby hadn't been the only person she'd thought about over the years.

Was it possible he still had feelings for her? Could they try again to make things work? They were both older and wiser and established in their careers. They weren't silly young college students who weren't responsible enough to take care of themselves, let alone a baby. *Was it possible they could rekindle their love and do things better the second time around?*

The thoughts had swirled around and around in her head in time with the frantic beating of her heart. And then he'd pulled away and apologized for kissing her.

It took all her courage to plaster a smile on her face and speak to him in a no-nonsense tone. It was a kiss, nothing more. Of course there was nothing between them. What they had was over. They were friends from the past and that's the way they'd remain. Nothing more, nothing less. And she was fine with that.

His look of consternation at her casual attitude had given her a tiny *zing* of satisfaction. She was glad he was put out by the fact she hadn't broken down in the face of his rejection. And make no mistake, he'd rejected her.

All his dribble about not looking to settle down and being unwilling to commit was just guy speak for "I don't love you enough to want to spend my life with you." Everyone knew that. Besides, she wasn't in love with him, either. Those feelings had died long ago.

Now, Morgan pushed her hair away from her face and lifted her gaze to his. "I think I might call it a night. It's been a long day. Thank you for dinner. It was lovely." She turned to head in the direction of the hallway.

"Let me show you to your room," he offered and walked ahead of her down the corridor.

The first door they came to was closed and she assumed it was his room. A bathroom and toilet stood on the opposite side of the hallway and a little further down on the same side as his was the spare room. Colt flipped a switch beside the door and the room was flooded with light.

"I brought your luggage in here earlier and left some clean towels on the bed. There are toiletries in the bathroom, if you need them. I'm sorry, but there's only one bath. I hope you don't mind sharing."

He flashed her a smile, but she wasn't in the mood for teasing. What she'd told him was right. It had been a long day. First on the train from Sydney and then the surprising discoveries that she had an uncle and her father had headed for the outback. It was enough to tire anyone out.

With a murmur of thanks, she closed the door on him and then flopped down on the queen-sized bed. Her gaze drifted around the room. The ceiling was white and nondescript and the walls were equally pale. They might have been a shade of gray, but it was hard to tell in the golden light of the lamp. Floral curtains in reds and oranges provided the only splash of color in the room.

While the kitchen and living room had been sleek and masculine, the spare bedroom looked more like it had been furnished out of a thrift shop. Still, it was clean and comfortable and apparently the only available room in town.

Darn the Lamb and Potato Festival! She'd arrived at a very inconvenient time. The festival was the only reason she found herself sharing a house with Colt Barrington. Once upon a time, she would have been beside herself with excitement at the thought of living with Colt – waking up every day in his bed, sharing breakfast, acting like a real, grown-up couple.

But this arrangement couldn't be further from the romantic notion she'd dreamed about from the moment she'd set eyes on him. He'd shown her to the guest room, but had no intention of joining her in bed. He'd made it more than clear whatever they'd shared a decade ago was over.

Colt leaned back against the wall beside the closed door that led to his guest room. He was still a little peeved at Morgan's blithe acceptance that what they'd had would never be again. The way she'd kissed him, clung to him – it had felt like she really cared, like she wanted to be with him, to know him, to be as close as two people could.

He should be glad she'd made it easy, that

they both saw eye to eye. It would be incredibly awkward otherwise. This way, things would be easy. They could go about their business and neither would get in the way. Expectations wouldn't be raised then doused because there were no expectations to be had.

Then why did the thought of her disrobing behind the very door he stood beside nearly drive him mad with need? That soft, supple body, naked between the sheets. At least, that's the way she used to sleep. His body hardened at the memory and he cursed beneath his breath.

This was ridiculous. She was an ex-girlfriend who needed his help for a day or two. That was it. She'd been quite open about the fact she was in the market for a husband. That she yearned for a child. He ran like hell from commitment. He couldn't bear the thought of suffering through the collateral damage when things didn't work out. People changed when they got married and as far as he could see, it wasn't for the better.

No, he needed to steer well clear of women like Morgan O'Brien. She wasn't looking for a fling or a no-strings-attached relationship. She'd just turned thirty and she was playing for keeps. He'd best remember that.

Morgan squinted against the early morning sunshine that filtered through the curtains she'd forgotten to close the night before. Rolling over in bed, she reached for her phone on the nightstand and checked the time. *Seven-thirteen.* She groaned.

If she were back in Sydney, she'd already be at work. It was funny how her body refused to get moving when it knew it didn't have to. There were no guesses as to the reason for her sluggishness. It had been way past late when she'd finally stopped tossing and turning over the complications that now crowded her life.

First on the list was her father and his abrupt departure from home. He'd emailed her and assured her he was fine, but a residual feeling of confusion remained. Next, there was the difficulty of facing Colt Barrington on a regular basis. When she'd accepted his offer of a room, she'd expected that it would be for no more than a night. But if his prediction about the availability of the hotel rooms in the city was correct, it would be the better part of a week before she could move out.

She supposed she could always stay at her father's place, but something about that idea held her back. Her uncle was a stranger. It didn't feel right cohabiting with him – at least, not without her dad.

She wondered which room Leslie had taken. It was only a two-bedroom house. He must be in her room. So, if she did move in, she'd be staying in her father's room. The very thought was too weird to contemplate. She'd never spent a night in her father's bed, even when her mom had died and they'd both been devastated with grief.

Besides, she hoped her dad would return now

that he knew that she was here. She'd email him again in a bit and tell him she was only in town for two weeks. If anything would get him to turn around and head for home, it was that. A knock on her door startled her and she pulled the sheets up to her neck before responding.

"Come in."

Colt appeared in the doorway. His dark hair was wet from the shower and he was freshly shaved. Dressed in a charcoal-gray suit, white business shirt and a red-and-gray striped tie, he looked every bit the smart professional. He tossed her an annoyingly cute smile.

"I have to be at work in fifteen minutes. If you want a ride downtown, you'd better hurry it up." And with that, he disappeared from view.

Morgan sighed and pushed back the bedclothes. The heat from the early morning sun could already be felt in the room. It promised to be another warm, summer day. Collecting her clothes and the towels Colt had given her the night before, she hurried to the shower.

The trip downtown was uneventful. Colt pulled up beside a coffee shop. "You can get breakfast here and they serve great coffee."

She murmured her thanks, collected her handbag from the floor and opened the door.

"I finish at six. We could go down to the Pink Pub for dinner, if you like." He threw her a quick grin. "I don't want to go overdoing it with the home-cooked meals."

She smiled reluctantly. "Sure. My treat. I owe you dinner, anyway."

He acknowledged her comment with a nod and another grin. "I guess I'll see you later. Have a good day."

She climbed out of the car and was about to walk away when he called out to her again.

"Give me your cell number, in case I need to reach you. If something unexpected crops up at work, I might be delayed. I'd hate for you to be sitting around worrying about me."

He gave her a wink and this time she laughed. Whatever the future held for them, she couldn't deny he had a sense of humor and knew how to keep her amused. She rattled off her number and he gave her his. With a final jaunty salute, he left.

Her spirits lifted from the doldrums she'd sunk into the evening before and she walked to the coffee shop with renewed vigor. All of a sudden, she was starving. Taking a seat at one of the empty tables that stood on the pavement outside, she ordered a full breakfast and a cup of black coffee.

She wondered vaguely about what Colt had eaten for breakfast. There hadn't been any dirty dishes in the sink. Either he'd cleaned up after himself, or he'd skipped it altogether. *Perhaps he planned to stop somewhere on his way to work?*

With an impatient snort, she forced her thoughts away from the man who had already consumed far too much of her time. She picked up one of the Sydney papers stacked neatly on a bookshelf near the door and spread it open. Immersing herself in national and international affairs was one way to get him off her mind.

The lead story dealt with a bushfire that was burning out of control in north eastern Victoria. It had been an unusually hot and dry summer in many parts of Australia and Victoria seemed to suffer severe bushfires more than most. It had been seven years since the fires that had caused Australia's highest ever loss of life from a bushfire. One hundred-and-seventy-three people had died and more than a hundred more were hospitalized, suffering from bad burns.

Those fires destroyed at least two thousand homes and damaged thousands more. Many towns northeast of the state capital of Melbourne were badly damaged or almost completely destroyed. The fires were still burning more than two weeks after they started.

She sighed. Black Saturday, as it became known, was a sad day for Victoria and for all the people of Australia. Morgan hated to think it could happen again.

Turning the page, she scanned the headlines and skimmed over a story on the Federal Government's proposal to increase the retirement age and another one on an assault and robbery in Kings Cross. The inner city Sydney suburb was a notoriously dangerous place after dark and she couldn't understand why people found the need to risk it. There was no way she'd take to the streets of Kings Cross on her own at night.

Her breakfast arrived in the hands of a cheery young waitress and Morgan set the paper aside. Liberally covering her bacon, eggs and sausages with ketchup, she began to eat. A woman's laughter snagged her attention and she glanced up and noticed a man sitting at the next table chatting with a young woman who looked enough like him to be his daughter. A pang went through her and she couldn't help but ponder the whereabouts of her father. He hadn't said how long he was staying in Tennant Creek, but it could have been only for the night. He didn't seem to have any concrete plans where he was going and when he'd return.

Pulling her iPad out of her handbag, she opened it up to her mail. A handful of new messages appeared, most of them spam. There was a message from Georgie Whitely checking that she'd arrived okay and telling her to enjoy her time at home. Morgan grimaced. She wasn't sure "enjoy" was the right word to use this time round. Still, all she could do was hope for the best and cross her fingers her dad would soon return. With that in mind, she sent him another email.

Hi Dad,

Thanks for letting me know you're all right. I appreciate it. After my surprise meeting with Uncle Leslie, I was worried. I can't imagine how it must have been for you to discover you had a twin. The very thought blows my mind.

Take the time you need, Dad, but I wanted you to know I'm only in Armidale for a fortnight. It was all the leave I had. I hope you find it within yourself to return before I leave. It would be good to see you again. I miss you, Dad.

Lots of love,

Morgan xx

With lips compressed, she sent the email into cyberspace and whispered a silent prayer heavenwards that her father would soon find Internet service somewhere along the road. His laptop was now several years old and didn't always connect to available Wi-Fi. She'd bought it for his birthday. She should have insisted he upgrade to an iPad. They'd talked about it only a few months ago. Yet again, he'd declined her offer to buy him one.

'Why do I need an iPad? The laptop works just fine. Besides, I'm familiar with the interface on this. I know where all the buttons are.' He'd laughed, indicating the laptop open on his desk at the time. 'Don't go confusing me with any more technology, honey. You'd only be wasting your money.'

Morgan hadn't been willing to let the matter go so easily. 'What about an iPhone, then?' she'd suggested. 'You could start out learning the ins and outs on that. Then, when I finally mange to persuade you to upgrade to an iPad, you'll have the technique down pat. The iPhone and iPad use the same interface and all the same commands. The only thing the iPad doesn't do is make phone calls, unless you're connected to Facetime and even then, the person you're calling needs to be on that, too.' She'd paused to catch her breath and looked at him. 'So, what do you think?'

Her father merely shook his head and chuckled. 'Facetime, iPads, iPhones... Where does it end? I'm perfectly content with my laptop. It does everything I need. Besides, why do I need a cell phone? I never go very far from home. The occasional day trip away with my golfing buddies is about all I do I these days. You know where to find me most of the time, honey. I don't need to be reachable twenty-four seven, especially now that I'm retired. It's one of the things I really enjoy, being able to get away from it all.' He'd looked apologetic.

'Not like you kids these days. You don't know what it's like to escape from the hustle and bustle of life every now and then.' He shook his head slowly back and forth. 'I don't know where you find the energy to be constantly switched on. It must get exhausting.'

Morgan had heaved a sigh of resignation and let the subject drop. If her father didn't want an iPad or a cell phone, then that was his business. It wasn't like he was in poor health with the need to contact emergency services at any time of the day or night. The more she thought about it, the more she'd agreed – he was probably right. He was content without a raft of technology complicating his life.

But that had been months ago, before he'd discovered he had a secret twin and had headed off into the outback, alone except for his dog. Things were different now. He wasn't just off for a day trip with his golfing buddies. He was on his own in the middle of nowhere. Anything could happen. She couldn't help but worry about him and all of a sudden, she wished she'd ignored his protests, and at the very least, had bought him a phone.

The sound of her cell ringing interrupted her thoughts and she pulled it out of her handbag. She checked the screen and her heart skipped a beat. The call was coming from her father's home.

Had he arrived back in Armidale already? Was that even possible? She didn't know exactly where Tennant Creek was, but she knew it was in the Northern Territory. Had he driven all night, after sending her the emails? Was he even now waiting for her at home? With her chest tight with expectation, she answered the call.

"Dad?"

"No, I'm sorry, Morgan. It's Leslie. Your uncle."

Disappointment flooded through her. "Oh... Uncle Leslie. I'm sorry. Dad's number came up on my phone. I just thought... Never mind. What can I do for you?"

"I understand this must have been a shock to you – arriving home to find your father gone and an uncle you didn't even know existed, in his place. I... I wanted to call and explain, seeing as your dad's not here to do it."

"Um...of course. I... I guess so. But, don't feel like you have to. I mean, it's none of my business—"

"Of course it's your business. I'm your uncle, your father's identical twin. You already know we were separated at birth, but there is a lot more to it."

Morgan's head spun. She wasn't sure if she was ready to hear his story. Though both her grandparents were now dead, they'd been an important part of her life. She had many fond memories of spending time with them. She still missed them. She didn't know how she'd feel if her uncle had less than flattering tales to tell about two people she'd loved and admired all her life.

"Um... I'm not sure I need to know the secrets of your childhood. It's enough that my dad's excited to have you in his life. I'm happy for him, for both of you. Can't we just leave it at that?"

"I appreciate your discretion, Morgan. I'm sure you've worked out my life wasn't quite as smooth sailing as your father's. I guess I just want to know that my less-than-stellar background doesn't matter to you."

Morgan swallowed. She wasn't sure how she felt about her long-lost uncle, but whether he'd lived a less privileged life didn't matter. She and her dad were alike in that. She never judged anyone on their looks or what they did or didn't have. It was their character that was important, the only thing that mattered. She hurried to reassure him.

"Of course it doesn't, Uncle."

"Then you'll come over for tea and let me tell you all about it."

After a moment's hesitation, she accepted.

CHAPTER 8

It felt weird knocking on the door to her father's house, knowing that he wasn't home. There had never been a time in her life until yesterday that she'd arrived at Butler Street without a single family member around to greet her. Okay, Uncle Leslie was family, but she'd known him less than twenty-four hours. It would take some time to come to think of him in that way. Her father urged her to accept his twin and spend time getting to know him. For her dad's sake, she was determined to do it.

She knocked a second time and was finally rewarded with the sound of footsteps on the other side of the door. A moment later, Leslie greeted her with a smile.

"Morgan! How lovely to see you again! Thank you for coming over."

He stood back to allow her to enter and she was once again taken aback by how closely he resembled her father. The hairstyle, the dimple in his cheek when he smiled, the way he dressed. He even *smelled* like her father! She hadn't noticed that the previous night.

She wondered if by some freak "twin synchronicity" they actually wore the same brand, or whether he'd simply borrowed what was in the bathroom cupboard. His clothing was also the same style her father wore.

Her father prided himself on his neatly pressed slacks and array of designer polo shirts. After her mother died, he'd paid a woman from the town to wash and iron his clothes. Prior to that he'd spent all his working life wearing suits, business shirts and ties and he found it hard to dress down, even in his retirement.

Her uncle wore a pair of tan-colored pants that could have been her dad's. He had teamed it with a green Ralph Lauren polo shirt, a brand her father favored. Her uncle had hinted at hard times, but it looked like his life had changed for the better now. She realized she was curious to hear more about the truth.

———————————

Leslie added bowls of cream and sugar and a plate of fresh banana cake to the tea tray and thought about the woman who waited for him in the other room. She was attractive and confident and her blue eyes – so much like her father's – exuded intelligence. She was a daughter any father would be proud to claim.

One of Leslie's many regrets was that he hadn't

fathered any children, at least, none that he knew about. Now that he was well and truly in the second half of his life, he wished he'd spent a bit more time looking for the kind of woman he might have wanted to be the mother of his child. Not that he'd ever been in a position to support a family.

"Do you need any help in here?"

Morgan's question startled him from his thoughts. He looked up as she came into the kitchen and acknowledged her query with a forced smile.

"Thanks, honey, but I have it all under control. It's been a month since your father went away. I think I've just about learned where everything is." He shot her another smile, hoping to set her at ease. He could only imagine how strange it felt for her to be in her father's house without him and with a stranger in his place.

She frowned and he could see she was still nervous. No doubt it would take time for her to come to terms with what had happened. He'd do all he could to help. It was the reason he'd invited her over, and after what had happened with her father, it was the least he could do.

With that thought in mind, he picked up the tea tray and headed back into the open-concept living and dining room filled with tasteful and expensive furniture. A fine oak dining table with eight matching chairs filled half of the space. A carved sideboard in matching oak stood against one wall.

On the opposite side of the room was a three-seater leather couch and matching recliners that faced a widescreen TV. Though the leather showed signs of age, especially one of the recliners, they were still nice pieces and would have cost a pretty penny. It was just another example of how far apart their lives had been.

A familiar wave of anger surged through him, but he forcefully thrust it aside. That part of his life was over. He'd done what needed to be done. He might not be comfortable with his motives, but he was sure pleased with the results. Leslie O'Brien had moved up in the world. Of that, there was no doubt.

Placing the tea tray on the dining table, he pulled out a chair and seated himself before reaching out for the pot of tea. "Do you take cream and sugar, Morgan?"

She took a seat opposite him and shook her head. "No, thanks. Black is fine."

He poured her a cup and handed it to her and then poured one for himself. Adding a generous amount of cream and two sugars, he stirred it before bringing it to his lips.

"Mm, just how I like it. Hot and sweet and creamy." He followed the comment with smile.

She smiled back. "Just like my dad. I still can't believe how much you look like him."

He shrugged. "Hey, we're identical twins. What more can I say?"

"Yes," she murmured and took a sip from her cup. "It's come as such a surprise."

"Your dad said something very similar. Would you like to hear my story? I'd very much like to share it with you. Perhaps then, you might feel more comfortable with me in your father's house."

A faint blush stained her cheeks. She opened her mouth to protest, but he held up his hand and cut her off.

"It's all right, Morgan. I understand. You arrived here expecting to see your father. Instead, you discover he's gone away without telling you and find me here in his place. To add to the confusion, I'm the long-lost twin nobody knew about. You're entitled to feel a little out of kilter." He laughed in an effort to ease the lines of tension that had gathered around her mouth.

She smiled hesitantly. "You're right. I... I am feeling a little like I've been hit head-on by a Mack truck. Dad and I keep in touch regularly. I haven't heard from him much over the past few weeks and I haven't spoken to him for nearly a month. He didn't call me for my birthday, or for the anniversary of Mom's death. They're dates he normally wouldn't miss. I was worried about him. It's the reason I hopped on a train and came up here. I wanted to see for myself that he was okay."

"Instead, you found me. I can understand how that hasn't helped ease your mind."

She gave him another grudging smile. "You're right. It kind of freaks me out a little when I look at you. You look so much like my dad and yet, you're virtually a stranger."

She blushed again and looked away and he could tell she was embarrassed by what she'd said. Her next words confirmed it.

"I'm sorry, Uncle Leslie. I didn't mean—"

"It's all right, honey." He hurried to reassure her. "I understand." He took another sip from his tea. "Like I told you, your dad didn't react much better. If I hadn't looked so much like him, I don't think he'd have believed me. We had a few tense hours early on, don't you worry."

"But you sorted things out, right?" she insisted. "You didn't have a falling out? That's not why he went away, is it?"

"No, of course not. It didn't take long to sort things out. I told him all about my past, how we'd been separated at birth. He was shocked and saddened and mad all at once and everything in between. He left because he needed some time to himself, to come to terms with things. He urged me to stay right here and make myself at home." He spread his arms wide. "So, I have."

She nodded and her face relaxed. She brought her tea cup to her mouth and sipped.

Leslie offered her the plate. "Would you like some cake?"

She reached over and took a piece and murmured her thanks. "Did you bake it?"

He chuckled. "No, though I've been known to bake every now and then. I bought it at the bakery downtown. It's good, though, don't you think?"

She took a bite and swallowed and then nodded. "Yes, it's good. And I bet I can guess exactly where you got it. Moxons, on Marsh Street, right?"

"It sounds like you know it well," he teased. "Do I take it you're not a cook?"

She laughed. "Good guess, Uncle. Despite my

mother's constant urgings, I was never interested in spending time in the kitchen. I preferred to be outside, riding my bike or playing with my friends down at the river. Even when I was in high school, Mom couldn't convince me to come inside and learn the art of baking a pie. I guess I just wasn't cut out for that kind of thing."

"You take after your father," he guessed.

"In almost every way," she agreed.

A comfortable silence fell between them. They both sipped their tea. A moment later, Morgan lifted her gaze to his. His chest tightened in anticipation. *Was this it? Had he done enough to win her trust? Was she finally ready to hear?*

"Tell me your story, Uncle Leslie."

Morgan pushed her cup of tea to one side and folded her arms in front of her. Being at the table, sharing food and stories in her home, brought back fond memories of life with her mom and dad. She couldn't count the number of meals she'd shared with her family in this very spot – and later, with just her dad. They'd talked and talked about everything, even when she was a kid. As an only child, she was loved and adored and they were interested in everything she did. She never resented their intrusion into her life. In fact, she enjoyed the attention. There were plenty of kids around her who didn't know what it was like to live with parents who cared.

Occasionally, they'd refuse to let her do something or to go out to a party with her friends, but there was always a firm, but loving explanation as to why they'd decided the way they had. The mutual respect and love they had for each other lived on into her adulthood. And then her mom got cancer and for a while, everything changed. For months, her mom was in and out of hospital, going for treatments here and there until at last, there was nothing more they could do for her and that was the worst thing of all.

All the time, during and after, Morgan had been attending university and did the best she could. Her mom had been gone nearly twelve months when she met Colt at a college Christmas party. The few short weeks they were together were a high point in her sorrow, and together were the most magical weeks of Morgan's life – and then she got pregnant...

If her mom had still been alive, she would have told her. Perhaps her mom would have even been able to convince her to keep the baby. But the timing was all wrong. Her dad was still consumed by the grief of losing his wife and was in no fit state to consult over something as momentous as an unplanned pregnancy with a man she barely knew. Besides, she still had another year of college. A baby was totally impractical...

She swallowed a heavy sigh and forced herself to concentrate on her uncle. No doubt life had also thrown him some twists and turns. All of a sudden, she wanted to hear them. Reaching across the table, she squeezed his hand encouragingly. He looked a little startled, but slowly began to speak.

"On the fifth of October, 1961, Ivy and Alan O'Brien became first-time parents to identical twin boys. They kept one and showered him with love and affection. The other one, they offered up for adoption."

Though he spoke calmly and without inflection, Morgan could see the hurt that shadowed his eyes even now, so many years later. Her heart ached with sadness.

As if sensing her distress, he gave her a little smile.

"It's all right, Morgan. Don't feel bad. I've had fifty-five years to get used to it."

She shook her head helplessly. "But why? Why would they do that? Why would they keep my father and give their other son away?"

Leslie lowered his gaze to the table and shrugged. "Who knows? They were young. They must have had their reasons. Unfortunately, they're dead. I'll never get the chance to ask them."

"Did you always know you were adopted?" she asked.

His face twisted into a grimace. "Yes. My adopted parents were only too happy to remind me of that every opportunity they got. What I didn't know until recently was that I had a twin."

She gasped in surprise. "You didn't know, either? Your parents never said?"

"No. They said lots of things about me, none of

which were pleasant, but they never breathed a word about your father."

"I take it you weren't adopted into a nice family," she murmured.

The pain in Leslie's face deepened. His eyes darkened with emotion. "No. There were a lot of ways to describe Bruce and Wilma Lexington, but nice wasn't one of them."

Morgan held his gaze, her heart filled with sympathy. "You refer to them in the past tense."

His lips twisted into a grimace. "Yes. They died in a house fire last winter. Good riddance, is what I say. Burning to death while they slept in their beds was too good for them."

Morgan was taken aback by the venom in his voice, but forced herself to continue. "How did you find out about my father?"

He sighed. "After the fire, I went to visit my parents' lawyer, to sort out their affairs. They'd left everything to a charity. I didn't receive a thing. The only thing they wanted me to have was a box containing my birth certificate and other official documents concerning my adoption. It was then that I discovered my biological mother had given birth to twins."

Morgan stared at him, her heart once again swelling with sadness. "It must have been such a shock to you – all of it. To be cut out of your parents' wills and then to discover you had a twin brother... I can't begin to imagine how you felt."

"About the same way you did when I introduced myself, no doubt." He chuckled and she marveled that he could find humor in the dreadful circumstances he'd been forced to endure.

"As for my parents being selfish and vindictive enough to leave all of their earthly belongings to strangers, that didn't surprise me one bit. They'd never shown me kindness in their lifetime. I didn't expect them to show any generosity of spirit in their death."

Morgan shook her head. "But... But, it's so awful for them to have done that to you! Did they have any other children? Do you have any other brothers and sisters?"

"No, thank God. I wouldn't wish my childhood on anyone."

"I wonder why they adopted you," she mused. "From what you've said, they didn't want you from the start."

"It's true," her uncle nodded. "Every now and then, when they were at their vitriolic best, I'd ask them, 'Why? Why did you take me home?' I would have been better off in the hospital."

"And what did they say?"

"They refused to answer. Instead, I usually copped another mouthful of how they wished they'd done just that. And finally, one night when my mom had called me every name under the sun and my dad had walloped me with a horse whip for refusing to eat my greens, I learned the truth."

Morgan clenched her hands tightly together, barely daring to breathe. She wasn't sure if she had the courage to listen to what he was about to reveal. Still, she'd asked the question. She owed him the courtesy of listening to his reply.

Her Uncle Leslie ran a hand tiredly through his closely cropped, gray hair. He lifted his tea cup, but set it down again without drinking. He picked at a scab on his forearm and cleared his throat and then scratched at his hair again. Finally, he looked up at her and she stifled a gasp at the sight of the pain that filled his eyes.

"You see, Bruce and Wilma Lexington really wanted a girl. They'd wanted a girl for as long as they could remember. Instead, they got me."

Emotion burned behind Morgan's eyes. She quickly scrubbed it away. Reaching over, she took her uncle's hand and held it, trying to convey without words just how much she felt for him and the sad, unloved child he'd been. And then her mind caught on something else he'd said.

"Your name was Lexington?"

He nodded and eased his breath out on a quiet sigh. "Yes. For fifty-four years I was Leslie Lexington. Wilma even spelled my first name in the manner of a girl. But when I discovered who I really was, I changed my surname."

"You found out about my dad more than six months ago. Why did it take you so long to find him?"

"For a few months after I found out, I wasn't sure if I wanted to. The existence of a twin brother explained so much – I'd gone through life always feeling like part of me was missing – but I'd put that down to growing up in a loveless family and being made to feel every day of my life that I didn't deserve to be there.

"When I found out about Rex, I was overjoyed

that I'd finally discovered where I'd come from and where I belonged, but I was terrified he wouldn't want anything to do with me, that he'd reject me, like my parents." He sighed again.

"Then there were the questions I had about my biological parents and the anger I felt at their actions. How could they have given me up into the life of hell I endured – and kept the other son? I wanted to rant and rave at them, but I was afraid of what they would say. I didn't realize they were no longer with the living, or I might have reached out to Rex sooner."

Morgan nodded in understanding. "My grandparents died a few years ago. First Grandad – he had a massive heart attack one night in his sleep. Less than a year later, Grandma died of breast cancer, like my mom. I'm sorry you didn't get to meet them. They were kind and generous and nice. I can't imagine how they came to the decision to give up one of their sons. I'm sure it wouldn't have been easy."

Her uncle shrugged, his lips compressed. She was sure it was difficult for him to accept his biological parents were good people. She was having a hard enough time reconciling the Ivy and Alan O'Brien he spoke of, with the grandparents she'd adored and now they'd never know why. Once again, she reached for his hand, roughened with work and age, and squeezed it.

"Thank you for sharing your story," she murmured and meant it.

He stared at her. Tears glinted in his eyes. With a

muffled oath, he swiped at them with the back of his hand and offered her a shaky smile.

"Thank you for listening," he replied quietly. "You're a good girl, Morgan O'Brien. Your dad must be so proud."

At the mention of her father, Morgan's chest tightened, but she managed a nod in return. At the same time, she sent another silent prayer heavenward that he was all right and that even now, he was on his way home.

Pushing away from the table, she set her empty cup back on the tray. "Thank you for the tea, Uncle Leslie. It was lovely."

"Are you leaving already?" he protested. "I was enjoying your company."

"Yes, and I have very much enjoyed yours, but I must be on my way," she replied, needing to get out of the house and have some time to think and reflect on all she'd learned. "Do you mind if I take a little look around outside? I haven't been home for a while."

"No, of course not. You're welcome to stay here, you know. I've moved into your father's room. He insisted I use it in his absence and to tell you the truth, I like having him near. His smell, his things... It makes me feel closer to him."

Morgan frowned and then noticed the embarrassed flush that stained her uncle's cheeks. Her initial discomfort at the thought of her uncle in her father's bedroom was replaced with a rush of tenderness. She couldn't imagine what it would be like to have an identical twin, but from everything she'd read about them, she understood they had an indelible bond that neither time nor distance could destroy.

Her uncle's need to be as close to her dad as possible wasn't weird or freaky, it was just the way twins were, nothing more, nothing less.

CHAPTER 9

Dear Diary,

I hope I've done enough to satisfy her curiosity. She's a smart girl. She asks a lot of questions. I've told her the truth, just not all of it. It's better for everyone that I don't. Nobody needs to know everything, not even Morgan O'Brien.

———————

Morgan scuffed at the ground with the toe of her Converse. With her hands jammed in the pockets of her shorts, she wandered around the side of her childhood home and headed toward the back. The house had been painted nearly twelve years earlier. She remembered the time well. She'd even chosen the color. Her mom was already sick and both Morgan and her dad had wanted her mom to have the final say, but her mom had merely smiled and insisted it was Morgan and her dad who needed to be happy with the decision.

Together, they'd decided on a sandstone color, with the trims painted in a crisp white. The end result was both fresh and modern. It didn't matter that the color scheme was now out of date.

Rounding the corner to the backyard, Morgan was pleased to see the flowerbeds awash with brightness. Pansies, petunias and white button daisies reached up toward the sun. Like the freshly mown lawn, it was obvious her uncle had made an effort with the upkeep. He must have known how much pride her father had in his garden and the appearance of his yard – or maybe her uncle just felt the same way about things.

She walked down the worn dirt driveway that led to the back shed. Pulling the doors open, she winced at the strident squeak of protest. Blinking, she waited for her eyes to adjust to the dimness.

Like she expected, the space where her father usually parked his pickup was empty. Still, she was hit with a wave of longing to have him safe and sound at home again. It had been months since she'd seen him and after all she'd learned about his twin, she wanted to put her arms around him and give him a reassuring hug.

With a soft sigh of resignation, she moved further inside. A mezzanine level had been added years earlier and was filled with items neither of them could bear to part with. There was Morgan's white cane bassinette she'd slept in as a newborn and the cot she'd moved into when she grew too big.

There was a highchair, covered in dust and cobwebs and a large wooden box. It was filled with mementoes and other bits and pieces she'd saved from her days at school. Awards and sports ribbons and trophies...and the only love letter she'd ever received. It had been written by a boy in the third grade. She'd been in grade two. Adam Charles, the love of her life. At least, he had been, back then. She smiled at the memory.

Leaving the shed and its nostalgia behind her, she wandered further down toward the back. Her father's house was on a large lot, nearly a hectare. When she'd been younger, she'd begged for a pony, claiming they had plenty of room, but her parents had refused, saying they didn't have the time to put into riding and looking after a horse. Instead, she'd had to settle for her pushbike.

The yard was well grassed over and green. It must have rained not too long ago. Either that, or her uncle had kept it watered. Sometimes, especially during the summer, the grass was browned off and yellow from the harsh Australian sun. Making her way toward the back fence, a pile of fresh dirt caught her eye. She wandered closer for a better look.

The mound was only a few feet long and less than a foot wide. Though the dirt piled high had crusted and dried in the heat, it was fresh enough that no grass or weeds were growing on top. If she didn't know any better, she'd have guessed it was a grave.

Once, when she was little, a baby magpie had

fallen out of its nest. Morgan had found it and had brought it in to her dad. He'd told her that it had gone to heaven and they should bury it out in the yard. She'd gone with him and had watched while he dug a hole deep enough that predators wouldn't dig it up. If memory served her right, the magpie's grave hadn't been far from this one.

Curious, she kicked at the dirt with her shoe. The sun glinted off something metallic. Frowning, she bent over and scraped away dirt with her hand. A silver buckle came into view, followed by a wide ribbon of woven blue fabric. Closing her fingers around her discovery, she picked it up and shook off the remaining dirt.

It was a dog collar... And then it hit her: It was Rusty's dog collar. *Or was it?* With her heart pounding, she set the collar back on the ground, brushed off her hands and pulled out her phone. Flicking through her photo gallery, she found the picture she'd been looking for.

It was a shot of her dad and Rusty, taken the last time she'd been home. Her dad sat in his usual seat on the front porch with Rusty at his side. The golden retriever looked at her with his pink tongue hanging low. Around his neck was a collar identical to the one she'd found.

She stared at the photo and then down at the collar that now lay at her feet. *Why would Rusty's collar be on top of a pile of freshly turned earth?* Rusty was with her father. He'd told her that himself. He wouldn't have lied about it. The dog couldn't possibly be in the ground. She was sure of it.

And then doubt began to assail her. *What if this was just another thing her father hadn't discussed with her?* She'd assumed his departure after the arrival of his twin had been done in haste and was totally unexpected. She understood why he hadn't told her. But what if he'd been distancing himself from her even earlier than she imagined? What if Rusty had died more than a month ago and he hadn't told her?

The very thought that her dad could have deliberately kept such things from her was distressing. What could be worse, was that he might have lied about taking the dog with him. *Was he ill? Suffering from a brain tumor? Was that the reason he'd kept things from her? Were there even bigger things he was hiding?* She couldn't bear the thought.

The sound of her phone ringing interrupted her feverish thoughts and she snatched at her cell in relief. The Caller ID showed it was Colt.

"Morgan, I'm due for a break soon and can come and get you if—"

"Colt!" she gasped, unable to help herself.

"Morgan? What's wrong? You sound like you're out of breath."

She sucked in another lungful and eased it out in a deliberate effort to get her heart rate back under control. "I'm sorry, I've..." She debated for a millisecond whether to tell him or not, and then came out with it. "I'm at Dad's place. I've had a bit of a shock."

His tone sharpened with concern. "What kind of a shock? Is your uncle still there?"

"Yes, but this has nothing to do with him."

"Then what is it?"

"I've found something near the back fence – a pile of dirt. It looks...like a grave."

Colt issued a bark of nervous laughter. "A grave? Don't tell me you think your father—"

"No! Of course not!" she interrupted. "That thought never entered my mind. I received a couple of emails from him last night, remember? He's in Tennant Creek. At least, that's where he was last night. He could be anywhere now. Anyway, it doesn't matter. The grave – if it is a grave – is only small. It couldn't possibly hold a human, but I found a dog collar just beneath the surface. The buckle was sticking up. I'm sure it belongs to Rusty. My father's dog."

"Did the dog die without your father telling you?"

"That's the thing," she said quietly. "I don't know. Dad told me he had Rusty with him. Twenty-four hours ago, I wouldn't have believed he'd lie to me, but then I discover he's gone away for who knows how long and he didn't breathe a word! To top it off, I find Rusty's collar buried in the dirt. I can't help but wonder if there's something else going on."

"Like what?"

"I don't know. Perhaps he has a brain tumor and he doesn't know how to tell me. Or maybe the tumor's interfering with his thought processes and he doesn't realize. I've heard that kind of thing can happen. I saw a documentary about it on *Discovery Health*. I—"

Colt chuckled on the other end of the line. "Morgan, stop. You're sounding ridiculous. Your dad had good reasons for taking off. He just found out he had an identical twin brother. That would rattle anyone. As for Rusty... Who knows? Maybe he died and your dad didn't want to upset you by telling you about it. Then again, maybe things are just as he said and Rusty's by his side. It could just be a coincidence you found the collar near what you think looks like a grave."

Colt's calm explanation helped to relieve her building fears. She took a couple more deep breaths and the tightness in her chest eased. Colt was right. There were many possibilities as to what might or might not have happened. Finding the collar didn't mean her dad had lied to her or, heaven forbid, was suffering from an inoperable brain tumor.

"You're right," she said, her tone almost normal. "I'm sorry. I overreacted. Of course Rusty's still with Dad. Where else would he be? He might be nine years old, but that's not exactly ancient. He's fitter than I am and nowhere near ready to die. Besides, Dad would have told me. I'm sure of it."

"See? Have you asked your uncle about the mound? He's been there a month. Perhaps he knows what's buried there?"

"No, I haven't. I'm still down the back."

"Okay. How about I come over and check it out?"

Morgan couldn't keep the hope from her voice. "Would you?"

"Of course. Give me ten minutes."

She breathed a sigh of relief. "Thank you, Colt. I'd really appreciate that."

"No problem. I'll see you soon."

Morgan ended the call and slid the phone back into the pocket of her shorts. Bending down, she collected Rusty's collar and headed back to the house. Once again, she knocked on the front door and waited for her uncle to answer it.

"Morgan! I take it you're done with looking around. Is there something else I can help you with?"

"I... I'm not sure. I... I found this down the back. It's Rusty's collar. I found it beside a mound of fresh dirt. Do you know anything about it?"

Her uncle frowned. "No, I don't."

The sound of a vehicle approaching reached Morgan's ears. She turned and was relieved to see Colt pulling up to the curb. His long stride ate up the distance between them and within moments, he stood by her side. She threw him a grateful smile.

"Thanks for coming over."

"No problem." He turned his attention to her uncle and held out his hand. "I'm Detective Barrington. We met last night."

Morgan's uncle shook Colt's proffered hand. "To what do we owe this pleasure, Detective?"

"I'm here as Morgan's friend. She found a mound of dirt at the back of the property. Can you tell us anything about it?"

"No, I can't. I just finished telling her," Leslie replied.

Colt eyed her uncle. "You arrived at your brother's place a month ago, is that correct?"

"Yes, thereabouts. I don't remember the exact date."

"Where are you from?" Colt asked, his voice filled with curiosity. Morgan swallowed a smile. Colt probably wasn't even aware how much he sounded like a cop.

Leslie looked away. "Here and there. I've moved around a bit over the course of my life."

"Where were you living before you arrived in Armidale?"

"Sydney. That's where I was born."

Colt nodded briefly in acknowledgement. "What do you do for a living, Mr O'Brien?"

"This and that. I left school at fifteen. I didn't learn a trade. I guess you could call me a handyman. Sometimes I do odd jobs for people, fix leaking pipes, squeaky doors, windows that won't open. Whatever needs doing, really; whatever someone will pay me for."

Colt shot her a glance, apparently satisfied with her uncle's answers. "Let's go and take a look at this pile of dirt."

Feeling slightly apprehensive, Morgan led the way down the back to where she'd found the earthen mound. Her uncle trailed behind them.

"It's right there," she said and pointed.

Colt kneeled and picked up a clod of soil that lay on the top of the pile. "It's dried hard. It's been exposed to the sun for a while. We haven't had rain all month. It's my guess it's been here since before Christmas."

Morgan frowned and looked at her uncle. "You're sure you haven't noticed it?"

"No. I haven't been all the way down the back. There's no reason to. I only mow to the edge of the lawn. There's nothing but dirt back here."

Colt stood and brushed off his hands. He faced Leslie. "Do you have a shovel?"

Leslie frowned. "What, you're going to just dig it up?"

"That's right," Colt replied. "How else are we going to tell what's under there?"

"But it mightn't be anything. It might just be a pile of dirt," her uncle protested.

Colt shrugged. "Could be, but I don't think so. This dirt's been formed up deliberately. It wasn't just dropped here. And Morgan's right. It looks like some kind of grave. Given that she found a dog collar here, it's my guess an animal's been buried here. There's only one way to find out. Do you have a shovel, or not?"

"Yeah, all right. Hold your horses. I'll get one from the shed." Leslie turned away and headed back in the direction they'd come. Morgan looked at Colt.

"What do you think?" she asked.

"Exactly what I told your uncle. I think someone buried an animal. From the size of the mound, I'd hazard a guess it's a dog."

"It can't be Rusty," Morgan said, not sure which one of them she was trying to convince. "He's with my dad."

Colt's lips compressed. "Yes, that's what you told me."

Leslie arrived back, carrying a round-nosed shovel. He handed it to Colt. A light sweat had broken out on her uncle's brow and his breath came fast. Morgan was reminded he wasn't a young man. She probably should have offered to go and get the shovel. The morning sun had warmed up and even she was feeling its effects. She hoped her uncle hadn't overdone it.

Colt pulled off his suit jacket and handed it to her before rolling up the sleeves of his shirt. She wondered how the crisp white fabric would fare after he'd dug up the pile of dirt and was grateful all over again that he was there, helping her – and to hell with his expensive clothes. This was probably the nicest thing a man had ever done for her.

Oblivious to her thoughts, Colt bent over the shovel and started digging. Load after load of dirt was removed until finally, the shovel scraped against something that looked like a piece of blue plastic. Morgan's heart leaped into her throat. She was sure it wasn't Rusty, but she didn't know if she was ready to see what the grave was about to reveal.

Colt scraped off another layer of dirt and more and more plastic was exposed. On closer inspection, it looked like a cheap tarpaulin – the type that could be bought from any hardware store. When the object concealed by the plastic was cleared of dirt, Colt set the shovel aside and bent over and lifted one side.

The smell hit her like a wall of putrid heat. She

covered her mouth and nose and tried hard not to breathe too deeply. Whatever it was had been there long enough to decompose. Barely daring to look, she peeked between her fingers. Bit by bit, the contents were revealed.

The first thing she saw was a golden yellow coat, but unlike Rusty's it was matted and dull. Still, her pulse picked up its pace. Colt pulled back more of the plastic, revealing the badly decomposed body of what had once been a large dog. He looked back at her and she could see the question in his eyes.

She shook her head back and forth with increasing vigor. "It's not Rusty. I'm sure it's not him."

Colt turned back to the dog and moved closer. Morgan wondered how on earth he could bear the smell. The stench was making her retch. Any moment, she expected to vomit and yet Colt was poking through the remains with a stick, as if looking for something.

"The decomposition's pretty bad. There's no collar or other identification that I can see, but he has a large white patch of fur under his chin."

Morgan froze. Rusty had a large white patch under his chin. But it couldn't be Rusty! He was with her dad. *Wasn't* he? She made a sound of distress in the back of her throat and Colt's gaze immediately zeroed in on her.

"Are you all right, Morgan?"

She bit her lip to hold back the tears and somehow managed to nod.

Colt's expression softened. "It's Rusty, isn't it?"

His voice was gentle, but his quiet words pierced her heart. *How could her father's dog be lying dead, buried in the ground?* Her father had told her only the night before that Rusty was with him. *Why would he lie?*

She would have understood if he'd told her he'd had to leave his beloved dog behind. He'd left in a hurry with no real destination in mind. Taking a dog along might not have suited his plans. After all, Leslie was staying in his home and was presumably willing to feed and look after the animal.

It didn't make sense that her father would leave him behind and then lie to her about it. And not only lie about having his dog, but withhold the fact that, far from being with him on his journey of self-discovery, Rusty had died. Perhaps he thought that if she believed his dog was with him she might not worry so much.

Though she tried hard to hold them back, hot tears filled her eyes. She clenched her jaw tight, but a sob escaped, followed quickly by another. Before she realized it, she was crying softly for Rusty and for her dad. She didn't know what the hell was going on, but she needed to talk to her father, to see him, to hold him, to assure herself everything was all right.

She suddenly remembered her conversation with her uncle only the night before. She turned to face him.

"I guess that's why you hadn't seen Rusty. He must have died before you arrived." She shook her head slowly back and forth. "I just can't understand why Dad didn't tell me and why he felt the need to lie."

Leslie looked stricken. "You mean, your father told you he had the dog with him? Is that what you mean?"

Morgan bit her lip against a fresh wave of emotion and nodded. "Yes. He emailed me last night. He told me not to worry, that he had Rusty with him and that everything was all right. But it's not all right! It's not!"

"I'm sorry, honey. I really am. I don't know what to say."

Her uncle looked so distraught, Morgan's heart went out to him. None of it was his fault. *Had Rusty died right before Christmas? Was that the reason her dad hadn't told her?* Perhaps he hadn't wanted to spoil her excitement over the holidays.

She'd always loved celebrating Christmas, even the times when she had to work. It was possible he was trying to protect her by withholding the sad news. The thought brought her a modicum of comfort.

Colt drew the tarpaulin back over the body and covered it again with dirt. Morgan felt like she'd been through the wringer and the day wasn't nearly done. She was grateful for Colt's assistance, but right now, she needed to be alone. She wanted to check her emails and see if her dad had replied. She wanted to call him, to hear his voice, to know that he was all right. She moved closer to Colt.

"Do you mind dropping me back at your place?" she asked quietly.

He stared at her a moment in silence and then nodded. "Of course. Are you sure you're okay?"

Drawing in a deep breath, she let it out slowly on a heavy sigh. "No, but I will be. Just as soon as I speak with my dad."

CHAPTER 10

After giving Morgan the spare key to his condo and dropping her off outside the complex, Colt headed back to the station. His thoughts immediately returned to Leslie O'Brien. It was obvious the man was a drifter with no fixed abode. Though he wore clean clothes and had recently shaved, there was a general air of neglect about him that came from years of living a life filled with instability and change.

Colt had seen it many times during his years in the police service. A fair percentage of the people who ended up behind bars had lived a transient life and though Colt hadn't wanted to draw it to Morgan's attention, there was something about her uncle that got Colt's radar humming. The man definitely warranted a closer look.

Then there was Rusty. Morgan's father had told her via an email the dog was with him and yet, clearly that wasn't the case. Either Rex O'Brien had lied to spare his daughter or he wasn't the person who'd sent the email. *And if not Rex, then who?*

Colt made a mental note to ask Morgan if someone else could have access to her father's username and password. Colt hadn't wanted to say anything to Morgan, but it was clear the dog hadn't died from natural causes. Despite the advanced decomposition, Colt had noticed Rusty had been shot.

Taking the set of stairs two at a time, he pushed open the door that led into the detectives' squad room and made a beeline for his desk. Nodding distracted greetings to the handful of officers that occupied the room, he pulled off his jacket and hung it over the back of his chair and took a seat. Dragging the keyboard of his computer toward him, he signed into the database that stored the names of anyone who'd ever been arrested in New South Wales. And then he entered Leslie O'Brien.

Almost immediately, the page filled with text. Scrolling through the information, Colt eliminated the first two entries purely on the basis of age. He wasn't sure how old Morgan's uncle was, but the man looked like he was in his late fifties or early sixties. Then again, it was obvious he'd lived a hard life. That tended to age people. Even so, he wasn't a young man and the first two Leslie O'Briens were under forty.

The next two entries were in the right age bracket, but both of them were women. It was the last entry that caught his attention. The file related to a white male, aged fifty-nine, whose last known address was in Sydney.

Colt's heart rate picked up speed. He continued to scan the text. There was only one offense recorded and it was more than a decade earlier. O'Brien had been convicted of common assault. He'd been given a two hundred-dollar fine.

Colt's excitement dimmed. If he was looking at the same Leslie O'Brien, there wasn't much to be found. A minor offense more than ten years ago. It counted for zilch. So much for his gut instinct.

With a disappointed oath, Colt pushed the keyboard away and contemplated what he knew so far. There was a lack of weeds on the grave and the advanced state of composition indicated the dog had died several weeks earlier. Leslie had been house-minding for a month. Morgan's uncle knew nothing about the dog or his death. Or so he said. Morgan's father had apparently told her the dog was with him. If he'd been the one to send the email, he was definitely lying. But was he the only one? And why had he lied to his daughter?

Movement out of the corner of Colt's eye snagged his attention. He turned to see his superintendent bearing down on him.

"Colt, I've just taken a call from dispatch. There's been an accident on the New England Highway, just north of Uralla. A car's gone into the river."

A familiar surge of adrenaline flooded Colt's veins. He was on his feet and reaching for his jacket even before his boss had finished speaking.

"How many occupants?" he asked.

"I'm not sure," Superintendent Troy Barwick replied. "The call came in from a passing motorist. He saw the vehicle leave the road."

"Who else is at the scene?" Colt asked, searching for his keys.

"I told Jared Buchanan to ride with you. Bob Coster and Jack Small are already on their way. They were in a patrol car on that side of town when the call came in."

Colt nodded, recognizing the names of the two highway patrol officers. Finding his keys at last, he snatched them from beneath a pile of paperwork and headed for the door, calling out for Jared as he went.

Colt saw the blue and white and red strobe emergency lights flashing across the field from nearly a mile away. A crowd of emergency personnel – paramedics, police officers, firemen – as well as the usual gathering of curious onlookers were scattered around the accident scene.

Someone had called a tow truck and an early model dark blue Mitsubishi Magna was in the process of being lowered back to the ground via a winch. Colt came to a sudden halt not far away and jumped out of the car. His colleague, Detective Jared Buchanan, followed suit.

Muddy water still poured from beneath the doors of the rescued vehicle. Colt located Sergeant Bob Coster and asked the highway patrol officer to bring them up to speed.

Bob scratched at his thick, gray hair and peered off into the distance, his expression grim.

"The car belongs to Anthony Adamson. He's over there."

Colt turned in surprise. He hadn't realized the driver had escaped unharmed. A long, thin man with unkempt hair and a straggly beard stood not far away, his clothes dripping. He looked to be in his mid-thirties.

"He got out okay?" Colt asked.

Bob grimaced and turned to spit on the grass. "Yeah. Too bad about his kids."

The words turned Colt's blood to ice. He forced himself to ask. "Kids?"

"Yeah," Bob replied. "There were two of them in the back, strapped into car seats."

Bob's words penetrated Colt's brain and all of a sudden, he felt sick. He stared at his colleague, willing him to take the words back, but the man said nothing. "You're fucking kidding."

Bob's lips thinned and his gaze turned to flint. "I wish I was."

A solid block of concrete settled in Colt's gut. With leaden feet, he forced himself forward until he stood beside the Magna. He put his face to the back window on the passenger side and spied a baby. It was blue and still.

With growing dread, Colt took hold of the door handle and wrenched it open. He gasped in horror. Another child lay dead on the opposite side. Like Bob had told him, they were both strapped into car seats. They hadn't stood a chance.

Bile rose up inside him and he pushed away from the car. He only managed to take a few steps before the contents of his stomach burned a path up his esophagus and poured out onto the ground.

Grabbing a hanky from his pocket, he swiped the back of his hand across his mouth, trying his best to wipe himself clean. His throat burned and all he could taste was vomit, but he reminded himself, this wasn't about him. Two children lay dead in their car seats, drowned in the most horrible way. He couldn't imagine how it must have felt for them, screaming, gasping, hollering; desperate for air that wasn't there.

He felt a hand on his shoulder and turned around to face his colleague. Bob stared at him, grim and sympathetic.

"It's all right, buddy. Take it easy."

Shaking off his hand, Colt drew in a deep breath and got himself together. He'd attended his fair share of traumatic accident scenes. This one was no different. He needed to shut out the emotion and simply get on with his job. That was the only way to cope.

He looked back at Bob. "What happened?"

"According to the driver, he failed to take the corner and ended up in the river. Said he was going way too fast. Wasn't familiar with the road. Didn't know about the tight bend. He hit it hard, tried to brake, but lost control. Next thing he remembers is the car hitting a wall of water. The vehicle filled up fast. It took him awhile to undo his seatbelt. He tried to release the kids. Their seatbelts jammed. There was nothing he could do."

"Jesus!" Colt breathed and fresh horror surged through him again.

"Yeah," Bob agreed. "That's *his* story. It gets worse."

The dread that had settled in Colt's gut spread like icy tentacles through his veins. "What do you mean?"

Bob looked over to where another man stood with a junior constable. The man was dressed in a suit and tie and looked like a lawyer or perhaps an accountant.

"See that man over there?"

Colt followed his line of sight and nodded. "Yeah. What about him?"

"His name is Simon Potter. He's an accountant with Wright and Westport."

Colt shifted his weight and tried not to let his impatience show. "What about him?"

Bob blew out his breath on a heavy sigh. His expression remained grim. "He told the constable he was traveling behind Anthony Adamson, on his way to see a client. He witnessed the accident."

"That's lucky. It will make our job easier."

"Yes. It does. Especially when our eyewitness says he never saw the brake lights come on."

Colt stared at his colleague. It took a moment for the words to sink in. He frowned.

"What do you mean, there were no brake lights? Adamson must have braked at some point. He was heading straight for the river."

Bob's somber gaze remained steady on his. "Yeah. You'd think so. Only, we took a walk back along the road in the direction he came from. There were no skid marks on the road."

Shock rendered Colt momentarily speechless.

Finally, he found his voice. "You mean... He did this on *purpose*? He *meant* to kill his kids?"

Bob shrugged. "The bastard said he braked, but the eyewitness gives another account. Take it however you like, but to me, that's what it looks like. I suspect it might have started out being him and the kids, but at the last minute, the asshole chickened out. He made sure he got out safe and sound and left his kids in there to drown." Bob shook his head and anger glinted in eyes that had seen far too much.

Colt stared at him, aghast. "I don't believe it! Nobody would do something like that! They're his kids, for Christ's sake! His fucking *kids*!"

"We made some calls," Bob said quietly, ignoring Colt's outburst. "Adamson's in the middle of a messy divorce. Yesterday, the court gave his wife custody."

Colt gasped. The shaft of pain that went through him nearly doubled him over. "*Fuck, fuck, fuck!* You can't be serious! He meant to do this? He *meant* to do this!"

Bob regarded him with a sad and weary expression on his face. "There are no brake marks on the road, Colt. You figure it out."

———

Morgan checked her emails for the hundredth time and frowned when there was no more word from her father. She'd lost count of the number of times she'd wished he had a cell phone, but there was no point wasting time on that. He didn't have a cell and she had no way of contacting him, other than through emails – and even then, she was at the mercy of decent Wi-Fi service in the middle of the outback and the whim of her father as to when he might actually check his mail.

She'd sent another email the moment she got back to Colt's place. She'd told her father about her discovery and pleaded with him to tell her why he'd lied about Rusty. She finished the message with her cell number and an impassioned plea for him to call. She needed to hear his voice.

But that was hours ago and she still hadn't heard a thing. She wished Colt wasn't at work. She needed someone to distract her from the endless questions that circled around her mind.

A feeling of helplessness surged through her. No matter how much she willed it to happen, there was nothing she could do. Her father would check his emails when it suited him, or when he had a decent Internet signal. His next contact could be a day or more away, depending where he was.

The sound of her phone ringing sent her heart leaping into her throat. *It was her dad! He'd finally received her message!* She snatched up the phone from where she'd left it on the kitchen counter and stared down at the screen. And just like that, she was deflated. It wasn't her father. It was Colt.

"Hi," she said, her tone dull.

"Hey," he said, his voice equally subdued.

"How are you doing?" she asked, remembering

her manners. It wasn't his fault she'd been waiting all day to hear from her father.

"Good. No. Not good… The truth is, since I dropped you back at home, my day's gone to shit."

His voice was raw with emotion. Morgan pushed her own troubles aside. Something was wrong and it sounded like Colt needed her.

"What happened?" she asked quietly and heard his heavy sigh.

"A car accident. It's not good."

"Fatalities?" she asked gently.

"Two kids."

"Oh, no! Colt! How dreadful! I'm so sorry!"

"Yeah. Me too."

"How terrible for you to have to deal with that."

"Hey, I'm a cop. It's what I do."

"Yes, but you're still human. Is there anything I can do?"

"No. I'm calling because I don't think I can face going out to dinner tonight."

"That's fine," she hastened to reassure him. "We don't have to go out. I can throw together something here. Don't worry about it."

"You hate cooking," he said and she detected the faintest sound of a smile.

"I don't hate it. It just isn't something I enjoy enough for it to take precedence over other things. Like cutting my toenails."

This time, he laughed and the sound of it warmed her through. She was pleased she'd been able to lighten his mood, even for a little while.

"What time will you be home?" she asked softly.

"I'm aiming for seven, but who knows? We're still interviewing witnesses, including other members of the family. It could be awhile."

"No problem. Don't worry, I'll have dinner ready whenever you get here."

"Thanks, Morgan. I owe you."

The warmth in his tone sent a glow of contentment rushing through her veins. With another reassurance for him to not concern himself about her, she ended the call.

CHAPTER 11

It was closer to eight than seven when Morgan heard Colt's key in the door. He entered the condo slowly, tiredly, as if he carried the weight of the world. His face was drawn and lined with fatigue. His eyes were dull.

Her heart went out to him. She couldn't imagine what the past few hours had been like. Two children dead. Relatives to console. Scattered fragments of the story to piece together. Questions asked. Answers given. Reports to be prepared. She believed being a police officer was one of the hardest jobs in the world. She admired him and all the other officers who did this every day.

"How did you do?" she asked softly, unfurling herself from the couch. She came toward him, intending to offer him comfort in whatever way she could.

His sigh was deep and heavy. Setting his briefcase on the kitchen counter, he went straight for the fridge and pulled out a beer. The sharp crack of the can opening filled the silence.

"I made some dinner," she murmured.

"Thanks," he replied, but she could tell food was the last thing on his mind.

"Do you want to talk about it?" she asked.

He was silent for so long, she didn't think he was going to answer. And then, he cursed under his breath. His eyes turned hard with anger.

"He did it on purpose, Morgan. The fucking prick did it on purpose! He murdered his own children! And the worst part is, he did it out of spite!" He rounded on her. His eyes burned with fury, his expression was fierce, but she held her ground. He was angry, but his anger wasn't directed at her.

"Can you *believe* it?" he continued, his volume increasing along with his fury.

It was a rhetorical question, but she answered him anyway. "No, I can't believe it. How about you tell me what happened? I'd like to know."

With another curse, he pushed away from the counter and began to prowl the modest space between the kitchen table and the couch.

"Anthony Adamson. What a hero!" Colt said, his voice filled with sarcasm. "The bastard had it all planned out, right down to the last second. The only thing was, at the last minute, he chickened out."

"What do you mean?" she said quietly.

"The plan was to drive into the river with him and his kids in the car. He intended for all of them to drown, but at the last minute, he couldn't do it – to himself, that is. As the car filled with water, he panicked and got himself free. The fucking coward swam to safety and left his kids to drown. They were strapped into their fucking car seats, Morgan. Their fucking *car seats!*"

His voice cracked with emotion and his eyes flashed once again with anger. Morgan stood nearby, frozen in shock, unable to comprehend how any parent could do such a thing. It was beyond belief, beyond explanation. It was the most horrible thing she'd ever heard. How anyone could do that to their innocent children... The thought defied belief.

"How... How old were they?" she whispered.

"The little boy was two-and-a-half. The baby was barely six months." He turned toward her, his eyes tortured, his face ravaged with fury and pain. "They didn't stand a chance, Morgan. They didn't stand a chance..." His shoulders slumped with defeat. He shook his head slowly back and forth, beyond words.

Without thinking, Morgan stepped forward and put her arms around his waist. Her only thought was to offer him comfort. He tensed momentarily, but then pulled her hard against his chest. He dropped his head to her shoulder and continued to pour out his distress.

"The cowardly bastard... No words can describe it... *How could he?* How could he swim away from that vehicle, knowing his children were locked inside? And then he had the audacity to tell us it was an accident, that he lost control of his car. That he hadn't meant to go through the fence and into the river. That it wasn't his fault..."

Morgan tightened her arms about him. When she spoke again, her voice was muffled against his chest. "How did you discover the truth?"

Colt lifted his head off her shoulder and stared down at her, as if only just becoming aware that they were holding each other. Dropping his arms to his sides, he released her and took a couple of steps back. Retrieving his beer from where he'd left it on the counter, he emptied it in just a few swallows and then cleared his throat, his composure restored.

"There was a witness to the accident. A man traveling behind Anthony Adamson's car. He saw the whole thing happen, including the fact Adamson didn't apply the brakes."

Morgan's breath caught in horror. "He didn't try to stop?"

Colt's lips thinned. "No, he didn't."

"Perhaps there was something mechanical at fault? Do you think that's possible?"

"It's always possible, but not this time. We made inquiries. Discovered Adamson was in the middle of a nasty divorce and the court had just awarded his wife the kids. In light of the evidence against him, Adamson finally broke down and confessed. He told us he meant for all of them to die – he was meant to die, too. Only, he got scared when the car filled with water and the cowardly bastard got himself out."

"Oh, Colt!" Morgan was devastated all over again.

The depth of evil that resided in some people's souls never ceased to amaze her. The thought of someone murdering their children as payback to the other parent was beyond abhorrent. She didn't know how society could begin to punish a person capable of such selfishness and depravity. *Was it even possible? Did the man even have an inkling of the evil he'd done?*

"How is he?" she asked, her voice rough with emotion.

"Adamson?"

"Yes. Has he expressed any remorse?"

Colt shook his head and his shoulders slumped on a weary sigh. "Not enough. Oh, he's sorry, but I got the distinct impression he's sorrier about facing a lengthy jail sentence than the fact his kids are dead. He ought to be paralytic with grief, beside himself with the horror of what he's done – and the sad truth is, he's not. No doubt it'll be a different story when it comes to fronting the courts and when the cameras are out in force."

She nodded grimly. It was amazing how sorry people could be when confronted with a healthy prison term. Too bad it wouldn't bring Anthony Adamson's children back. She couldn't bear to think how their mother was feeling.

With another sigh, Colt tossed the empty beer can into the recycling box that stood in the corner of the kitchen. He reached into the fridge and pulled out another and then paused. He glanced at Morgan.

"Would you like one?"

"No, thanks. I'm good. I'm not much of a beer drinker."

He nodded. "White wine, right?"

"Yes, I guess so. Or vodka. You can't beat a decent vodka martini."

"Shaken, not stirred, right?" The tiniest grin tugged at the corners of his mouth.

Morgan smiled back at him. "Right."

It was much later when Colt agreed to have something to eat and Morgan heated up bowls of spaghetti bolognaise. They ate together on the sofa, like they had in Morgan's college days. Back then, it had been out of necessity. Neither Colt nor Beau had owned a kitchen table, but tonight, after the trauma of the day, it seemed more comfortable to relax on the couch.

Colt set his empty bowl on the coffee table and sat back. He sighed quietly and looked at Morgan. "How did you do with your father? Did he explain about his dog?"

Morgan swallowed her last bite of spaghetti and shook her head. "No, he hasn't replied to my email yet." Colt frowned and Morgan hurried to explain.

"He's out in the middle of nowhere. He only has sporadic Internet service. He's got an old laptop and a dongle. It's fine to use in the city and towns, but in the outback... Who knows? And public phone booths are few and far between."

She shrugged. "I'm sure he has an explanation. No doubt he was trying to spare me the upset and worry, and he's right. Losing Rusty is upsetting. It was bound to happen someday, but he was only ten. I didn't expect it to be so soon. I'm totally unprepared. It's different when you have an old dog that's near the end of his life. You brace yourself for it to happen. It's the way life is. But Rusty..." She shook her head.

"I gave him that dog after Mom died. Rusty was only a puppy. Dad needed a distraction and Rusty was only too happy to steal his attention as often and for as long as he could. He grew up faithful and loyal. He was always by Dad's side. Dad knew I'd feel relieved knowing he had Rusty with him. I guess that's why he lied."

Colt nodded in understanding, but his expression remained grim. He opened his mouth and then closed it, as if unsure whether he should speak. Morgan set her bowl down on the coffee table and frowned.

"What is it, Colt?"

His lips compressed into a thin line and once again, he appeared to be debating about what to say. She sat forward on the couch and stared at him.

"What do you know? I can tell you know something I don't."

Colt's gaze remained steady on hers. A moment later, he blew out his breath. "All right, I'll tell you, but only because I want you to be safe. There's something about your uncle that concerns me."

Morgan's frown deepened. She shook her head in confusion. "Concerns you? In what way?"

"I'm not sure. That's why I wasn't going to say anything, but it's obvious how much you love your dad. I think you have a right to know."

Morgan's confusion deepened. "Know what?"

Colt drew in another deep breath. "Rusty didn't die of old age. He was shot."

Shock ricocheted through Morgan. She gasped and her hand came up to her mouth. "He was...shot? Are you sure?"

"Yes. I saw the bullet hole in his skull. There's no mistake."

Morgan's mind whirled with so many questions, she couldn't think straight. *Who would kill her father's dog?* She couldn't imagine her dad had done it. He loved Rusty almost as much as he loved her. There was no way he would have done such a thing.

But the dog was buried at the back of her dad's place. Her father must have known about it... So why had he lied and said Rusty was with him in the outback? So much didn't make sense.

"I couldn't tell if the dog was ill – did your father say anything about that? That Rusty was suffering from a terminal illness? That he might have to put him to sleep?"

Morgan was shaking her head from side to side before Colt was even finished. "No! No, of course not! He never mentioned a thing! We haven't spoken for quite a while. The first time he mentioned Rusty was in the email I received last night."

"When he emailed you and lied about having the dog with him," Colt finished. "The question is, was it your father who sent the email and if so, why would he mislead you?"

Morgan frowned. "Of course my father sent the email. It came from his account."

Colt's gaze remained steady on hers. "Who else has his login details?"

Morgan stared at him, her thoughts in a whirl. "No one that I know of. What are you getting at?"

Colt shrugged. "I'm just throwing up possibilities. You're at a loss to understand why your father wouldn't tell you the truth about Rusty. You're relying on the fact you were advised by your father that the dog was with him. All I'm saying is that it might be possible it came from someone else."

"You mean, someone else could have written that email? How could that be? Dad was a lawyer. He knew all about confidentiality. I can't imagine he'd ever disclose his login details – and certainly not to one of his friends. It doesn't make sense." She slumped back against the couch, her thoughts too jumbled to interpret.

"What about to your uncle? Is it possible your dad gave his login details to his brother?"

Morgan stared at him. "I doubt it. He'd only just met the man. Is that what you meant when you said you think this might have something to do with my uncle?"

Colt's nod came reluctantly. "After discovering Rusty had been shot, I decided to do a little investigating into Leslie's background. It's obvious he's a drifter who's been down on his luck more than once. I was curious about him. So I ran his name through the police database."

Morgan's heart skipped a beat. After all, what did she really know about her father's twin? "Did it come up with anything?"

"Yes, but nothing important. A minor assault more than a decade ago. It was dealt with by way of a fine. Like I said, it was nothing."

"Oh, I guess that's a good thing."

"Yes, but I must admit, I was expecting more. There's something about him... I've been a cop a long time. You get a sense of people... This time, it didn't pan out."

Something caught in Morgan's memory. She frowned. "What name did you use?"

Colt turned to face her. "What do you mean?"

"I mean, when you put his details into the system, what name did you use?"

"Leslie O'Brien. I guessed him to be somewhere in his late fifties or early sixties. It helped to eliminate a few others."

She pursed her lips. "He's fifty-five, actually, the same age as my father. But his name's not Leslie O'Brien. At least, it didn't used to be. He told me he recently changed it. He used to be Leslie Lexington."

Colt's eyes narrowed and she could almost see the thoughts running through his head. Leslie Lexington might very well have the criminal background he sensed. The thought sobered her.

Still, it didn't change the fact he was her uncle and the identical twin brother of her dad. Though shocked at the discovery, her father's email had reassured her he was happy to have Leslie in his life. It didn't sound like he had any reservations, especially not the kind Colt had. *Unless the emails hadn't come from her dad...*

"What are you going to do?" she murmured.

"I'm going to run another criminal history check. I want to be certain this guy is who he says he is."

"Of *course* he's who he says he is. He looks just like my dad! Nobody could fake that, not for all the plastic surgery in the world and he doesn't look like someone who could afford surgery. Besides, why would he pretend to be someone he isn't? Dad might be comfortable in his retirement, but he's not a millionaire. You'd think if Leslie was targeting someone, he'd make sure it was worth his while."

Colt looked thoughtful. "Yes, you're right. Still, I'm going to follow it up, if for no other reason than to reassure myself that I can still rely on my gut."

All of a sudden she was tired of Colt's conspiracy theories. A surge of impatience rushed through her. Leslie Lexington was her uncle. There was no denying it. She pushed away from the couch.

"And what if you do find something?" she cried. "What difference does it make? It won't change the fact he's my father's brother, the only other blood relative I have."

Colt regarded her steadily, his expression remaining calm. "You're right. It won't make any difference to that, but I'm a cop. I need to know the truth. I need to know if someone's hiding something because the next question will be why. Nobody does anything in isolation. There's always a cause and effect. For every action there's an equal and opposite reaction. Basic physics, right?"

His grin pulled up the sides of his mouth, but failed to reach his eyes. Morgan stared at him, unconvinced, her lips set in a mutinous line. And then, just as suddenly as it had erupted, the anger went out of her. *What did it matter if Colt poked around a little?* He was a cop. It was what he did. She didn't really have a problem with that.

"I'm sorry," she said quietly and regained her place beside him on the couch. "I didn't mean to shout at you. I'm just anxious about Dad. This whole thing is weirding me out – no birthday or anniversary call, a twin brother I never knew he had, and now Rusty... I need Dad to call me, or at the least, email me back."

Colt held her gaze. "I get it, Morgan. I do. And I wish there was some way I could help. You said last night he was at Tennant Creek. I could call the local police station and ask them to take a look around. If he's still there, they might be able to find him and tell him to give you a call. Do you know what kind of vehicle he's driving?"

Morgan was filled with a surge of hope. "Yes, of course! A white Ford Ranger. A 2015 model."

Colt nodded. "Okay, I'll see what I can do. It's a fairly common kind of pickup, but you never know. He's traveling on his own. In the outback, most people don't – especially not tourists. That kind of thing stands out. Someone might have noticed."

Morgan could barely contain her excitement. She grabbed hold of Colt's hand. "Do you think so? Do you think the police might be able to find my dad?"

She watched Colt stare down at the place where their hands touched and all of a sudden, she was filled with a rush of warmth. Awareness shot through her and just like that, tension filled the air. Their earlier embrace came rushing back and her heart thumped double time.

His cologne, fresh and clean and woodsy, filled her nostrils. He must have showered before he left work. A pulse fluttered in his neck. The blue of his irises darkened to almost black. Her lips parted on the tiniest breath and heat flared in his eyes. She leaned forward, trance-like, and touched her mouth to his.

He tasted cold and yeasty, with a splash of spaghetti sauce thrown in. The five o'clock shadow on his cheeks and chin tickled her skin. She kissed him again, softly, curiously, needing more. And then it was over.

He pulled away and turned aside and it was like he'd doused her in a barrel of ice water. She gasped and tried to catch her breath. Her cheeks burned like they were on fire. She'd kissed him in a wordless promise that offered everything and more and he'd turned her down. Again. *Did it get any more humiliating?*

"I'm sorry, Morgan. It's me, not you."

"Oh, please," she scoffed in an effort to hide her embarrassment. "Don't give me that lame old line."

His gaze was filled with turmoil. A spurt of satisfaction went through her. At least he felt something.

"It's true," he said quietly, his eyes pleading with her to understand. "We want different things, Morgan. You want a husband, a family. You're ready to settle down. I don't know that I'll ever be in that place. And after today, after witnessing the horror of just how wrong marriages can go, I'm even more certain I don't ever want to go down that path."

Morgan shook her head, aghast at the thought. "You can't possibly think you could drown your children, just because your marriage fell apart? You're nothing like that man! You're good and kind and—"

"How do you know?" he interrupted, his voice harsh with emotion. "When they were in love, before they had those kids, could she have seen his weakness? Was it even there then, or did they change? How do any of us know what we're capable of?"

She stared at him and her heart filled with sadness and regret. The awful events of the day were still too fresh. This wasn't the time to reason with him. She got that. Swallowing a sigh, she got to her feet.

In silence, she collected the dirty dishes and headed for the kitchen.

Chapter 12

Colt stared at the blank computer screen in front of him and cursed under his breath. For the past hour, he'd been trying to complete the paperwork on Anthony Adamson's arrest. The man had been brought before the courts earlier that morning.

Given the circumstances of his arrest, most people assumed he'd be on suicide watch, but according to the corrections officers the prisoner was behaving normally and so far, his behavior behind bars hadn't raised any concerns. Adamson had been refused bail and for that, Colt was grateful. It meant that the hordes of media camped outside the police station could finally disperse. They wouldn't be getting camera shots or a sound bite from Adamson anytime soon.

Unbidden, Colt's thoughts turned to Morgan and her certainty the night before that a nasty divorce could never result in him murdering his children. He'd done some digging on Adamson's background. The man was employed in middle management in a local insurance broker's firm. He was liked and respected by his peers. In the ten years he'd worked there, no one had ever heard him raise his voice. Every person Colt spoke to expressed shock and disbelief that their friend and coworker could have done such a thing.

And yet, he had.

Whether it was the stress from his marriage breakdown, or something else, this normally calm and mild-mannered executive snapped and in that instant, made the fatal decision to drown his children. The horror and sadness of it was overwhelming, but despite Morgan's assurances, it was like Colt had said: How could anyone know how they'd react if placed in similar circumstances?

He wanted to shake his head in adamant denial. There was no way he could contemplate such a thing. Children were the innocent victims when a marriage fell apart. They weren't pawns to be bargained for, or worse, stolen from the other parent.

Colt understood how excruciating it might be for a man to love his children so deeply and have to come to terms with the fact a court decided they were best off with his estranged wife, especially if he no longer thought she was the best person to raise them, or worse, that she was vindictive and malicious enough to turn them against him.

That was Adamson's argument. He told Colt his wife had already spread lies about him to his kids. 'They were only babies! Too young to know wrong from right! Too young to be able to separate her lies from the truth.' He'd believed he'd lose them anyway, and just as surely as if they'd died. In fact, he claimed they'd be better off dead than be filled with the poisonous words issued by his ex.

Adamson's explanation only made Colt feel even more sad and depressed. There were no winners here. Not Adamson, not his ex and certainly not their kids. The whole tragic scenario only reinforced his opinion that when a marriage went off the rails, it left everyone devastated.

He wasn't obtuse enough to accept that all marriages ended in divorce, but the stats were there for all to see and they were damning. He was sure not a single one of his buddies who'd gone through a broken marriage had, on the day they stood before the altar with their bride, thought things might end that way. And yet they did. Over and over again. He didn't know why and that was just as frightening. He couldn't avoid the same pitfalls if he didn't understand what caused things to fall apart.

He wished he weren't so jaded. With all his heart, he wished that things were different. That he could look to a future filled with love and laughter with the girl he'd chosen for his wife, like his mom and dad and so many other couples of that generation.

What was it about those people? What did they have that younger generations didn't – that allowed them to stick things out and make their marriages work? He thought of beautiful, sweet

Morgan and the kisses they'd shared and wished he knew.

He left for work early that morning, before she surfaced from her room. He hadn't spoken to her since the night before. He thought she'd appreciate his forthrightness, but she hadn't seen it that way. She'd stacked the dirty bowls and utensils in the dishwasher in silence and with a muttered goodnight tossed in his general direction, had headed off for bed.

With a sigh, Colt pulled the keyboard toward him and signed into the police database. As much as he wanted to push thoughts of Morgan O'Brien out of his mind, the whole situation with her uncle still intrigued him. He'd been surprised and disappointed to discover the man had nothing much on his record. Now, knowing he'd changed his name a short time ago, the game had completely changed. Right from the outset, his cop radar had sensed there was much more to Leslie O'Brien – aka Leslie Lexington – than met the eye. It was time to prove himself right.

Typing in the name Leslie Lexington, Colt waited, a little on edge. Fortunately, he didn't have to wait long. Only two Leslie Lexingtons were in the system and one of them was a woman. The other one fit O'Brien's profile – height and weight and date of birth all checked out. Better still, there were several mug shots, taken over the course of Lexington's life. It was obvious Colt had found the right one.

The first photo was taken when Lexington was just fourteen. Though crimes committed when the offender was a child couldn't be used against them as an adult, the records remained on the database for any investigator to see. From the string of entries under Lexington's name, it was clear he'd started on his life of crime at an early age.

The adult offenses were just as lengthy. Most of them were for theft, break and enter and assaults. There were only minor drug convictions recorded, which was a little surprising considering there were at least two dozen different addresses listed in Lexington's profile. Every time he was charged, he'd been residing somewhere new. In Colt's experience, that kind of transient lifestyle often indicated drug abuse. Often, drugs took over, to the exclusion of everything else. Rents went unpaid, tenants were evicted and the whole sorry situation repeated itself over and over again.

But Lexington didn't appear to have a drug problem, so it was something else that had caused his transient lifestyle. Colt studied the information on his screen a little more closely and all of a sudden, he was pretty sure he knew what it was.

Among the assaults and break and enters, he found a number of fraud offenses. Nothing too serious – most had only resulted in jail terms of six or twelve months. But each time a fraud offense occurred, Lexington offered a new address. Colt guessed if the man were stealing from an employer or a friend or colleague, upon its discovery, he'd be forced to relocate.

Pursing his lips together, Colt contemplated his discovery. It gave him a certain grim kind of satisfaction to discover his instincts had been right. Leslie Lexington was a career criminal who'd been in trouble with the law from an early age. Now Colt was faced with the issue of whether or not to tell Morgan, and if so, how much to tell.

The night before, when he'd raised the issue that her uncle might not be all that he seemed, she hadn't reacted favorably. It was obvious she was a little sensitive about her family, especially – as she'd quite rightly pointed out – there was no way Leslie wasn't her father's twin.

Still, the extensive criminal history that stared back at him wasn't something he could easily dismiss. The man probably wasn't dangerous, despite the handful of assaults, but there was no denying he was dishonest and frequently willing to break the law. Not exactly the kind of man most people wanted to spend time with, or allow to get too close. It made him uncomfortable thinking Morgan might very well want to do that.

As far as she was concerned, the guy was her long lost uncle – the prodigal brother returned. Even her father had encouraged her to think of her uncle that way. Colt couldn't help but wonder if Rex O'Brien knew anything about his brother's shady past. Surely not, or he wouldn't have been so quick to encourage his daughter to accept her uncle into her life.

And now he'd apparently gone off on some trip to find himself, or at least to contemplate his life, and his daughter had been left to sort things out on her own, including how she felt about her new uncle.

No, Colt sensed it was up to him to help her navigate the murky waters that were Leslie O'Brien. Morgan needed to know there was more and possibly less to the man than met the eye and she needed to be on her guard, even a little. With his mind made up, he tugged out his cell and dialed her number. He was relieved when she answered after only a couple of rings.

"Colt, how are you doing? How is the day treating you?"

She sounded her normal cheery self and Colt was filled with relief. After the way they'd parted the night before, he wasn't sure what mood he'd find her in, but it was as if the morning had brought with it a clean slate. She didn't sound like she harbored any ill will.

"I'm doing fine, thanks. Tying up loose ends with the Adamson case and seeing to a few odds and ends. What about you?"

"I was just thinking about going to see my uncle again. I still haven't heard from Dad. I thought I might take the opportunity to get to know him a little better, while I can. I won't be able to hang around forever – I only took a fortnight's leave. I emailed Dad and told him I was on vacation and I'm hoping that news might bring him home sooner than he originally planned – if he had any plan."

Colt compressed his lips, wishing he had better news. He'd contacted the local Tennant Creek police as promised and they'd driven around the town. They'd made some inquiries at the local caravan parks and the few motels in town, but nobody fit Rex's description and no one remembered seeing him the night before. They'd hit a dead end. He told Morgan as much and listened to her disheartened sigh.

"Why won't he call me? Or at the very least, answer my emails?" she asked with a little catch in her voice.

Colt grimaced and wondered if now was a good time to tell her about her uncle. He wasn't sure if she could handle any more bad news. Still, she was heading over to see the man. It would be best if she knew the truth.

"I'm afraid I have something else to tell you that you're not going to like," he said.

Her voice grew wary. "What are you talking about?"

"It isn't about your dad. It's...Leslie O'Brien, aka Leslie Lexington."

"You found a criminal record. Is that what you're going to tell me?" Her tone was curt.

Colt took a deep breath and held on to his irritation. He'd done the search for *her*. He wanted her to know exactly who she was dealing with. Didn't she get that? Okay, he'd been curious about the guy too, and wanted to confirm what his gut told him, but his primary reasons had been for Morgan. All he'd been doing was looking out for her, like he would for any friend.

Except she was more than a friend – just like she had been in the past – and he knew it. The question was, what was he prepared to do about that?

Thrusting the irritating thoughts aside, he

answered her in a voice that remained deceptively calm. "Yes, I found his criminal record and it's quite extensive. He's spent much of his life in and out of prison. The majority of them are offenses of dishonesty, including several short prison terms for fraud. It makes me wonder what he's doing here, with your dad."

"We spoke about this last night, Colt!" she exploded. "You've seen his birthdate, right? Same as Dad's, I'm sure. Didn't you listen to a word I said? The man looks identical to my father. There's no way he could fake that. He's my uncle, my father's brother. Okay, he looks like he's grown up on the wrong side of the tracks. So what? He told me about his childhood. It wasn't pretty. That wasn't his fault."

"Nobody forced him to become a criminal," Colt pointed out calmly, refusing to back down.

"No, but until you've walked a mile in someone else's shoes, how do you know what you're capable of?"

The words were said quietly, in stark contrast to her earlier outburst. He also held that view about life and that view influenced his feelings about marriage. So, against his better judgment, but knowing he had no choice, he retreated. She wasn't in the right frame of mind to hear anything bad about her uncle. Colt could only hope she kept the knowledge of Leslie's criminality in the back of her mind the next time she came into contact with him.

"Do you need a ride to your uncle's?" he asked, hoping to ease the tension.

"You mean, my dad's," she replied, her voice dry.

"Yes, of course, your dad's place. I can swing by and pick you up. It would save you walking."

"Thanks, but I'm fine. It's a nice day out and it's not too far away. I'm looking forward to the walk."

"Okay, well, let me know if there's anything I can do," he said, unwilling to end the conversation. He enjoyed talking to her, looking out for her.

"Yes, I will. And if you're not busy later, I might get you to collect me afterwards. The walk home to your place will be mostly uphill."

He laughed and assured her he'd be happy to give her a ride whenever she was finished. All she had to do was phone. On that note, and with a smile still on his face, he ended the call.

CHAPTER 13

Leslie O'Brien stared at the emails that filled the inbox of his brother's mail program. A few were from businesses offering golfing supplies, magazine subscriptions and holidays, but the majority of them were from Morgan. Reading through them, he frowned. She was getting increasingly concerned and she kept going on and on about the stupid dog.

He cursed aloud, angry at himself for his sloppiness. He should never have buried the animal on the property. If he'd taken the dog to a dumpster, like he'd originally planned, Morgan would never have been the wiser. She would have accepted the explanation in her father's email that the dog was with him and would have gone on her merry way.

But at the last minute, Leslie had panicked. A lot of shops these days had security cameras around their back and front entrances. A dog with a bullet hole in his head would have attracted attention and Leslie would have been captured on camera dumping the body. If any of the shop owners had taken the footage to the police, he'd have been quickly identified and then the questions would have come at him faster than the time it took for him to formulate his lies.

It was a risk he hadn't been willing to take at the time, so he'd buried the dog down the back. And now the decision was coming back to bite him. He thought he'd planned it all so well and then Morgan had shown up. She'd thrown everything into disarray and had put his plan at risk.

It served him right for being so greedy. After being initially taken aback, Rex had welcomed him with open arms and a more than generous heart. But that welcome hadn't been enough and now Leslie was paying the price. He was being backed into a corner and had to do something to reassure Rex's daughter, to throw her off the scent.

Perhaps he could call her? He sounded enough like his brother that he could probably pull it off. But what if she asked him things and he didn't know the answers? A call could be fraught with danger and he probably didn't need to put himself at such a risk. No, better to stick with the emails. They seemed to be working well enough for now.

Pulling the laptop toward him, he shot off another email from her father, apologizing for not being upfront with her about Rusty and begging her forgiveness. The dog had been suffering from cancer. It had happened right before Christmas.

After what had happened to her mom, he hadn't wanted to tell her. Then it was her birthday and the anniversary of her mom's death. There didn't seem to be a good time. He was sorry. He should have simply told her. He hadn't meant to lie. *Blah, blah, blah.*

Leslie's fingers moved slowly over the keyboard, typing one letter at a time. He was careful to check the spelling. He was sure his learned brother wouldn't spell anything wrong.

I'm on my way to Darwin, the email continued. *Try not to worry. I'm perfectly fine on my own. I'll do my best to be back before you have to leave. Take care. I love you, Dad.*

Leslie re-read the message and satisfied, clicked on the send. He hoped it was enough to keep Morgan happy. Later in the week, he'd make sure Rex emailed his daughter explaining there was a delay in his plans. Perhaps he'd get caught in a monsoon and be flooded in. Of course he'd be fine, but he wouldn't be able to make it back home in time to see her. He'd be very sorry, but he'd catch her next time... And on and on.

It didn't really matter what excuse Leslie used. Anything to have Rex's daughter return to Sydney without too many more concerns. Leslie needed her gone to put his final plans into action. Leslie O'Brien would cease to exist and in his place, Rex would return.

A knock on the door startled him from his musings. Looking over his shoulder, he could see the outline of a woman standing on the porch.

The knock came again, and this time the unexpected visitor called out his name.

"Uncle Leslie? Are you home?"

Morgan was just about to knock on the door for the third time when it opened. Her uncle greeted her with a smile.

"Morgan! What an unexpected surprise! Please, come in!"

Once again, she was taken aback by his resemblance to her father. She wondered if she'd ever get used to it. Today he wore a white polo shirt and a pair of navy slacks. The clothes looked suspiciously like her father's.

Not that it mattered. It had been obvious Uncle Leslie was down on his luck and she was certain her dad wouldn't mind. He'd always had a generous heart and would be the first one to encourage his brother to make himself at home, even if that meant borrowing a few of his clothes.

Her uncle stepped back to allow her to enter and Morgan caught a whiff of his cologne. It was the same one her dad used. *Or maybe it was her dad's?* Once again, she couldn't help but wonder.

She walked into the open-concept living and dining room and dropped her handbag on the table. Looking around her, she took in the familiar surroundings. The leather recliner where her dad liked to sit in the evening and watch TV. She'd often sit beside him in the matching armchair. The bookshelf that contained her mother's collection of Royal Doulton figurines. There they were, grouped together like they had been for many years. Except...a couple were missing.

Morgan frowned and moved closer. Yes, there were definitely two missing. A woman in a beautiful crimson ball gown with cream-colored overlay and another woman in pale blue, lifting the skirt of her dress to show her white petticoats beneath. There were even clear spots amidst the dust on the bookshelf, showing where the statutes used to be.

She wondered where they were. There was no way her father would have gotten rid of them. Every single one of her mother's collectibles remained where they'd always been, scattered throughout the house. He'd told her once that seeing them helped him feel close to her and after all, what would he do with them? They'd belong to Morgan when he died.

Her gaze continued to wander around the room. Her father's writing desk stood underneath the window on the wall opposite the TV. If he wasn't watching one of his favorite shows, he was often on his computer. She noted the laptop was in its usual spot on the desk. The lid was down, but the power was connected. She could see a blue flashing light at the front.

Something stirred in her memory and she frowned, trying to figure out what it was.

"Would you like a cup of tea or coffee? I can put the jug on."

Uncle Leslie's query interrupted her train of thought. She turned to face him and offered him a smile. "That would be lovely. I'll have tea, thanks."

"Black, no sugar, right?"

She smiled wider, pleased he'd remembered. "You have a good memory," she said.

He gave her a wink before turning away and heading toward the kitchen. She heard him whistling as he went. Intent on offering him her assistance, she started off after him.

"Have you heard from your father lately?" her uncle called from the other room.

"Yes, he emailed me the night before last. He was at Tennant Creek. I emailed him back and asked him about Rusty, but I haven't heard from him since then."

She walked into the kitchen where her uncle was filling the electric jug. "I checked earlier this morning, but there was nothing. I can only assume he doesn't have any Internet service. Whatever possessed him to head off into the outback with no way of staying in regular contact, defies common sense!"

Her uncle chuckled and set the jug to boil. "I'm sure he's fine. He'll contact you when he can. He won't want you to worry and he knows you will."

Morgan nodded grimly. "Yes. I made it very clear the last time I emailed him that he needs to call me. I—"

Morgan stopped mid-sentence and frowned. She'd emailed off her iPad. Her father had the laptop. The laptop she'd given him. But...the laptop was sitting on the writing desk in the living room.

Dread swirled in her stomach and her heart took off in a rush. *What was her dad's laptop doing in the living room? Surely he'd taken it with him? How else was he sending her emails?* He hadn't said anything about using public computers. She'd just assumed he had his own. She looked up at her uncle who was busy loading a tea tray.

"Uncle Leslie, why didn't Dad take his laptop? I just realized it's still here. I don't understand how he's been emailing me all this time. Do you know anything about it?"

Her uncle frowned in thought. "I'm not sure, honey. He didn't mention it to me, but he did leave in kind of a hurry. I guess the shock and all of having me suddenly appear... Perhaps he bought another one somewhere along the way? Or some other fancy gizmo – what do they call them? A tablet? That's it! What a strange name for a device that works pretty much like a computer." He shook his head. "I wouldn't know one end from the other. Can't say I've ever had much use for them."

"No, no. Dad wouldn't have bought a tablet. Not so long ago, I wanted to get him an iPad. He wouldn't hear of it. Said he was happy doing things the old-fashioned way, from his laptop. He knew his way around it and didn't want to have to spend time learning something new."

Dread continued to fill her stomach. She couldn't imagine her father heading into an Internet café just so that he could check his emails – and that was only if there were such places in the outback. She'd never been, but from what she'd seen on television, the towns out there weren't overrun with technology. Perhaps that was the reason his emails were so few and far between?

She blew out her breath on a heavy sigh. There were too many questions and no answers. It was *Groundhog Day* all over again. The situation was doing her head in. She felt so helpless, sitting around, waiting for him to call, to email, to reassure her everything was all right...

"Right, the tea's made. Let's go and enjoy a cup."

Her uncle's announcement interrupted her thoughts and she forced them to the back of her mind. Following him out of the kitchen, she once again took a seat at the dining room table and accepted a cup of tea.

Her handbag sat where she left it. The corner of her iPad peeked out of the open compartment where she'd stored her wallet, tissues, lip gloss and a myriad of other things. It drew her eye over and over, urging her to open it.

She glanced at her uncle who sat across from her and wondered if it would be rude to check her email again. Yes, of course it would. She'd come over to spend time with him, to get to know him better. After all, he was family. Dragging her gaze away from the temptation her handbag afforded, she gave him a friendly smile.

"Thank you for the tea. It's lovely."

"No problem, honey. Try some banana cake. It

was fresh from the bakery the day before. I'm sure it's still good."

"Yes, Moxons. I remember." She leaned across and picked up a piece of cake. It smelled delicious. She took a bite. It tasted as good as it smelled.

"Tell me a little bit more about your life, Uncle. I know you did it hard. I'm sorry your adoptive parents weren't kinder. I'd really like to hear how you fared. Did you finish high school? Go to college?"

Her uncle chuckled softly and set down his cup of tea. "My, you ask a lot of questions!"

Morgan looked down, embarrassed. "I'm sorry, I don't mean to be nosy, but you're my father's brother, the only family I have. You look so much like him, it makes me feel like I know you and then I remember I don't know very much about you at all." She shrugged and continued on, her voice gentle. "You've hinted at a tough life and Colt told me you'd spent time in jail... I don't care about that, Uncle. As far as I'm concerned, that's all in the past. You're here now and I'd like to get to you know better."

Her uncle regarded her solemnly and Morgan wondered if she'd said too much. Perhaps she shouldn't have mentioned the fact she knew about his record? Still, he'd told her the day before that life hadn't always treated him kindly. It hadn't been too much of a stretch at the time to imagine that might mean a run-in or two with the law.

He continued to stare at her. His lips had thinned and tension lines had appeared around his mouth. She was upset at the thought she might have shamed him when she mentioned his time in jail and she hurried to reassure him again.

"I'm sorry, Uncle Leslie. I shouldn't have said anything about your past. It's none of my business. I'm just glad you're here. We have plenty of time to get to know each other. It doesn't have to be right now. I—"

"It's all right, Morgan," he interrupted, his tone mild. "I'm far from proud of my history, but I have nothing to hide. I'll tell you whatever it is you want to know, but first, will you please check your email? You haven't stopped looking at your handbag since we sat down. I'm assuming you brought the device that will allow you to check your mail?"

Morgan ducked her head, embarrassed. Heat crept up her cheeks. She hadn't realized she'd been so obvious with her furtive glances toward her bag.

"Thanks, Uncle. Yes, I have my iPad. I can also check them on my phone. I just prefer to do it on my iPad. The screen's bigger and I can type faster. Are you sure you don't mind? It won't take a second. I promise, if there's nothing from Dad, I'll close it right up and we can get back to where we were."

Her uncle smiled indulgently. "Take all the time you need. I'll sit here and enjoy my tea."

———

Leslie watched Rex's daughter pull a tablet from her handbag and quickly set it up in front of her. He couldn't see the screen from where he was sitting, but he didn't need to. He'd composed the email less than thirty minutes earlier. He knew exactly what it said.

Her confession that her cop friend had confirmed his criminal record had startled him, even though he shouldn't have been surprised. Cops seemed to have the ability to sense a criminal in their midst. It was the same with other criminals. They all seemed to know when they were in the company of someone who'd done time. He was no different.

He'd have to be extra vigilant and watch everything he said. Morgan had told her father she was only in town for two weeks. Two weeks. That's how long he had to keep his lies straight and not raise anyone's suspicions, particularly the cop's.

Cops were bad news. They saw beyond the façade. They saw things nobody else did. A nosy cop could undo him and ruin all his plans. He wouldn't let it happen. There was no way he was giving up his new life.

Morgan gasped in surprise and pleasure and he guessed she'd found the email from her father.

"What is it?" he asked, keeping up the pretense.

"It's Dad! He's finally responded to my messages! He says he's sorry for not telling me about Rusty and that everything is fine. He's on his way to Darwin, but he's going to try and get home before I leave."

She looked up at him with eyes that shone with

relief. Leslie tamped down a surge of guilt and forced a smile.

"That's great, honey. I'm glad he's doing okay. Now you can put your mind at ease and not be so worried all the time. He's a big boy. He knows how to look after himself. He'll be home before you know it."

Leslie offered her another reassuring smile and picked up the pot of tea. "Now, would you like a refill before I regale you with a few more of the ups and downs of my life?"

CHAPTER 14

Colt glanced at the clock on the wall and stretched out in his seat. His shift was almost over and he had yet to hear from Morgan. She'd told him she was spending the day with her uncle. She was supposed to call him for a ride home. He'd just tugged out his phone, intent on phoning her, when the device rang in his hand. He glanced at the screen and smiled.

"Mom, how are you doing?"

"I'm well thanks, Colt. You're sounding rather cheery. I take it you had a good day at work?"

"Yeah, I guess. The truth is, I thought you were someone else." The moment the words were out of his mouth, he wished them back. He grimaced and hoped his mother wouldn't notice his slip. He should have known better.

"*Really?*" she asked, the single word full of emphasis and innuendo. "Do I know her?"

Colt bit back a curse. His mother wouldn't let it go until she had an answer. He decided to go with the truth.

"Yes, as a matter of fact, you do. Morgan O'Brien's back in town. She's paying her father a visit."

"Morgan O'Brien? As in the college girl you dated back when you were still in the Academy?"

"Yes, Mom. That's the one."

"You seemed to really like her, Colt. I never understood why things didn't work out. Even though you didn't go out for very long, I had a sense she was the one. I was very put out to discover my mom radar was so far out of kilter. You never did tell me why things didn't work out."

"And I'm not about to tell you now. That's all in the past, Mom."

"And yet, you were expecting her call. I'm very intrigued, Colt. It seems to me there's more to this than you're saying."

Colt suppressed a groan. "Stop making this into something it's not, Mom. Morgan and I are old friends. That's it."

"Well, good," his mom replied. "Invite her to the anniversary party we're holding on the weekend. It would be lovely to see her again and I'm sure your brothers and sisters would feel the same way. I seem to recall she met everyone once at a family barbecue. Yes, that's right. It was a New Year's Eve party. We held it in the backyard. Do you remember?"

"Yes, Mom. I remember," Colt replied through gritted teeth. *How the hell had he gotten himself here?* As quickly as he could manage, he extricated himself from the conversation and ended the call.

Before he could return the phone to his pocket, it rang again. Tensing, and anticipating being on the receiving end of yet another conversation with his mom, he answered the call with a brusque, "Yes?"

"Oh, h-hi, it's Morgan. Have I caught you at a bad time? It's all right. I can find my own way home. I'll just call a cab and—"

"Morgan, I'm sorry," Colt hurriedly interrupted, gathering his thoughts. "My mind was on something else."

"It's okay, Colt. You're busy. I'll call a cab."

"No," he cried. "Don't go doing that. I'm almost finished here. I'll swing by and pick you up. You're at your father's place, right?"

"Yes, but only come by if you're free. I don't want to put you out."

"Of course you're not putting me out," he protested. "Like I said, I was just finishing up."

"Okay, that would be good. Thanks."

He could hear the gratitude in her voice. He smiled. It felt good to be needed. "How about we go out to dinner tonight? I'm sure neither of us feels like cooking."

She chuckled. "You're right there. We could always go to the Pink Pub."

"Sounds like a plan. I'll be there shortly."

"So, how was your day?" Colt asked, taking a sip from his beer. It was cold and refreshing after the hot day.

Morgan set down her wineglass and acknowledged his question with a nod. After a quick shower at his condo, they were enjoying pre-dinner drinks at the Wicklow bar, while waiting for a table to come free.

"It was pretty good, actually. After reading Dad's email, I calmed down a lot and enjoyed the time I spent with my uncle." Her expression grew sad. "He had a terrible childhood, Colt. His adoptive parents were horrible. They wanted a girl and they got him. They never let him forget he wasn't their first choice."

Anger flashed in her eyes. Colt remained silent and let her continue. It was obvious she wouldn't take kindly to a reminder from him that Leslie hadn't set aside the trials of his childhood and lived a law-abiding life. Nobody had forced him to become a criminal, especially after he was an adult and well away from the influence of his parents.

"Can you imagine?" she continued, her voice rising in volume and strength. "Being told every day how worthless and unlovable you were? After awhile, you'd have no choice but to believe it. It was like that for my uncle."

Once again, Colt wisely chose to remain silent, only offering her a slight nod before taking another mouthful from his beer. To his relief, her monologue was interrupted when a waitress told them their table was ready.

As Morgan slid off the barstool, Colt did his best not to let his gaze linger on her long legs. She wore a skirt that reached mid-thigh and left plenty of tanned skin on show. He wondered if she had any idea the effect she had on him – and on an ample number of the other men in the room, if their ogling stares were any indication. A couple of them had even approached her and asked if they could buy her a drink. He'd been sitting right beside her. *Were they blind?* Just because they were only friends didn't mean he wanted other men hitting on her.

Colt frowned at the thought and was immediately annoyed by the surge of possessiveness that flooded his veins. It was like he'd told his mom – he and Morgan were friends, nothing more. He had no hold on her. He wasn't even her boyfriend, let alone something more permanent and he was happy about that. He didn't do commitment. It wasn't his thing.

Still, he couldn't help feeling protective of her. He wanted to keep her safe – whether it be from drunken men making unwanted advances, or an uncle who might not be all that he seemed. It didn't mean that his resolve was weakening or that he had a soft spot for her. It merely meant he was behaving like a gentleman, in the way that he'd been raised. His parents would be proud.

"Colt Barrington! Fancy seeing you here!"

The throaty voice caught his attention and he turned in time to see Rachel Florence bearing down upon him. A moment later, he was enveloped in warm female flesh and spicy perfume that filled the air. She pressed herself against him in the guise of a friendly hug.

"Rachel," he managed and did his best to

extricate himself from her arms. "It's nice to see you."

Seemingly unperturbed by Morgan's presence, she leaned in and kissed him full upon the mouth. "And you, too, you sexy thing! Where have you been hiding? It seems like forever since I saw you!"

Morgan watched the exchange with interest. A slight frown marred the smooth skin of her forehead. He cursed silently. Of all the luck, to run into one of his ex-girlfriends.

They'd split up more than six months ago, but Rachel insisted on trying her luck with him every opportunity she got. He'd given her the same story that he gave all of them when they started getting way too serious: He wasn't into commitment. It was him, not them. He wasn't the marrying kind. They were better off finding a guy who wanted the same things they did, settling down, having kids... *Blah, blah, blah.*

Rachel put her hand on his arm in a proprietary gesture and Morgan's frown deepened. She caught him watching and immediately turned her head away. A moment later, she excused herself and disappeared into the crowd. Despite his best efforts, Rachel remained plastered to his side.

"It's great to see you, Rach. You're looking fabulous, as always," he managed and extricated his arm.

She smiled widely and flipped her hair, her eyes beaming with satisfaction. She pressed herself even closer and opened her mouth to speak, but he cut her off, not wanting to give her the wrong impression.

"I'm sorry, Rachel, but…I'm here with someone else."

Disappointment turned down her mouth and clouded her gaze. "Oh. I see. Well, anyway, it was good to see you again. Take care now."

To his relief, she moved on without further ado and he hurried in the direction of the dining room. Morgan was seated at a table with the menu up to her face. He took the chair beside her.

"I'm sorry," he began. "That was an old f—"

"Flame?" Morgan supplied, her gaze fixed on the menu.

Heat crept up Colt's neck. "I was going to say friend, but okay, it's true. We used to date."

"For how long?"

———

Morgan heard the words fall out of her mouth and instantly wished them back. Why should she care if they ran into one of Colt's old girlfriends? She was an old girlfriend, too. They'd split up a decade ago. She had no hold on him. He dated who he pleased. It was none of her business.

And yet, she still wanted to know…

She tightened her lips in irritation. Colt Barrington was her past and that's where he would stay. He'd been more than upfront with her about his future. It didn't include a wife and child and they were the things she yearned for, that were important in her life. She wanted a husband and a family to call her own.

She couldn't imagine having her family die with her, to be the last of her line. It was like it had been for Uncle Leslie. All of his life, he thought he had no one and then he'd discovered he had a brother. It wasn't any wonder he'd been driven to find him...

She looked around at the crowd of people that filled the dining room. The Wicklow was fondly known by the locals as "The Pink Pub" because of the bright pink paint that covered its façade. It was a favorite hangout for college students and young professionals. It had undergone a substantial makeover since the days when she hung out there with her friends and it was now a stylish and modern place to dine and relax.

Too bad she was wired as tight as a guitar string. She only had herself to blame. It was the girl who'd thrown herself at Colt who had her out of sorts. No, that wasn't fair. It had nothing to do with the girl, even though she was the type of confident, brash, sexy woman Morgan had learned to dislike on sight.

The fact was, she didn't like the thought of Colt dating anyone and that was plain stupid. Just because he didn't want to settle down, didn't mean he was celibate. He was young and sexy and intelligent; he was fit and in his prime. Of course he'd date other women. It was just her stupid heart that wished things were different. *Get over it, O'Brien. He isn't the one for you. Accept it and move on.*

"What looks good on the menu?" he asked, breaking the silence that had fallen between them.

She looked up and offered him a slight smile. "I think I'll have the scotch fillet," she answered. "They always did a great steak here."

His face filled with relief at her light conversational tone and she was pleased she'd let go of her tension. She vowed silently to enjoy the night. She was seated beside the sexiest man God ever put on the Earth. No matter what else they were, they were friends who got on well and she intended to make the most of it.

———————————

Colt drew in a surreptitious breath and eased it out on a quiet sigh of relief. He'd been worried that his run-in with Rachel would ruin the rest of the night. Morgan's face had looked like a thundercloud when she'd turned away from them and he'd been nervous about what he'd find when he finally caught up with her.

But, once again she'd surprised him. There was no sign of her earlier disapproval or the irritation that had narrowed her eyes. Instead, she spoke as if nothing had happened; like they were two friends out to dinner, eager to enjoy the night.

Her mature attitude suited him fine and she grew in his estimation. A lot of girls would have flown off the deep end in a similar situation. But not Morgan. She was a great girl and would no doubt one day make some lucky guy a great wife.

He had a sudden image of her waiting by the

front gate for the man in her life, surrounded by three or four kids. The picture filled him with an unexpected surge of yearning. It seemed so happy and joyful and right. What would it be like to come home to someone like Morgan? Someone who was happy to see him at the end of a busy day? He didn't know and sure as hell didn't have the courage to find out.

"I almost forgot to tell you!" Morgan cried, interrupting his thoughts.

"What is it?"

"It's about Dad! He replied to my emails! He apologized for not telling me about Rusty. The poor dog had cancer. Dad didn't want to upset me, seeing how Mom died that way. I guess he had to put him down."

Colt smiled, relieved by the news. "That explains why Rusty had a bullet hole in his skull."

"Yes. Dad's owned a handful of guns for like, forever, including an old .22 rifle. I remember when he used to take me out to the rifle range on the weekends to get in some target practice. I must have been all of six or seven. At least Rusty didn't suffer. Dad would have made sure of that." She paused and then added, "Anyway, Dad's on his way to Darwin and then he's coming home. I'm so relieved everything's all right."

Colt nodded his agreement. He hadn't wanted to tell her that his concerns about her uncle had been growing. The circumstances surrounding Rex O'Brien's hasty departure were strange enough, but he'd been gone a month and from all accounts nobody along the way had seen or heard from him. As well as sending information to the police at Tennant Creek, Colt had taken the liberty of giving a description of Rex and his vehicle to some of the other stations he'd have passed through on his way. None of them could recall seeing Rex or his truck.

"Hey, that's great news," he said. Without thinking, he reached over and gave her hand a quick squeeze.

It was meant to be a sign of reassurance and encouragement, but she reacted like she'd been burned. She snatched her hand away and concealed it under the table. He hid his embarrassment behind the menu.

What the hell was he doing? He had no right to touch her. They were friends. That was it. He'd best remember that. It irritated him that it wasn't the first time he'd had to remind himself. In an effort to draw attention away from what had happened, he pushed away from the table and stood. "I'll go and give them our order. You like your steak medium rare, right?"

She nodded and smiled and he was relieved that once again, she hadn't turned an uncomfortable situation into a scene that would have ruined the night.

"Fries and salad, or vegetables?" he asked.

"Fries and salad," she replied.

He nodded. "I'll be right back."

Lining up with the queue of people who waited to be served, Colt glanced back toward their table. Morgan had her iPad out and was staring at the screen. Many other patrons were playing with their phones, even ones who sat at crowded tables.

It was a sign of the times. He didn't blame them. Technology was taking over. People spent more time communicating online than they did in real life. Whether it was a good thing, or bad, Colt didn't know. It was just the way it was. Still, there was something to be said for socializing the good old-fashioned way. Out to dinner, talking across the table, spending quality time with friends.

He was reminded of his mother's invitation and the anniversary party on the weekend. He wondered if he should invite Morgan and if he did, whether she'd come. She'd met his family years ago, when he and she had dated. His brothers and sisters used to like her, and so had his mom and dad.

She'd met his cousin Chase, before, too and although she hadn't met Chase's wife, Josie, Colt was sure they'd get on just fine. Josie also came from a big family, with five older brothers and a younger sister. She knew what it was like to be surrounded by people who loved and annoyed you at the same time.

It might be fun for Morgan to catch up with everyone again. It might get her mind off her dad and it would stop the endless questions from well-meaning relatives about when he was going to settle down. With Morgan by his side, all but his immediate family would assume they were together. It was a perfect solution. He silently thanked his mom for thinking of it.

An attractive college student with a coquettish

smile and promise in her dark eyes stood behind the counter. Once upon a time, not so very long ago, Colt would have been interested in her unspoken offer. But tonight, her flirtations left him unmoved. After placing the order, he paid for their meals and returned to their table.

Morgan closed her iPad and looked up at him. "How did you do?"

"Good. There's a twenty-five minute wait on the steaks. I hope you don't mind a bit more old-fashioned conversation? Or perhaps we could pull out our phones and let them occupy us for a while. It looks like that's what most people are doing."

She laughed and the sound of it warmed him through. It was the first time he'd heard her laugh properly since she'd arrived back in town. He was pleased that the news she'd received from her father had finally set her mind at ease.

"So, your dad's still traveling?"

"Yes." A moment later, she frowned. "Darn it! I forgot to ask him about the laptop. I need to send him another email."

"What about the laptop?"

"It's the strangest thing. He left it at home. I saw it on his writing desk when I went around to visit Uncle Leslie. It's where Dad always used it. I mentioned it to my uncle, but he didn't know anything about it. He said my dad left in a hurry and must have forgotten to take it. I meant to email Dad and ask him how he's been accessing the Internet." She frowned again and shook her head. "It's all a bit weird."

Colt nodded and then said gently, "Everything about this thing with your dad and his brother has been a bit weird."

"Yes, you're right. When I think about all that's happened, it feels a bit surreal. I'm glad Dad's okay and enjoying his travels, but I can't wait for him to come back home. I want to see him again. I want to see for myself that he's all right."

"I know what you mean. My family drives me nuts half the time, but I wouldn't give any of them up. In fact, the whole family's getting together on the weekend to celebrate my mom and dad's wedding anniversary."

Morgan smiled softly. "How many years?"

"Thirty-five. It took them a few years to start their family. Once they started, they didn't know when to stop," he joked.

"There are eight of you, right?"

"Yep. Five boys and three girls."

Morgan shook her head and smiled a little wistfully. "Wow."

"Yeah, it's fun, I guess, although we've had our share of squabbles," he added with a laugh.

Their meals arrived and they fell silent as both of them began to eat. Colt's steak was cooked to perfection and Morgan appeared to be enjoying hers, too. She ate with enthusiasm and when she was finished, the only things remaining were three pieces of cucumber.

He raised a querying eyebrow. "What's with the cucumber? Not to your liking?"

She chuckled. "I'm sure it's very fresh – and for some people, no doubt it tastes delicious – but

I've never been fond of cucumber. Not even when I was young."

Colt reached over and plucked the thin slices off her plate and tossed them into his mouth. Crunching loudly, he finished them off in a few bites.

"*Mm*, you were right. Fresh *and* delicious."

Her smile reached all the way to her eyes. He stared at her and all of a sudden, he couldn't catch his breath. Her mouth was partly open, her lips were moist and pink. A soft blush had stolen up her cheeks, highlighting her features. *She was beautiful*. There was no other way to describe her.

His heart increased its pressure and his chest felt tight. Blood rushed to his groin. He cast around for something witty to say and came up with nothing. The silence lengthened. Heat crept up his neck. With an act of will, he tore his gaze from hers and reached blindly for his beer. Too late he remembered he'd left it at the bar. *Why hadn't he noticed that until now?* It just went to show how completely the woman who'd agreed to share her evening with him, had captured his attention. *This was not good.*

"Talking about weird things, I noticed a couple of Mom's porcelain statues are missing from the bookshelf in the living room."

Her words were so far removed from his sudden wild fantasy of taking her in his arms and kissing her senseless, he blinked like he'd been doused with a bucket of ice. "Excuse me?"

"Mom had a collection of Royal Doulton figurines. There were eight in total. They're quite valuable. She kept them on a shelf in the living room. When I was at home today, I noticed two were missing. You can still see from the dust that had gathered around them where they stood."

Colt cleared his throat and fixed his thoughts firmly on the conversation. "Would your father have moved them?"

"No, I don't think so. Why would he? They've been on that shelf forever. Each time Mom would buy another one, she'd add it to the collection."

"Perhaps a couple got broken?" Colt suggested.

Morgan shook her head. "That doesn't make sense. If something hit the shelf by accident, you'd think the whole lot of them would have been damaged and the bookshelf's not exactly in harm's way. Besides, Dad lives on his own. He's hardly going to do something careless like bumping into valuable items in his house and it's not like he has a houseful of grandkids running in and out."

She said the words lightly, but he sensed an undertone of strain. She didn't need to explain and he found himself imagining himself in the role of her partner, even for a short time.

This time, the thought didn't send a shaft of panic flooding through his veins. In fact, he remained quite calm. His unexpected reaction was more frightening than the usual feeling of terror that rushed through him whenever thoughts of marriage, kids and commitment filled his head.

"Did you ask your uncle about the figurines?" he asked and surprised himself again by speaking in a tone that was calm and conversational.

What the hell was happening to him? He ought to be in a lather of panic. The very thought of maintaining a conversation with a woman looking to settle down usually had that effect on him. *What was it about Morgan that had him thinking otherwise for the first time in his life? And why did he have an uneasy feeling about Leslie and the figurines?*

"No, I didn't get around to it. We spoke about Dad's laptop and then I ended up checking my emails and found the one from Dad. I kind of got sidetracked after that. Things didn't seem quite so out of whack. Dad was fine and promised to be back soon. I felt a whole lot more relaxed. Uncle Leslie talked to me about his past and I learned a lot about him. He's had a tough life, but he's come through it. I couldn't help but feel proud of him."

Once again, Colt chose to remain silent on the subject of her uncle. He still wasn't convinced Leslie O'Brien was the harmless prodigal twin he appeared to be. Still, as long as he treated Morgan right, it wasn't Colt's to call. This was between Morgan, her Uncle Leslie and her dad.

Besides, he didn't want to spoil the easy camaraderie that had sprung up between the two of them. He couldn't remember the last time he'd enjoyed the company of a woman he hadn't been trying to get into bed.

The thought sobered him. Hadn't he only a moment ago been fantasizing about kissing her until both of them were gasping for breath? And in his fantasy, he'd had no intention of stopping there. *What was this nonsense about enjoying the company of a woman he didn't want to sleep with?* Of course he wanted to sleep with her! It was all the complications that came with it that he shied away from.

The best thing to do would be to stay the hell away from her, but for the life of him, he couldn't do it. He was drawn to her. He had been from the first moment he saw her across the common room of a frat house at the University of New England in Armidale.

Colt had only just arrived at Beau's from the Academy. He was on his Christmas break. The last thing he'd wanted to do was go to a party, but Beau had dragged him along anyway. He'd spotted Morgan right away and knew he had to meet her. She'd ended the night in his bed.

The memory of their first time together hit him full force in the gut. His body surged with remembered lust. His heart thumped. His hands clenched into fists. He sneaked a glance in her direction, but she appeared oblivious to his predicament and for that, he was relieved.

Needing to escape the close confines of the table, he pushed back his chair and stood. Morgan looked up at him in surprise.

"Are you ready to leave?" he asked.

Her eyebrows rose higher at his abruptness and he cursed silently under his breath, but she stood and gathered her handbag without comment and followed him out the door. The night was pleasantly warm after the air conditioning inside the bar. He glanced up at the sky and noticed the heavy clouds that obscured the stars. He could almost smell the rain and the realization lifted his spirits. From his earliest memories, he'd always loved the power and might of a storm.

"It feels like rain," he murmured and saw Morgan tense beside him.

"What is it?" he asked.

"I don't like storms."

"Really? What's not to like? The howling wind, the crack of lightning, the rumble of the thunder. It gets my adrenaline pumping just thinking about it. Unless you're stuck out in it. I can understand that it's not so great then."

"It isn't anything like that," she replied softly.

"Okay, so now I'm intrigued. What is it about storms that you don't like?"

She was silent for so long, he wasn't sure she was going to answer. When she did, her voice was a low murmur. "There was a terrible storm the night my mom died. She was home, of course, not out in it, but it was awful just the same. I can still remember the howl of the wind and the crash of lightning in the sky. It played in rhythm with Mom's silent cries of pain as the cancer slowly won the battle."

She turned to face him. Her eyes were huge and sad in her face. Colt's heart catapulted with the need to comfort her and without giving it any more thought, he drew her into his arms.

Her head came up and his came down. Their lips met in the middle. Warm and pliant, hers moved beneath his and he greedily took all she offered. A moment later, she wrenched herself away. She stared at him in the dimness, her breath coming fast.

"What are we doing? What am *I* doing? This is such a bad idea. You don't do commitment."

He shot her a cheeky wink. "Who said anything about commitment?"

The moment the words were out of his mouth, he wished he could take them back. She recoiled as if he'd struck her and shock and anger flooded her face. The mouth that he'd kissed so well was now set into a thin line. The feeling of disappointment he felt was mirrored on her face and that cut him to the quick.

"I'd like to go home," she said, her voice low and vibrating with anger.

In silence, they returned to his condo. Colt moved into the kitchen and filled the jug. "Would you like a cup of tea?"

She stared at him and slowly shook her head. "No, thank you. I'm still full from dinner. I think I might turn in. Goodnight."

And without another word, she turned and left.

CHAPTER 15

The crack of lightning right outside Morgan's window brought her awake with a start. With her heart pounding, she sat up in bed and listened. The storm that had been hanging around since early evening had finally hit. Another flash illuminated the night sky visible through the open curtains that framed the window. It was quickly followed by another rumble of thunder. A moment later, the heavens opened.

Her heart continued to pound and sweat broke out on her brow. She tried to get a grip on her panic. She was safe and warm inside Colt's house. She couldn't come to harm. The reassuring self-talk should have calmed her, but it had little effect. Like it always did at times like this, common sense and logic deserted her. All she could see was her mother, moaning softly in her drug-induced stupor as the cancer ravaged her body and all along, the storm continued to rage.

Morgan didn't realize she was crying until she

felt the dampness on her cheeks. Even after all these years, memories of those final moments of her mother's life upset her. And now, her dad had gone away on a trip of self-discovery and she was left all alone. She had no one. Except her uncle, and he didn't really count. She'd only met him a couple of days ago and she was still coming to terms with the fact her father had a twin, let alone that Uncle Leslie was now part of her family.

Another bolt of lightning cracked in the distance and she cried out and covered her ears. A moment later, the door to her bedroom was flung open and Colt stood there wearing nothing more than a pair of boxer shorts.

"Morgan! Are you all right?" he asked in a tone that was filled with concern.

She shook her head, beyond words. She thought the storm had abated and there was nothing left but the rain, but it had somehow circled back again with renewed ferocity. The thunder and lightning crashed and banged and she jumped each time it sounded. Colt came closer and bent over and switched on the lamp that stood on the nightstand near her bed.

He took one look at her and cursed softly under his breath. Moving to sit beside her, he cradled her against his chest. She breathed in deeply of his woodsy cologne, taking comfort from his warmth and strength. Clinging to his waist like he was a lifeline, together, they rode out the storm.

"*Shh*, it's okay, Morgan," he murmured against her hair. His hand stroked her tenderly, rhythmically, soothing her fear. "It's just a storm. It will pass soon and everything will be all right again."

Drawing comfort from his presence, Morgan tightened her hold around his waist. The storm continued to vent outside but somehow, having Colt close beside her, helped her keep her memories and fear at bay. She lifted her head to thank him.

Their gazes locked. Her mouth was inches from his. The golden glow from the lamp cast shadows across his handsome face. His eyes were dark with longing and the need she saw there stole her breath. Despite her better judgement, with a pounding heart, she turned up her face and kissed him softly on the lips.

As if dry tinder had been ignited, heat rushed through every pore. His mouth opened under hers and their tongues tangled in a frantic, fiery dance. She buried her fingers in his hair and held his head in place, needing to kiss him, to taste him over and over again.

His hand stole down her side, skimming over one of her breasts. Desire shivered down her spine and centered in her core. Her nipples tightened, almost painfully, beneath the satin of her pajamas. She groaned and pressed herself awkwardly against him, yearning for more.

Pushing her back against the pillows, he immediately followed her down. She reached up and clung to his shoulders. Firm, hard muscles bunched beneath her fingers, sending a thrill of need coursing through her. Moving lower, she splayed her hands over the bare skin of his pecs.

He was as beautiful and perfect as she remembered – even more so. His body had filled out and strengthened, fulfilling the promise of his youth. His broad chest was still mostly hairless and glinted gold in the soft light. She marveled over the taut muscles across his stomach.

Another clap of thunder sounded right outside the house. She jumped. Colt leaned over and kissed her again, gently on the mouth. Taking her with him, he turned on his side and nibbled his way to her ear. His tongue, warm and moist, dipped into the curves and crevices, driving her wild.

She groaned again and moved until their legs were entwined. His erection pressed against her belly, thick and hard. Without thinking, she reached down between them and slipped her hand beneath the waistband of his boxers.

Her fingers skimmed over the head of his cock and then circled his impressive length. Squeezing rhythmically, she elicited a groan.

"You're a witch, Morgan O'Brien and I am totally beguiled," he murmured and reached out to cup one of her breasts. Pinching her nipple between his fingers, all of a sudden, it was her turn to gasp.

"Colt!"

"You don't like it?" he muttered, burying his face against her neck.

"I like it too much," she admitted.

A voice in the back of her head reminded her that she and Colt were all wrong. They wanted different things. He was about today. She was about forever. It would never work between them. *Why the hell was she complicating her life?*

The thoughts went round and round in her head until the noise nearly drove her mad and then, as their kiss deepened once more, it no longer mattered. She was there, with Colt, needing him, wanting him. She'd take whatever he offered, even for just a night. And in the morning, she'd get her life back on track and satisfy herself with the memories.

Mentally, she rehearsed how it would be – being friends in the morning light. The thought filled her with sadness and disappointment.

As if reading her mind, Colt drew slightly away and tilted her chin up to face him. "Are you sure you want to do this?" he asked, his voice soft and serious.

She stared at him and her brain fired a thousand reasons why sleeping with him was a very bad idea, but she ignored the turmoil in her head and nodded. "Yes," she said.

He groaned and kissed her hard on the mouth and then pushed her gently away. "Don't go anywhere. I'll be back in a minute." And with that, he stood and left the room.

Morgan had hardly enough time to register his absence before he was once again by her side. A flash of something in his fingers caught her eye and she realized he held a condom. She was relieved he had thought of it and was being responsible. One thing they didn't need was another unplanned pregnancy.

Not that she'd ever have another abortion. The first one was a sad and depressing experience and one she never wanted to repeat. Besides, she was in different place now – they both were. They were no longer in college with nothing to offer a child.

"Are you still okay with this?" Colt asked quietly and Morgan was grateful for his consideration and attentiveness.

"Yes," she replied and pulled him hard up against her.

Kissing him with all the feeling she'd stored up inside her for so long, she imprinted the taste and feel of him on her mind and body. His thick hair smelled clean and fruity, like it had been freshly shampooed. The stubble on his chin was scratchy, but she liked the way it felt: strong and masculine.

His lips were full and firm and were delicious to the taste. She traced the outline with her tongue and then slipped her tongue between his teeth. He kissed her back with feeling and she could have sworn they were still in love. Though they'd only been together a few short weeks, right from the very start, there had been fireworks when they came together. This time was no different.

Colt angled his head and deepened the kiss and she moaned softly under her breath. Fresh need spiraled through her, heating her blood. With murmurs of encouragement, he slid his hands beneath her pajama top and found her naked skin. His hands cupped her breasts and skimmed over her nipples, eliciting another gasp. But still he wasn't finished his torture and as his hands slid under the waistband of her shorts she braced herself against the intimate contact.

Warm and rough, his fingers caressed her mound and slid between her folds. Slick with need, her legs fell open as he prodded her heated flesh.

"You feel so warm, so wet," he muttered.

His words sent another shaft of desire coursing through her and she tightened her hold on his shoulders. The storm fell away and there was only Colt, surrounding her, consuming her, filling her with need.

"I want you, Colt," she whispered, her voice husky and low.

Needing no further encouragement, he reached over for the condom on the nightstand and quickly rolled it on. Settling himself between her legs, his cock prodded her entrance and then eased inside her, one agonizing inch at a time.

"Please, Colt," she begged. "It's been so long. I need you."

Emotion flared hotly in his eyes and she was rewarded with a sudden thrust. He filled her with his heated flesh, stretching her muscles wide. She gasped at the feel of him deep inside her and clung to him with all her might.

His breath came shallow and fast in her ear, as if he were straining to hold himself back. Her arms tightened around his neck, drawing him close. She lifted her hips in silent encouragement and slowly he began to move. He withdrew almost all the way and then glided smoothly back in. In and out, over and over, until she was mindless with need.

Fire burned hot in her belly and even hotter between her legs. Her breasts felt heavy, her clit tingled and pressure built way deep inside. She clung to his shoulders like he was a lifeboat and she was being tossed about in a stormy sea. Her fingernails dug into his skin, but he continued his sensual onslaught.

Faster and faster, he plunged in and out of her and she moaned and gasped in rhythm with his strokes. Higher and higher she climbed, her orgasm just within reach. Nearing the precipice, she tensed and gasped and cried out as she toppled over the edge. Her breathing was harsh in the silence as she slowly drifted back to earth.

Colt stared down at her, his expression unreadable, although she glimpsed satisfaction in his eyes. She'd barely managed to catch her breath when he began to move again. This time, his strokes were short and fast and moments later, he yelled out in triumph.

He collapsed against her and Morgan took his weight, relishing the feel of his spent body against hers. The moment didn't last nearly long enough. He lifted his head and then came up on his elbows before rolling over on his side. He reached for her and drew her against him and she sighed.

A torrent of confusing emotions flooded through her. There were a million reasons why what they'd just done was a completely terrible idea, but right here, right now with the storm abated and only the sound of gentle rain falling outside, she'd never felt more content.

Colt woke well before his usual time, and for a moment, lay still in the bed and tried to get his bearings. As the sun peeked over the horizon, he recognized the furniture of his spare room. He glanced sideways and saw Morgan, still asleep beside him.

Memories of the night before flooded over him. Feelings of peace and contentment were immediately replaced by guilt. He'd slept with her. Despite all his inward arguments and the logic of staying the hell away – he'd gone and slept with her.

What the hell had he been thinking? She deserved so much better than that, better than him. She deserved to get all she wanted out of life and none of those wants coincided with his.

Still, he didn't regret what had happened. Sex between them had always been magical and last night had been even better. It was like their lovemaking had gained a maturity it hadn't had before. Not that it changed the way things were or the fact they weren't right for each other. Too bad he hadn't listened to the voice of reason the night before. It was too late for regrets. He only hoped Morgan would feel the same way.

With another glance in her direction, he forced himself to slide out of bed. It would be less complicated for both of them if he were gone by the time she woke. Collecting his boxers and the used condom from the floor, he padded quietly out of the room and headed straight for the shower.

The water was hot and steamy and Colt was grateful for its punishing sting. Rinsing the soap off his body, he wondered for the hundredth time what he'd say to her when he saw her again. Whether it was before work or after, he'd have to face her and talk about what had happened and they'd have to agree on where they went from here.

His head insisted nothing had changed; his priorities remained the same. It was far safer to avoid the possibility of a long-term relationship altogether; to avoid the hurt that would ultimately follow. So far, that premise had served him well.

But that was before Morgan O'Brien had arrived back in his life. She turned his world upside down. She smiled and the day seemed brighter. Her laughter filled a room. She made him want to be a better person; to look out for her, protect her and keep her safe. But could he give her what she wanted? A lifetime of love and happiness?

And what if he did marry? Would he spend every day analyzing their relationship, putting it under the microscope, wanting to spot the very moment things began to drift off course? Would it be like that? Would he drive himself, and any wife he had, absolutely mad?

By the time he was finished with the conditioner, he still hadn't made up his mind. The arguments circled around inside his head until he wanted to shout long and loud. He stepped out of the shower with the beginning of a headache pounding behind his eyes. What a great way to start the day. He couldn't wait to get to work.

To Colt's consternation, Morgan was already in

the kitchen when he emerged, dressed, from his room. She had her back to him and was busy at the stove and didn't immediately notice him. He took the time to appreciate the sight of her in a pair of cutoff denim shorts and a shirt that ended just below her bra. A wide swathe of tanned flesh was bared to his gaze.

Memories of her smooth, soft skin bombarded him and his body tightened reflexively. Her butt was cupped gently by the denim and he remembered his palm holding her just the same way. Her hair was in a ponytail that swung jauntily to and fro, making her look younger than her thirty years.

The smell of brewing coffee teased his nostrils. As if on cue, toast popped out of the toaster. She turned to him and offered him a smile filled with sunshine and his gut somersaulted. He wanted to steal himself against the rush of feeling that flooded through him, but he was awfully afraid it was too late. He was falling for her and falling fast and he wasn't at all sure he had what it took to resist – or if he even wanted to try – and that was the scariest thing of all.

CHAPTER 16

Dear Diary,

I went down to the post office this morning and the lady behind the counter greeted me as if she'd known me forever. She even called me Rex. Admittedly, I wore his hat and sunglasses and of course, another set of his clothes. Slowly but surely, my plan is working. The next test is the bank. Once I've convinced the tellers of my identity, I shall be set.

Morgan sipped her coffee and scanned the contents of the morning paper that had been delivered to Colt's door. He'd already left for work and the house was still and silent. She missed his company and the camaraderie they shared.

She'd deliberately chosen to act normal around him, despite what had happened the night before. She could tell he was relieved when she didn't draw attention to the fact they'd slept with each other. Instead, the two of them had enjoyed a few pleasant moments over toast and cereal and eggs.

He mentioned again his parents' upcoming anniversary celebration and then surprised her by asking her if she wanted to go. She'd stared at him across the breakfast table, too taken aback to speak. He'd filled the sudden silence with an uncomfortable chuckle that was immediately followed by a rush of words.

"It probably doesn't sound as exciting as a night out in the city, but my brothers and sisters will be there and my cousin, Chase, and his wife. You haven't met Josie, but she's pretty good value. She's a child psychologist. I'm sure you'll get on well. And of course, there'll be plenty of country music. It's Country Music Festival time in Tamworth. I wouldn't be surprised if Mom's conned one or two buskers from Peel Street to give impromptu performances. I can't remember if you like country music. It's not my favorite thing, but Mom and Dad like it and—"

"It's all right, Colt. I'd love to come," she interrupted, smiling gently.

He stopped mid-sentence and stared at her. "Are you sure?"

"Yes, of course I'm sure. I haven't seen your family for a long time. It would be nice to catch up. And as for Chase – I'm pleased to hear he's found a wife. I seem to remember he ran with a wild pack there for a while. Even so, he was very popular among the female college students."

She softened her words with another smile and Colt nodded in agreement. "Yes, you aren't the only one surprised to discover he's put down roots. Mom and Dad despaired of him ever settling down."

"And yet he has," she said lightly, not wanting to make a big deal of it. She knew Colt's feelings on the subject of marriage and it was strange to talk about the taming of his cousin without transferring it to him. Sharing a magical night together didn't change anything, no matter how much she wished things were different.

Sneaking a peek at him over her coffee mug, Morgan was relieved to note Colt's expression was merely thoughtful, not closed and defensive. She wished she had a clue what was going on in his head and then was pleased she didn't. Some things were best left unknown – at least for now. She wanted to cherish the memories they'd made last night and bask in their warm glow while she could. There had been plenty of time after he left for work to analyze and dissect and examine what had happened... And accept that nothing had changed.

The buzz of her phone interrupted her thoughts and she set aside the paper to answer it. She glanced at the screen and smiled. It was Georgie Whitely.

"Georgie! How are you? It's good to hear from you!"

"I thought you must have fallen off the face of the earth!" Georgie replied with a laugh. "I emailed you a couple of days ago, but I didn't hear back."

Morgan felt a shaft of guilt. She hadn't called any of her friends since she'd left. It was probably because her life had been off kilter from the moment she'd arrived. With all that had happened in such a short time, it wasn't any wonder her head was in a spin.

"How are things in the country?" Georgie added.

"They're fine. At least, not too bad," Morgan amended.

"What's that supposed to mean?"

With a sigh, Morgan filled her in on what had been happening, all the while sitting through her friend's *oohs* and *ahhs* and curious questions, in particular when it came to the mention of Colt.

"I see," Georgie replied when Morgan mentioned she was staying with her ex-boyfriend from way back. "Is he still single?"

Heat crept up Morgan's neck and she was relieved Georgie couldn't see her discomfort.

"So, is he?" Georgie's gentle chiding reminded her she still hadn't given her friend an answer.

"Yes, he's still single," she managed.

"Cute, or has he gone to fat?"

Morgan choked. An image of Colt as he'd been the night before in all his lean, naked glory flooded her mind. "No, I think you could say he's... He's managed to keep himself quite fit, considering."

"Well, it has been ten years," Georgie replied sagely. "Time has a way of adding a few pounds."

"You can say that again," Morgan chuckled.

Georgie scoffed in disbelief. "You're kidding, right? You look fabulous! I didn't know you in college, but I can't imagine you looked any hotter than what you do now."

Morgan laughed. "You're so sweet, Georgina Whitely. Cameron Dawson's a lucky man."

"And doesn't he know it," Georgie quipped.

A comfortable silence fell between them. Georgie broke it with another question. "So, when are you coming back to Sydney?"

"I have another ten days of leave. Dad said he hoped to make it home before I have to go back. I'm going to stay for as long as I can, or at least until he returns. It's been way too long since I saw him. I want to satisfy myself that he's all right."

"I understand. From what you've told me, things have been a little weird. I can't believe he has a long lost brother, and an identical twin at that! The very thought blows my mind!"

"You're telling me. If Uncle Leslie didn't looked so much like Dad, I don't think I would have believed him. It was a real shock."

"I can well imagine. Still, it sounds like you're coming to terms with it," Georgie said.

"Yes, you're right, and the more I get to know my uncle, the more I like him. He's had a difficult life, but he's come through it and seems to have himself together. He's a really nice man. I'm glad he's found Dad. They can make some new memories together, make up for lost time."

"It must be difficult for him to accept how well your father fared from birth."

"Maybe you're right. Dad's led a very comfortable life."

"Is your uncle resentful of that?" Georgie's voice was full of curiosity.

Morgan paused to consider the question. "No, not that I can tell. He speaks quite openly of his unfortunate past, even of his time in jail. He doesn't seem to blame my dad for what happened in the past. He's staying in my father's house and has the run of the place. He seems right at home. I think he's just happy to finally know the truth about his past and to connect with his twin."

"It's a nice story, isn't it?" Georgie asked.

"Yes," Morgan replied. "I'm so pleased they discovered each other in time. The truth could so easily have died with both sets of parents without either brother being any the wiser."

"Yes, it's like you said: The more I think about it, the more amazing it feels. Twin boys separated at birth. One twin kept by his biological parents; the brothers reunited more than fifty years later. It sounds like something out of a Hollywood blockbuster." Georgie laughed.

Morgan smiled in agreement. It felt good to see the light side of the whole thing. For days, she'd been surviving in some kind of funk, worried about her father, confused about what had gone on; the death of Rusty, the lies her dad had told. They were so out of character.

But he'd finally replied to her emails and had explained most of the weirdness away. She still had to ask her dad about the laptop and the missing statues, but with the knowledge he'd soon be home, those things didn't seem to matter so much.

The sound of a baby crying interrupted her musings and she smiled into the phone. "It sounds like your son needs attention."

"Darn!" Georgie replied. "He's only been down an hour. That's not long enough, I'm afraid."

The crying increased in intensity and Morgan chuckled, even as she suppressed a stab of yearning.

"I'm going to have to go, Morgan. James refuses to be ignored."

"Give him a kiss from me, won't you?" Morgan replied and after an assurance from Georgie that she would, Morgan ended the call.

Setting her phone back down on the table, she reached for the newspaper once again. Her hand paused midway and she reached for her iPad instead. She'd already checked her emails and there hadn't been anything new from her dad, but that didn't mean she couldn't email him. She'd ask him about the laptop and the figurines. She was curious, that's all. There was nothing wrong with that.

———————

Leslie read the email that had just come in from Rex's daughter. From her tone, she appeared to be less stressed over his sudden decision to go traveling across the outback, but she was still asking questions.

He cursed again at the thought of the laptop. He'd been working on it right before she'd knocked. He'd been startled to find her outside the door and had forgotten to hide it.

Then there were the statues. He should have known they'd hold special significance and their disappearance would be noticed. But he'd needed cash and they'd seemed like the easiest things to hock. They'd fetched a pretty penny, too. He looked forward to selling the rest.

But Morgan had noticed two of them were missing and now she wanted to know why. He didn't know what he could tell her, what excuse she might buy. He didn't know what she did for a living, but it was clear she was bright and perceptive. He'd have to watch himself if he didn't want to slip up.

Leslie re-read her email. He'd take some time to consider his reply. He didn't want to respond in haste and regret his word choice. He had to say something that would appease her; something that would keep her suspicions at bay. Any more stupid mistakes could cost him dearly and bring his well-laid plans crashing down.

He'd have to return to the sewer he'd crawled out of, never to be seen again.

That was simply not an option.

Chapter 17

Morgan applied a second coat of cherry-colored lipstick and stepped back to assess the results in the mirror. Her honey-blond hair hung loose and shiny after a wash and blow dry and for once, the long waves fell neatly into place. She didn't normally wear a lot of makeup, but tonight, she'd applied eye shadow and eyeliner with care. She looked good. She looked relaxed and confident. Too bad she didn't feel that way.

She'd woken that morning nervous about meeting up with Colt's family again. She didn't know what he'd told them about the reasons for their parting. She only hoped he'd said nothing about the baby. His parents had been nice to her all those years ago and had seemed to like her well enough. She couldn't help but wonder if they still felt the same way.

The chime of a new email hitting her inbox snagged her attention. Turning away from the mirror, she scooped up her iPad from where it lay on her bed. It had been five days since her father's last email. She wasn't as concerned as she would have been had he not assured her he was okay the last time, but still, he wasn't exactly young and he was traveling in isolated and unfamiliar country all alone. She was still concerned about him traveling without his laptop, having to deal with Internet cafes and unfamiliar technology, and would be pleased when he arrived back home.

Flipping her iPad open, she entered her passcode and then scanned through her mail. Her heart skipped a beat. There was a new email from her dad. She opened the message and eagerly read over the words he'd written.

Hi Morgan,

Good to hear from you. Glad you're spending time with your uncle. He's a good bloke. I'm looking forward to getting to know him better.

I forgot to tell you I left my laptop behind. It was stupid of me, I know. I was halfway to Broken Hill before I remembered and by then, it was too late to turn back. But it all worked out. Some travelers in one of the caravan parks told me about Internet cafés. I'd never heard of such things, but they explained it all and it wasn't too complicated.

So, I've become a little more tech savvy and I've been forced into the twenty-first century. The only downside is having to find the café. They're not as thick on the ground as I was led to believe – at least, that's the way it's been for me. It's the reason my contact with you is so sporadic. Some towns offer such a service, but there are just as many out here that don't.

You asked about your mother's Royal Doulton figurines... I'm really sorry, Morgan. I should have told you. I know how much those statues mean to you. The truth is, I dropped them. First one and less than a week later, the other. I was admiring them one night while I watched the television. They simply slipped from my hands and shattered. I picked up the broken pieces, but there was nothing I could do. The first time it happened, I was shocked and saddened. It was like a part of your mother had been destroyed. I never imagined it could happen a second time...

I can't seem to hold onto things like I used to. My fingers just don't want to work. I'll have to go to the doctor when I get home and get checked out. Please don't worry. I'm sure it's nothing sinister.

You're smiling now, aren't you, because I know you better than anyone. Of course you're going to worry. You worry about everything. And I love you for it.

You'll be glad to know I'm nearly done with my travels and hope to return home soon. I've been warned about the wet season up here. I don't want to get caught in a monsoon.

Take care, honey and know that I'm well. I'm looking forward to seeing you again and I hope this finds you the same.

That's it for now. Dad xxx

Morgan swiped at a drop of moisture that had found its way into her eyes. She sniffed. It was good to hear from her father, but it only made her miss him more. It had been so long since she'd seen him, hugged him or heard his laughter ring through the house. She was glad he'd soon be on his way home. It couldn't come quick enough.

"Are you nearly finished in there, Morgan?"

Colt's question, accompanied by a knock on the bedroom door, broke into Morgan's thoughts. Glancing down at her sheer, short robe, she quickly gathered her makeup supplies, hairbrush and blow dryer before responding.

"Um, yes. I shouldn't be too much longer."

His reply was muffled behind the closed door and she pulled it open a crack. He looked down at the pile of things in her hands with a quizzical expression on his handsome face.

"I-I'm sorry, I didn't catch what you said," she stammered, intensely aware of her near-naked state. He might have seen her without clothes on, but this was different and even more so after they'd both agreed their night together was a one-off and wouldn't be repeated.

"I said, we'll be leaving in fifteen minutes. It will take us an hour to drive to Tamworth and Mom will have my head if we're late."

Laughter glinted in the bright blue depths of eyes that seemed to see into her very soul. Her heart skipped a beat and then pounded fast, stealing her breath. Not for the first time, she wondered if accompanying him to the family gathering was a good idea. His friends and relatives might get the wrong impression, read more into it than there was. *What if someone asked her if they were a couple? What would she say then?*

Something of her growing panic must have shown on her face. Colt frowned in concern.

"What is it, Morgan? Are you all right?"

She shook her head and gave a helpless shrug. "What are we doing, Colt? We're going to this party together. Assumptions will be made. I don't think it's fair on them or me to give them the wrong idea. Your family—"

"Will understand," he interrupted. "I'll be sure to tell them you're here as an old friend. I've already made it clear to Mom. I'm sure she's spread the word. Besides," he said, smiling disarmingly, "would it be so terrible for my great aunts and uncles to think we're an item?"

She stared at him in confusion. Anger stirred low in her stomach. "Of course it would! It's deceitful and totally unfair! I like you, Colt. A lot. I always have. But we want different things and I'm not prepared to compromise. It's not wrong of me to want a family of my own and I refuse to apologize for it. In fact, it's completely normal for someone my age to have the urge to settle down. The fact that you feel differently is neither here nor there. Do I wish you wanted the same things I do? Of course, but you've made it quite clear it's not going to happen and I'm through with wasting time. I—"

"Morgan. Stop."

Once again, he interrupted her and this time, he pushed open the door. Intensely conscious of the sheer robe, she crossed her arms over her front and stared him down.

He cursed softly. "Okay, I get it. I'm being a prick. I'm blowing hot and cold like a teenage girl and it feels like I don't know what the hell I want. I've told you how I feel and the kind of future I want. It all used to seem so clear." He dragged a hand through his hair and grimaced like he was in pain. Morgan held her ground, refusing to show him any sympathy.

"The truth is, Morgan, ever since you arrived back in town, you've turned my life upside down. I thought I had it all planned out, my path well and truly laid out. Now, I'm not so sure."

Her bark of laughter was devoid of humor. She shook her head in disbelief. "Oh, so you expect me to—"

"I don't expect you to do anything." His lips twisted again. "Shit, I'm not explaining myself very well."

He looked at her and her heart skipped a beat at the frank emotion on his face. Still, she refused to be swayed by the unspoken plea in his eyes. She wanted to hear him say the words, to be upfront about how he felt. She sensed a change behind his words and though her heart wanted to leap with hope, she wouldn't believe it until she heard him say it.

His shoulders slumped on a sigh. "I've spent almost all of my adult years believing I'd go through life on my own – and that's exactly the way I wanted it. Too many times, I've seen marriage and long-term relationships go down the toilet and everyone involved suffers. I didn't want to be the one inflicting that kind of pain, recovering from wounds so deep. It seemed easier and safer to avoid it altogether and forge onward solo.

"But now you've crashed back into my life and I can't help but wonder if I have things right. I think about spending my life with you, having kids, being there for each other and the thought doesn't terrify me quite like it used to. The difference is *you*, Morgan. I've never felt this way with anyone else and I'm pretty sure I won't feel it again. It still scares the hell out of me and I'm still not totally convinced, but... Would you like to give it a go? See where it leads?"

As far as proposals went, it fell vastly short of her expectations, but Morgan's heart still leaped with hope at the intent behind Colt's words. She'd always been in love with him, even if she'd refused to acknowledge it and it seemed like he might feel the same way, provided they could overcome his ingrained reservations that every relationship ended in pain.

She smiled tremulously and nodded and was gratified when his face lit up with excitement and joy.

"You mean it?" he asked, still grinning. "You want to give us a go?"

She rolled her eyes at him and shook her head. "You make it sound so romantic, Colt Barrington. How's a girl to refuse?"

He had the grace to look embarrassed again, but his grin remained firmly in place. He put his arms around her and lifted her off her feet. She made a grab for her flimsy robe, but the silky fabric gaped apart. Colt appeared oblivious to her wardrobe malfunction. Instead, he laughed and spun her around, before finally setting her back down on the floor.

His enthusiasm was infectious and Morgan's heart took off in flight. She hadn't come back to town looking for love, but she was more than happy about how things were working out.

As if only just becoming aware of her scanty attire, Colt's gaze drifted slowly over her. Moving from head to toe and pausing noticeably at her heaving bosom barely concealed beneath the fabric of her robe, his eyes darkened with desire.

An answering jolt of need went through her, but they were very nearly running late. She didn't want to be responsible for any sour looks from his mother because their tardiness had ruined her plans. So, as much as she longed to press herself against him, she tactfully took a step back.

"We're leaving in fifteen minutes, remember?" she reminded him and softened her words with another smile. "There'll be time enough for...this kind of thing after."

Colt looked like he wanted to argue, but a moment later, offered a reluctant nod. "You're right. Mom wants us there in plenty of time. She'll have my head if we walk in late. It's the first time in a long time she has all her children home. She means to make the most of it."

Morgan accepted his comment calmly, but inside she was a bundle of nerves. It had been more than ten years since she'd had anything to do with Colt's family. A lot had happened in that time. *Would she like them as much as she had a decade ago? Would they like her?* It was impossible to know and there was only one way she was going to find out.

———————

Colt snuck another look at Morgan where she stood on the other side of the crowded auditorium and his breath halted in his throat. She was laughing at something his sister, Ashleigh, said and her face glowed with warmth and natural beauty.

She wore a forest-green dress made of some kind of stretchy fabric that clung to her luscious curves. The plunging neckline revealed her generous cleavage. Her breasts bounced and jiggled with her mirth and he tensed, expecting them to burst free from their confines any moment, but it didn't happen and then he was both relieved and disappointed.

Though they'd arrived together and he was sure the majority of the people in the room assumed they were a couple, he had yet to make any sort of announcement to his family or confirm the unspoken questions in their eyes.

He shifted his weight, a little uncomfortable with the direction of his thoughts. Of course, he'd meant what he'd said to Morgan... But the decision to take the headlong plunge into a relationship still filled him with unease. He needed time to get used to the idea. That's all it was.

"Don't tell me that's Morgan O'Brien?" Beau murmured, his gaze fixed firmly on the woman that had kept Colt enthralled all night.

Dragging his gaze away from her, Colt frowned at his twin. "Yes. She came with me. What about it?"

Beau eyed him quizzically and Colt looked away. His brother knew him far too well. Beau would see something in Colt's eyes that he wasn't sure he was ready to acknowledge and then there'd be hell to pay. His twin would question him mercilessly and Colt wasn't up to that either. Not for the first time that evening, he wondered what he'd been thinking when he'd invited Morgan along.

"You dated her for a while, back when I was still in college, didn't you?"

Colt kept his tone disinterested. "Yeah, for a month or so. We were just kids. Things didn't work out. We went our separate ways."

"You never did share the details with me," Beau replied.

"And I'm not going to share them with you now," Colt replied, his voice brusque.

Beau raised his eyebrows, his gaze filled with curiosity. Colt cursed silently under his breath.

"It sounds like it's a touchy subject," Beau teased. "Don't tell me she broke your heart."

Colt made an impatient sound in the back of his throat and looked at his brother. "Don't be stupid."

Laughter glinted in Beau's blue eyes – eyes that

were identical to his. Colt braced himself for another sly comment. His brother didn't disappoint.

"This just keeps getting more and more interesting," Beau drawled. "How long has it been since you've seen her?"

"I haven't seen her since we broke up."

Beau nodded, his expression calculating. "That was at least a decade ago and now you've brought her to Mom and Dad's anniversary celebration. A party packed wall to wall with curious family and other relatives. You must have known this would cause quite a stir, especially among our sisters."

Beau turned and directed his gaze meaningfully to where Morgan stood surrounded by Ashleigh and Darcy and Emily, all of them staring at Morgan with varying degrees of interest and curiosity.

Colt grimaced. "I guess I didn't think it through," he muttered. "We were having breakfast and...it was nice. The party came up in conversation. I invited her to come."

Beau's eyes widened in surprise. "Breakfast, did you say? You mean, like the-morning-after-the-night-before breakfast?"

Embarrassment heated Colt's cheeks. He fixed his gaze on the floor. "Something like that."

Beau pounced. "How long's this been going on? I spoke to you a fortnight ago and you didn't say anything about a girlfriend – certainly nothing about Morgan O'Brien. Now I find out she's sleeping over and sharing breakfast. This sounds serious, little brother. I think we need to talk."

Colt chuckled at the faux-serious expression on his twin's face. With a sigh, he filled his brother in on what had happened since Morgan had arrived in town, though for some inexplicable reason, he held back the part where he'd invited her to be part of his life. When he finished, Beau stared at him and shook his head.

"Wow, that's amazing! First of all, running into her like that after all these years and then that stuff about her father... A twin brother he never knew he had... Like... Wow."

"Yeah and then her dad left before Morgan could even talk to him about it," Colt added. "It's all been a bit weird."

"So the brother's living in her family home on his own?"

"Yes. He's looking after the place while Rex is away. I'm not sure what the guy's plans are after Rex returns. Morgan didn't say anything, but I could tell she wasn't comfortable staying there alone with her uncle. She doesn't know him or anything much about him. All the hotels are full with the visitors to the Lamb and Potato Festival, so I offered her a room." Colt shrugged as if the matter wasn't of consequence, but his twin wasn't deceived.

Beau threw him a droll look. "Yeah, right. Don't come over all innocent with me, Colt. You've never offered your house to anyone, not even for a week or two. And I've been watching you tonight. You haven't taken your eyes off her all evening. There's no point denying it. She's special to you. I can see it all over your face."

Colt compressed his lips and remained silent, wishing again that he hadn't said anything to Morgan about the party. He'd invited her because he wanted to spend more time with her and after their night together, he'd wanted it even more. Morgan O'Brien had gotten under his skin and there was nothing he could do about it.

"You've got it bad, little bro," Beau chuckled, punching Colt lightly on the arm. "So much for your vow to remain single for the rest of your life. This woman's got you so twisted up in knots, you don't know which way to turn."

Colt frowned at his brother. "Do you think so?"

Beau's expression sobered. "Yes, buddy. I do. I think you care a great deal for her and you're not sure what to do. You were hell-bent on a certain course and now fate's brought her back into your life and thrown you for a spin. At the moment, you're like a rudderless boat, bobbing up and down on the ocean."

Colt frowned. Beau wasn't painting a very positive picture of his situation. His twin must have read something of Colt's dark thoughts in his face, because he hastened to reassure him.

"It's not all bad, Colt. I'm sure you'll come through it. You'll talk to Morgan and confirm that she's been bitten by the love bug as much as you and the two of you will live blissfully happy from then until the end of time."

Colt chuckled at his brother's ridiculous antics and slowly shook his head. "You're an idiot, you know that?" he said, giving his twin a fond smile.

Beau grinned. "Of course! Why do you think I'm

still single? It's not for want of trying! Unlike you, I don't have an aversion to marriage. In fact, I'm quite looking forward to it. But alas, word seems to have gotten around the Sydney Harbour Hospital that the brilliant neurosurgeon, Doctor Beau Barrington, is not the marrying kind. I'm not sure what I did to deserve it, but there you have it. Nobody but females only looking for a good time will go out with me." He shook his head and sighed dramatically. "Women can be so shallow."

This time, Colt laughed loudly and drew his brother close for a hug. It felt good to be with his twin again, to be connecting on every level. He thought fleetingly of Rex and Leslie and for the first time, felt sorry that they'd lived half their lives apart. And not only apart, they hadn't even known the other existed. The possibility of not having Beau in his life was unimaginable.

Colt gazed across the room and once again found Morgan. Still surrounded by his sisters, she seemed oblivious to him. And then she lifted her head and turned slightly in his direction. Her gaze found his and locked and held. His heart thumped so hard, he could barely breathe. Perspiration dampened his palms.

She smiled at him and it was so happy and soft and intimate, his knees weakened. It was ridiculous how a woman could have such an effect on him, but there was no denying she did. Like Beau had said, he was in a bad way. Now, all he had to decide was what he was going to do about it.

"What are you two looking so chirpy about?" Chase Barrington asked, his lips twisting in a grimace.

Colt turned to greet his cousin, surprised at Chase's surly mood. "It's good to see you, too, cousin. What's put you in such a bad mood?"

"Yeah, Chase," Beau added. "We're at a party. The beer's free and flowing, the food is great and even the music's passable. What do you have to complain about?"

Chase eyed the brothers with a churlish expression on his face. "Spoken by a couple of die-hard bachelors. Neither of you can understand the vagaries of women when you haven't found the courage to take the plunge and tie yourself down."

Colt frowned and his gaze sharpened on his cousin. "What are you talking about, Chase?"

"Trouble in paradise?" Beau teased.

Chase scowled. "It's Josie. Lately, it seems like I can't please her. It doesn't matter what I do, it's never enough. She complains I work too much, that I'm never around for our son. He's two. He barely knows when I'm home. He's in bed when I leave for work and in bed when I return. It's not my fault I work twelve-hour shifts. That's just the way it is."

He glanced at Colt. "You know how it works, Colt. Being a cop in a country town is tough. There are never enough staff to go round. We do what we have to do. Sometimes it means working a double." He shrugged.

"Josie used to understand. It's not like

anything's changed since we got married. I was a cop when we got together. I worked long hours then, too. It's just that now that Clancy's arrived, it seems she wants me home more and more. I don't know what to do about it and the whole situation's getting me down."

Colt stared at Chase and icy fear crawled through his gut. It was obvious Chase and Josie, who seemed ideal partners when they wed, were struggling now. *Hell, was their marriage on the rocks?* Colt had been a groomsman at their wedding only a few short years before. He'd never seen two people so in love. And yet, here they were, arguing over something Chase had no control over. *Didn't Josie get it? Didn't she love Chase like she once had?* Would theirs become like all the other relationships he'd watched go down the toilet?

He cursed under his breath. He'd been a fool to think he and Morgan could be different. If even his cousin couldn't make it work, what more proof did he need? People changed when they got married and it wasn't for the better. He hated the thought of Chase and Josie heading for divorce, but if the two of them couldn't sort out their differences, it seemed like a real possibility.

The sludge of dread weighed heavily in his veins. His boots felt like they were fixed to the floor. He should never have given Morgan hope they could have a future. He should have trusted his gut all along. It had served him well for more than thirty years. He'd best forget about wild possibilities and concentrate on the cold hard truth. More than forty percent of marriages ended in divorce. He refused to add to the statistics.

––––––––––––––

Morgan brushed back a lock of hair from her eyes and tucked it behind her ear. Taking a sip of wine, she surreptitiously surveyed the room. She kept sneaking glances in Colt's direction, but as far as she knew, he hadn't told his family about the two of them. The anniversary party was in full swing, with the auditorium filled to capacity. Two musicians played country music that had her toe tapping and she noticed several other partygoers had taken to the floor.

"So Morgan, tell us about the city. What's it like living there?"

Morgan forced her attention back to the women who surrounded her. It had been that way almost from the moment she arrived. She could understand Colt's sisters being interested in a woman their brother had brought to a family function. She'd never had siblings, but she had a lot of good friends. It was natural to be curious about who they were seeing, or weren't.

She smiled at Colt's youngest sister, Darcy, and answered the question. "The city's great. It has such a vibe. The streets are noisy and crowded. There are so many people going somewhere, always in a hurry."

Darcy pulled a face. "It doesn't sound like much fun to me."

Morgan laughed and Colt's oldest sister, Ashleigh, laughed too. "You've never lived anywhere else but Armidale, Darcy. Of course it sounds unattractive. Armidale and the New England area are so beautiful and peaceful, with everyone moving at a slower pace, but it doesn't mean crowds can't be exciting." Ashleigh looked at Morgan expectantly. "Right, Morgan?"

"Right. The hustle and bustle just adds to the excitement and there's so much to see and do! I work at the Sydney Harbour Hospital. It's only about five miles from the city. I spend most of my leisure time going to exhibitions, concerts and live shows." She laughed deprecatingly. "I never have any money, but I have a really good time."

The girls around her laughed, and Morgan felt a rush of warmth. Colt's sisters were so warm and welcoming, interested and polite. Darcy was in college and still lived at home. Her experience had been limited to a large country town, just like Morgan's had been at that age.

Still, Ashleigh was right about Armidale. It was a beautiful place to live. Each season was distinct and perfect, from the frost and snow in winter, to the heat of a wide blue summer sky. Morgan hadn't realized how much she loved the area until she'd returned this time. Most of her visits up until then had been for only four or five days.

"Would you ever move back?" Ashleigh asked quietly, as if she could read Morgan's mind. Darcy and Emily waited for her answer, identical expressions of expectation on the faces.

Morgan took a moment to think about her

reply. It would be nice to be closer to her father and with Uncle Leslie now living here… They were the only family she had.

Her thoughts flicked to Colt and her heart skipped a beat. He'd asked if she'd give them a go, but there was still so much to work out. She had a life in Sydney. He lived in the bush. *Would they do the long distance thing?* She couldn't bear the thought. *But was she prepared to sell her condo and relocate from the city for a man? What if things didn't work out?*

It was like Colt said – there was no guarantee of a happily ever after. *Was she prepared to turn her life upside down to find out?* She didn't have the reservations he did about love and marriage, but still…

"Morgan?"

The sound of Ashleigh's voice broke into Morgan's thoughts and she forced herself to focus on the young women who stood around her with questioning looks on their faces. Realizing she hadn't answered Ashleigh's question, she flushed.

"I'm sorry, Ashleigh. I was thinking about how best to reply. I guess I wouldn't rule out a return to the country. I grew up and went to college here. My father still lives here. It would be nice to be able to spend more time with him. But I love my life in the city, too. I have great job and a nice condo… It's hard to say."

A calculating gleam entered Ashleigh's eyes. "What if you met a country boy who just couldn't bear to drag himself away from his roots? Would that make a difference?"

Once again, heat stole across Morgan's cheeks. She wasn't sure if Ashleigh was hinting at the relationship between her and Colt, or if the girl was even aware of the history between them, but the woman's gaze seemed to see right through her, to her heart beating frantically within.

She wasn't sure if she should say anything about their recent decision to give things a go, or if she should wait for Colt to break the news. She was saved from answering because Colt arrived just then and even though his presence did nothing for her equilibrium, she was pleased for the interruption.

"Morgan, I hope my sisters aren't boring you to tears with their endless questions." The affectionate smile Colt bestowed on the women in his family softened his words.

Morgan licked her suddenly dry lips and answered him. "No, of course not. It's been lovely getting to know them."

"Good, but seeing as the speeches are over and the cake's been cut, I thought we might call it a night. We have a long drive back to Armidale."

Morgan blinked at the brusqueness in his tone, surprised that he wanted to leave while most of the guests were still there. She looked at him, trying to gage his mood. She'd barely spoken to him during the party. For most of the night, he'd been surrounded by his family and friends, while she'd been left to answer questions from many of the curious guests, including his sisters.

Still, she'd expected him to find her at some

point during the night, even if it was to ask her to dance. The music had been playing for most of the evening and she'd looked forward to taking a turn on the floor. But one look at the closed expression on his face and she knew they wouldn't be dancing anytime soon.

"I'll get my bag," she murmured and excused herself from the group. All the time, fear congealed in her heart.

CHAPTER 18

Colt glanced at Morgan where she sat in the passenger seat of his car, dreading the conversation he needed to have with her. The tension in the air was palpable. She looked confused and wary, and rightly so. He was acting like a jerk. She deserved an explanation.

Thoughts of his buddies and their broken lives, fighting over the kids – the anger, the animosity; the tragedy that at some time in the not-too-distant past, these people loved each other and were now hell-bent on destruction. And now he could add Chase and Josie to the list.

He didn't wish that kind of pain and heartache on anyone and he sure as hell didn't want it for himself. He glanced across at Morgan again. *How was he going to tell her? What was he going to say?*

"Are you all right?" she asked quietly.

He could hear the uncertainty in her voice and cursed under his breath. He wished he could reassure her, but the words just wouldn't come.

"Morgan... I'm sorry."

She stared at him, her eyes wide. "Sorry?"

He winced and hunted around for the right words. *Were there any right words in this kind of situation?*

"What's the problem, Colt?" Her gaze was now narrowed and her tone was edged with anger.

He grimaced again. "I shouldn't have said there could be something between us," he said in a rush, keeping his gaze fixed on the road ahead.

"*What?*"

The shock in her voice reverberated around the tight confines of the car. He squirmed in his seat, feeling like the gutless shit that he was.

He shot her a quick look. "I thought I could overcome the fear, but tonight it overwhelmed me once again. Chase told me he and Josie are having problems. They used to be so much in love." He shook his head in defeat. "If they can't make it, nobody can."

"You're a coward, Colt Barrington!"

Her accusation rang through the air. Colt remained silent. He couldn't deny it. She spoke the truth. He was a coward and she was better off without him. He was only glad they'd arrived at this point before too many feelings got involved. He wished with all his heart things could be different, that he could put faith in Morgan and their love, but the doubts and fears kept resurfacing. It was no way to go into a marriage.

"Tell me, Morgan," he said quietly, "how many people do you know who are happily married?"

In the dimness, he saw her lips purse in thought. She didn't offer a reply.

"See, I rest my case."

"Your parents have just celebrated thirty-five years," she said, her eyes flashing.

"Yes, but they're from a different time. Nobody does commitment like that these days."

"You're wrong. I have friends who are married, and very happily."

He shot her a droll look. "Give them time."

Once again, she narrowed her gaze at him. "What are you afraid of, Colt?"

Her question was made even more deadly for its quiet delivery. His heart skipped a beat and then took off in full flight. His gut burned with dread. She was right. He *was* afraid. No, he was more than afraid. He was terrified. He didn't want to end up like his buddies – despising the women they once vowed to love until death they did part.

As far as he was concerned, the end of the happily ever after, was a death, just not in the literal sense. He bet none of his friends thought on their wedding day that there would come a time when they couldn't stand the sight of their bride. It was all so terribly sad and depressing.

"I... I don't think I'm ready to give you what you need, Morgan. I wish I could. I want to. I want to so much, but...I can't."

They rode the rest of the way in silence and every tense mile ate into Colt's gut. Morgan sat quiet and still beside him, staring out the window into the dark. An hour later, he turned into his driveway and switched off the ignition. He hardly dared to look in her direction, but finally found the courage.

She stared at him, her eyes wide with devastation. Tears coursed down her cheeks. His jaw clenched. He felt worse than he'd ever felt in his life.

"Thank you for the evening," she murmured, "and just so you know, you can find someone else to play your stupid games. I'm done." With that, she climbed out of the car and with her head held high, she walked slowly in the direction of his condo.

Colt cursed and tamped down the instinct to go after her. She needed time to herself. Time to think through his about-face and to come to terms with it. Time to accept that Colt Barrington was a cowardly prick and she was better off without him.

———————

Morgan used the pillow to muffle her sobs. She'd used the spare key to get inside Colt's condo, unwilling to wait for him to let her in. He'd stared at her so calmly and told her there was no future for them, after everything they'd been through. She still couldn't believe it.

Oh, he'd told her at the outset that he wasn't the marrying kind. She'd known his stance as well as he knew how much she yearned to have a husband, a family of her own. And she'd believed him, as he'd believed her. But then, he'd slept with her and asked her to give them a chance. He'd even invited her to his parents' anniversary celebration, knowing all of his friends and family would be there. What else was she supposed to think, but that he'd been making a public declaration?

She wasn't stupid and neither were the people who gathered in that room. Most of them would have assumed they were a couple. It was Colt who'd turned cowardly, who'd backed out of their deal. She couldn't believe he'd done it, yet again.

A fresh wave of anger rushed through her and she pounded the pillow with her fist. She was angry at him for leading her on, but she was just as angry with herself. She'd known from the outset that he disdained commitment and for all his pretty words earlier in the evening, fear such as his didn't just go away. It served her right for thinking any different. She'd fallen for him and that was nobody's fault but hers.

The knowledge filled her spine with steel. She was made of sterner stuff. She'd been through some tough times before and come out the other side. The death of her mother had devastated her and yet she'd continued her studies and graduated from college with honors. She'd forged a successful career, had good friends, a condominium near the beach. She had much to be thankful for and as soon as her dad arrived home and she satisfied herself he was all right, she'd head back to the city.

That was her *real* life. The city, her job, her friends. Colt Barrington was her past and it was best for everyone that he stayed there. Now, if his sisters asked her their questions, the answers would come easy...

Colt glanced at the cheap government-issued clock that hung on the wall opposite his desk and rubbed his gritty eyes. It was barely nine in the morning, but already he'd had enough. The office was quiet. Even the phones hadn't rung. That happened on a public holiday. He ought to be out celebrating the national holiday, like everyone else. Instead, he was at work trying hard to summon the enthusiasm he needed to follow up on a few witness statements to the Anthony Adamson case.

The night before, he'd followed Morgan into his condo and had heard her crying behind her bedroom door. He'd wanted to go and offer her comfort, but he forced himself to stay away. Nothing had changed in the moments between when he'd torn her hopes apart and then and there was nothing he could say or do to make things better. Her door had still been closed when he left for work that morning.

He thought of Marie Adamson, the mother of the murdered children, and his chest went tight. That woman would spend the rest of her days knowing her ex-husband had murdered her children because he couldn't stand the thought of her having them. *How did someone come back from that? How did they manage to go on?* It was inconceivable that they could – and yet, Marie Adamson had no choice.

A fresh wave of sadness and irritation surged through him and he cursed under his breath, wishing he had something else to focus on, something that didn't involve putting a brief together against a father who'd deliberately drowned his kids.

The phone in his pocket vibrated and he sighed, welcoming the interruption. Glancing at the screen, he was tempted not to answer, but even talking to his brother had to be better than stewing on what had happened the night before.

"Beau, what do you want?" he muttered.

"My, my, my! Who's woken up tired and cranky? It's not my fault you've been up all night doing the horizontal samba."

Colt grimaced, wishing a long and mutually satisfying lovemaking session with Morgan was the cause of his irritation and fatigue. The night could have ended that way, if he'd kept his mouth shut. It just went to show what a dick he was.

"Shut up, Beau. It's none of your business."

Beau sounded taken aback. "Wow, okay. I take it the night didn't end as well as you expected."

"You've got that right," Colt muttered.

"Dare I ask what happened?"

"*I* happened. I told her there could never be anything between us."

"What the hell are you talking about, Colt? You're crazy for her. Anyone can see that."

"It's not that easy, Beau. She wants to get married, have a family. You know how I feel about all that. For a while, I thought maybe I could give it a go, see where it all led, but then Chase came over complaining about Josie and I panicked. What chance have I got when a couple like Chase and Josie can't make things work?"

Beau sighed on the other end of the phone. "Shit, Colt. You're overreacting. Chase was just having a bad night. We've all been there. All couples argue. It's natural. It doesn't mean their marriage is about to fall apart."

"More than forty percent of all marriages in Australia end in divorce, Beau. You know the stats as well as I do."

"Exactly!" Beau replied triumphantly. "The other sixty percent survive! You're looking at it all the wrong way, Colt. It's glass half-full kind of stuff. Not every marriage ends in divorce. Look on the bright side, little bro. It's nearly two-thirds full."

Colt compressed his lips. He hadn't looked at it like that. It seemed like he'd only seen the worst of it, the havoc that could be wreaked when it all went so wrong. Like with the Adamson family and countless others that filled the pages of the police files.

"If you think it's such a noble institution, how come you've never taken the plunge?" Colt threw at his brother.

"It's not for the same reasons as you, let me assure you," Beau replied. "The divorce rate doesn't scare me off. It's finding the right woman. I fully intend to get married and I plan on staying that way from the day the vows are made. I want what Mom and Dad have. Thirty-five years and still counting. I want forever, Colt. I just haven't found my forever woman, yet."

"It can't be that hard," Colt muttered. "You're a good-looking guy with a passable sense of humor. You're a neurosurgeon in one of Sydney's most prestigious hospitals and I'm led to believe you're rather good at your job. What are you doing wrong, bro?"

"It isn't that easy, Colt and you know it. After all, it's taken you all this time to realize Morgan O'Brien is darn near perfect and you even knew her from before. What hope have I got? I don't have the kind of time it takes to weed out the good from the bad and like I said to you before, I seem to have gathered a bit of a reputation for not playing for keeps. You must be influencing me subconsciously. Some days, it feels easier to forget about it and just get on with saving lives."

Beau's sigh was over dramatic, but Colt's mind had snagged on something else. "What do you mean Morgan's darn near perfect? Do you think...? Do you think she's my forever girl?"

"What, are you *blind*? Do you have a brain at all between those ears? Of course she's your forever girl! I thought she was ten years ago, but for some reason, the two of you parted ways. I wasn't at all surprised to see her at the party last night. I knew you'd end up together again."

"Did you talk to her?" Colt asked.

"No, apart from saying hello. The girls had her

tied up for most of the night. Then you left so abruptly... All I'm saying is, don't let her get away. You connect with her in a way I've never seen you do with any other girl. She's smart, pretty and she has substance. It's an uncommon combination. I think she's a keeper, bro, but I guess that's for you to decide."

Morgan stood on the porch outside her father's house, a suitcase in either hand. She should have called ahead, warned Uncle Leslie she was moving in, but she hadn't thought about it. After waking that morning and realizing Colt had already left, the only thing she wanted to do was pack up her things and get out of there.

She'd called a cab and had arrived at Butler Street without giving it too much thought. And here she was, hoping her uncle wouldn't mind a guest for a handful of days. It wouldn't be longer than that. She had to be back at work in five days. She only hoped her father would be home before then.

She wished for the hundredth time that she knew where he was. He'd told her in the email she'd received yesterday that after Darwin he was ready to head back home. She hadn't heard from him since, but her hopes were high that he was well and truly on his way. If all went well, she expected him either that day or the next.

Still, there was nothing she could do at the moment except knock on her father's door. She wasn't prepared to spend another night at Colt's place and the thought of hiding out in a hotel room was worse – if she could find one. She wanted her dad. She missed him so much. She needed to be surrounded by his things. Uncle Leslie was the next best thing.

Taking a breath, Morgan rapped on the panel beside the screen door and waited. The house was quiet and still. She glanced at her watch. It was nearly ten. *Surely he wasn't still sleeping?* Maybe he was a little hard of hearing? She remembered the last time she'd called on him unannounced, it had taken him awhile to answer the door.

She knocked again and called out and a moment later, was rewarded with the sound of footsteps. The door opened and her uncle greeted her with a friendly smile.

"Morgan! How lovely to see you! What brings you around this fine sunny morning?"

She stepped forward and pecked him on a grizzled cheek and breathed in the familiar scent of her father.

"Uncle Leslie, I'm sorry to arrive like this, but I need somewhere to stay. Do you mind if I spend a few days with you?"

"Of course, honey!" he said with a smile. "I'd love to spend more time with my niece!"

He reached down and took her largest suitcase and then headed back into the house. "Come in, come in. I was just about to have a cup of tea."

Taking hold of her other bag, she followed him.

"I'll put your things in your old room," he offered. "That way you'll feel right at home."

She threw him a grateful smile, thankful he hadn't peppered her with questions. "It will only be for a few days, I promise," she said and followed him down the hall.

"Stay as long as you want, honey. After all, this is your home."

"Thank you, Uncle. Your kindness means a great deal. As soon as Dad gets back, I'll be sure to tell him how lovely you've been to me."

Her uncle opened the door to her old room and set the suitcase on the floor. Morgan was pleased to see it looked almost like it always had, although the heavy, antique oak dresser that had stood under the window for as long as she could remember was gone.

She frowned and looked more closely around the room. Two matching, limited edition Peter Schuster prints that had hung over the bed were also missing. She couldn't understand why. Her father had mentioned nothing about the changes. *What was going on? Was he that short of money that he had to sell some of their things? Why hadn't he said anything?* She was determined to have a full and frank discussion with him when he returned.

"I'm sure you know where everything is," her uncle said, interrupting her thoughts.

"Yes, I'll be fine and thank you for letting me stay."

He opened his arms expansively. "Like I said, this

is your home. You don't have to ask permission, and especially not from me."

She was touched by his humility and thanked him once again. It was such a shame she hadn't met him earlier. She was sure they would have been close. Still, she had an opportunity now to make up for lost time and staying under the same roof would be even more conducive to that.

"Do you fancy a cup of tea, honey? I put the kettle on not long ago."

"Thank you, uncle. A cup of tea sounds lovely."

He led the way into the kitchen and Morgan followed him. It was the first time in a long time since she'd been all the way into the room. She looked around and noted other little changes.

There was an empty ashtray on the small table that took up most of the space in the cozy breakfast nook. As her father didn't smoke, she could only assume it belonged to her uncle. She hoped he hadn't been smoking in the house. Her dad hated the smell of smoke. It was one thing the twins didn't have in common.

A new rug, slightly askew, ran half the length of the galley kitchen. Its garish colors and cheap quality seemed out of place with the other tasteful, expensive pieces of furniture that filled the room. She wondered when her dad had bought it and why. It was so *not* his style.

He loved the polished floorboards that comprised most of the rooms in the house. It was only in the bedrooms that he'd made a concession to the winter chill and had laid carpet. Over the years, Morgan had complained lightheartedly that he needed some floor rugs; that her feet always got too cold. The next time she visited, she was surprised and touched to discover her dad had arranged for in-floor heating to be installed.

"Here you go."

Her uncle handed her a cup that was filled with black tea. She murmured her thanks and took it from him. "Where shall we sit?" she asked.

"How about just here," he replied and headed for the breakfast nook.

Her glance strayed again to the ashtray. Her uncle noticed the direction of her gaze. He jerked to a halt and then threw her an embarrassed look. Hastily reaching for the ashtray, he shoved it in the pocket of his pants.

"Sorry. Filthy habit. I really should give it up."

She forced a smile. "Yes, you should. Your body will thank you for it. It's never too late to quit."

"You sound like the last doctor I attended," her uncle chuckled. "It was the middle of winter, a couple of years back. I had such a bad chest, I thought I was going to die."

"Perhaps you should have listened to him," she said lightly.

He eyed her curiously. "What is it that you do, Morgan?"

"I'm a nurse at the Sydney Harbour Hospital."

His eyes gleamed with understanding. "Ah, now the comment about quitting makes even more sense."

"Yes, unfortunately, the wards are filled with far too many people with chronic diseases that have been caused by smoking. Quitting's a far better option, and cheaper, too." She smiled again in an effort to soften her words.

"So, you like living in Sydney?" her uncle asked, leaning forward, lifting his cup to his mouth and taking a sip of tea.

"Yes, I do. It's very different from life in the country, as I'm sure you'll agree. You were living in Sydney before you came looking for my dad, weren't you?"

"Yes, although I'm not sure I'd call it living. Existing's probably a better word. I left home a long time ago and moved around a lot. I've lived rough without a roof over my head for more nights than I care to remember."

He glanced at Morgan who felt a renewed sense of sadness when she considered the life her uncle had led.

He shrugged deprecatingly. "Don't feel sorry for me, honey. It was what it was. We can't all be born lucky."

Like her dad...

He didn't say the words, but he didn't have to. She could see it in the shadows that darkened his eyes and in the hint of anger that tightened his jaw. She thought of her conversation with Georgie and for the first time considered if her uncle could harbor feelings of resentment toward her dad.

She understood his reaction, if he did. It must hurt to know that his twin had not only been raised by his parents, but had been lavished with love and other material blessings throughout his life – the kind of things her uncle had never known...

"So, tell me, Morgan. Do you have your own place in Sydney?"

"Yes. I've been lucky. Dad helped me get into a one-bedroom condo in Bondi. It's small, but it's in a nice complex and I have a view of the beach."

"It sounds lovely."

Her uncle bestowed a beatific smile upon her and sipped from his cup again. Setting it back down on the saucer, he sighed with contentment.

"It's such a beautiful day outside. It seems a shame to waste it indoors. Would you like to go for a walk? You could tell me all about that boyfriend of yours and why you've turned up on my doorstep. I take it you had an argument; is that it?"

Morgan felt a stab of surprise. "Colt's not my boyfriend. We knew each other years ago. We...used to date a long time ago."

"Ah, so he *is* a boyfriend, just not a current one. It looked to me that he was still very much interested, the way he hovered over you that first night. I assumed you were a couple. He seemed very protective."

"Yes, well, he's a detective. I think they're born that way," Morgan replied dryly, unwilling to pay any heed to what her uncle thought he sensed. After all, he barely knew her and he didn't know Colt at all.

Her uncle said nothing, but threw her a knowing look. She grimaced and lowered her gaze. She wasn't sure she was comfortable discussing her love life with a man she'd only just met, uncle or no uncle. But he appeared oblivious to her reservations. Pushing away from the table, he picked up his cup and headed toward the exit.

"Come on, let's take a walk. You can bring your tea with you. I think it's time you and I had a little talk."

"Of course. I'll be right with you. Just as soon as I straighten this rug. It's been annoying me from the moment I spotted it. Hold on a moment, I'll be right there."

Morgan stood and walked into the kitchen. Her uncle headed out the door. Bending low, she took hold of the fringed end of the rug. Up close, it was even more hideous. Giving it a tug, she frowned when it remained firmly in place. Tugging harder, she realized it had been nailed into place.

How curious... She couldn't imagine why her dad would fix a rug permanently to his floor. It was downright strange. Just another anomaly in a list of unusual things that were beginning to pile up...

It had to be a brain tumor. It was the only thing that made sense. Her father had an inoperable tumor taking over his head. It was the reason so many things were out of kilter and why from the very first moment she returned home, she'd felt strange.

The sad conclusion weighed like concrete in her belly. The very thought of losing her beloved father way before his time was almost something she couldn't cope with and so, with a determined effort, she pushed it aside. She refused to think about it another moment. She'd wait for him to return and set her mind at ease. Until then, she'd enjoy the time with her uncle. If her theory about her dad's health status was right, before too long her uncle might be the only family she had.

CHAPTER 19

Leslie held the front door open for Morgan and waited for her to precede him. The faint scent of her perfume wafted toward him. She was a beautiful woman, full of confidence and charm. He could see why the young detective was all in a lather about her. He wondered what had driven Morgan out of his arms and into her uncle's domain. Well, into her father's – at least technically… Soon all that would change.

His plan had been masterful and had gone almost as smoothly as he'd imagined. He'd overcome Rex's initial reservations and within days of Leslie's arrival, the two of them were fast friends. On the surface, at least.

Leslie had no intention of befriending his long lost brother. From the moment he'd learned the truth surrounding the circumstances of his birth, he'd been livid with rage. It was unfortunate his biological parents were no longer of this world. It meant that the only one left to take the brunt of his anger was his twin. And rightly so. After all, the man had been given everything – parents who loved him unreservedly, an illustrious career, a very comfortable life. It wasn't fair and someone had to pay. Too bad for Rex, he was the first and only person in line…until now.

Within days of his arrival, he'd disposed of his long lost brother and had set about turning himself into the upstanding Rex O'Brien. He'd cut his hair in the style favored by his twin, took to wearing his shoes and clothes and other accessories. He even used the man's cologne. In the short time they'd been together, Rex had told him about his daughter, Morgan. Leslie had been lucky to notice the girl's birthday marked on the calendar and had sent her a birthday card, in an effort to maintain the charade.

But then he'd screwed up over the anniversary of her mother's death and the next thing he knew, Rex's daughter was standing on his doorstep. His plan to steal his brother's identity had to undergo a change.

So, he'd turned his attention to Rex's laptop. It was easy enough to guess his brother's password. It had only taken two tries. From then, it had been simple enough to put Morgan off the scent by sending her emails from her dad, assuring her that everything was all right. Pretty soon – probably tonight – he'd send her another explaining that her "dad" had been caught up in a monsoon. It was wet season in the tropics, after all, and last Morgan knew, her father was headed for Darwin…

Leslie hadn't planned on killing his niece, but

now it seemed like a much more fitting end to what he'd once thought was the perfect plan. Morgan was a liability and she simply knew too much. And now that he'd stumbled across a copy of Rex's will... There was nothing else for it. Both O'Briens needed to meet with premature deaths.

Leslie had spent some time planning how they'd occur. Rex's death was easy. After all, everyone knew he'd gone away. It wasn't beyond reason that he might die on the road. The people of Armidale would be saddened to hear their friend and long-term member of the community had passed away. Leslie would make sure the townspeople knew his brother had died doing what he'd always wanted to do: visiting the outback, creating some memories, experiencing the Australian bush.

He was sure no one would ask too many questions. After all, elderly people went missing and died in the outback all the time. Okay, maybe not all the time, but it happened. People underestimated the isolation and the long distances between towns and fuel stops. Unaccustomed to the harsh conditions, it was easy for them to succumb to the heat and vast emptiness, get confused, dehydrated, wander off...never to be seen again.

Morgan's death was a little trickier, but now that he knew she owned an expensive property, he was eager to see it done. With both Rex and Morgan out of the way, he was the closest living relative. He'd inherit everything in his own right. Life didn't get any sweeter.

All he had to do was make sure he got the timing right. It was imperative she die before her father, or at least, before her father's death became known. That way, Rex would inherit from his daughter and the whole lot would come to Leslie upon his brother's sad and unfortunate end.

It was a perfect plan and fitting revenge against the man who had lived so long with everything Leslie didn't have. The best thing was, he was well on the way to seeing it to fruition. The gods had been looking down on him that morning when Morgan stumbled into his lair.

He wondered again how he might do it. Rat poison would probably do the trick. There were boxes of it in the shed. He'd seen them there. Yes, he'd bake her a cake and lace it with poison. If he got the dosage right and made sure she ate enough, her death was as good as guaranteed. And after all, it had been her birthday only a few weeks ago. He'd made sure he'd sent her a card. He bet she hadn't had a cake and everyone deserved a cake on their birthday... Didn't they?

Colt stared at the screen on his phone where it sat so innocently on his desk and swallowed a lump of nerves. For the past twenty minutes, he'd been trying to scrounge up the courage to call Morgan. He'd replayed his conversation with Beau over and over again in his head and had finally accepted that it was time to put aside his cowardice and get on with living his life – a life he very much wanted Morgan O'Brien to be a part of.

The thought of her with someone else, married to someone else had become unbearable and he was seized with a feeling of urgency that if he didn't act soon, it would be too late. A woman like her wouldn't wait around forever and he was sure there were plenty of willing applicants just waiting for a chance to claim her for their own.

But what if she turned him down, tired of his indecision? Wasn't interested in his declarations of love. Love? Was he in *love* with her? All the signs pointed in that direction.

He'd always enjoyed her company. She was intelligent, beautiful and funny. They shared a similar sense of humor and both worked hard at their careers. They were certainly sexually compatible. There was no question there. The night of the storm he'd burned with a need so great he'd been surprised he hadn't been consumed.

But it had been less than twelve hours ago that he'd told her he could never give her what she wanted. *What if she refused to believe him? How was he going to convince her that he'd changed his mind and that this time, he really meant it?*

Colt sighed and his gut twisted once again with nerves. *Had he blown it with her forever? Had his fear and cowardice pushed her out of his reach?*

There was only one way to find out. He picked up his phone.

―――――――――――――

Morgan rinsed her hands in the bathroom sink after coming in from outside. Her walk around the perimeter of her father's property in the company of Uncle Leslie had been pleasant, but it had only served to highlight the fact her dad was still not home. She missed him and it had become an almost physical ache.

It was probably because here, in Armidale, she had so much more time on her hands and being in her hometown reminded her of him. She'd never visited without staying with him, spending time with him in the garden; down the street having coffee at a café; watching movies; playing cards; talking about anything and everything. She missed all of it and was more than ready to see his Ford Ranger turn into the drive.

Reaching for the hand towel that hung from a hook near the sink, she noticed the toothbrush that stood in a charger near the faucet. It was her father's toothbrush. She'd bought it for him for Christmas. An electric one, with all the bells and whistles.

He'd laughed when he'd unwrapped it and declared he'd always wanted one. She'd made sure it was in his favorite color – blue. Surely her uncle couldn't have the same one? She'd heard all about how in tune twins were, and identical twins even more so, but to own the same toothbrush? *Was that taking the twin thing too far?*

But what other explanation was there? Her father had gone away. It was obvious he'd planned to be away for some time. He'd been gone more than a month already. There was no way he'd leave without packing his toothbrush.

Unless he simply forgot it or took a travel toothbrush that didn't require electricity? She hated that she didn't know, that he wasn't there to answer yet another question – questions that were piling up. On impulse, she walked into his bedroom and strode over to his closet. Pulling open the doors, she scanned the racks of clothes and shoes, all neatly arranged on the shelves.

Nothing appeared out of the ordinary. Her shoulders slumped on a sigh. She didn't know what she was looking for, but unease had been gnawing away at her belly. It wasn't any single thing that had caused it, but a host of little things: the missing figurines, the furniture, the laptop, the missing pictures, Rusty...and now the toothbrush. She didn't know what to make of it and she wished once again her dad were there, safe and sound, laughing away her fears.

And then it struck her. Her father's closet looked the way it always had and therein lay the problem. He'd gone away. There should have been empty hangers, vacant spaces left by clothes and shoes he'd taken with him. She looked up to the ledge where he stored his suitcases and noticed both were still there.

Her sense of foreboding grew and with it, icy

tentacles of fear. They crept insidiously along her veins, prickling her skin as they went. She shivered and rubbed her arms in an effort to force them away.

She was being ridiculous. Of course her dad was away. He was traveling across the outback. He'd even told her so. It had to be true. There was no other possibility. Because if it wasn't, it meant—

No, she refused to go there. He was traveling, clearing his head, and soon he'd be home. She was sure of it. In fact, she'd go and check her emails right now and see if he'd sent a new message.

Hurrying from the room, she headed down the hall to the living room in search of her handbag. Turning the corner, she came up short. Uncle Leslie was at her father's desk, typing on the computer. Confusion flooded her mind.

"Oh, Uncle Leslie... I'm sorry. I... I didn't realize you were using Dad's laptop."

Her uncle spun on the chair like he'd been shot and immediately closed the screen. Morgan caught a glimpse of the mail program and became even more intrigued. Slowly, she walked further into the room, her heart hammering against her ribs.

"I thought you told me you didn't know one end of a computer from another?" she murmured, keeping her voice calm.

Her uncle laughed, but there was tension around his eyes. "Did I tell you that, honey? I might have exaggerated a little. I took a few courses here and there over the years. I'm not exactly proficient, but I guess I know enough to get by."

Morgan swallowed her surprise. Another surge of unease flooded through her veins. She wondered how many other things her uncle had exaggerated about.

"Don't look so worried, honey." He chuckled. "The truth is, I've never had much of an opportunity to work with computers. When I arrived here, your dad was surfing on the net. I was curious and he showed me how it worked. I couldn't believe the kind of things you could discover with just a few keystrokes. It blew me away."

His eyes sparkled with delight, like a small child on Christmas morning. Morgan's dread eased. She was worrying over nothing. It was just the fact she hadn't spoken to her father for so long and her nerves were frayed from worry. Toss in the crushing disappointment with Colt and it was no wonder she was more than a little on edge.

"In fact," her uncle added, "it was probably my fault your father left his laptop behind. He'd been showing me something right before he left. I think he walked out the door and didn't even think about it."

Morgan sighed and nodded. "He was probably so fixed on his upcoming trip, he didn't give anything proper consideration. He didn't even pack his toothbrush."

She thought her uncle paled, but it could have been a trick of light. Just then, her phone buzzed in her pocket and she pulled it out of her shorts.

She glanced at the screen and her heart skipped a beat.

Colt.

What could he possibly have to say to her? Perhaps he'd gone home for lunch and had discovered she'd left. Her luggage was missing. It wouldn't take him long to realize she'd moved out – and why. It couldn't have come as a surprise.

She debated about letting the call go through to voicemail, but her uncle was looking at her with a curious expression on his face and she had no choice but to answer it. Turning away, she headed back down the hall toward her bedroom. She pulled the door closed behind her.

"Colt, what can I do for you?"

Her tone was barely warmer than frosty and she didn't feel the slightest bit guilty. He couldn't lead her on, then dash her hopes so spectacularly and not expect a little punishment, even if it were only a lack of desire to encourage conversation.

"Morgan, I... I wanted to apologize for last night."

"There's no need to apologize, Colt. In fact, I'm a little tired of your apologies. You said what you needed to say. In fact, I should thank you for being so forthright. Again. It would have been much easier to let me continue to believe you'd changed your mind about commitment and marriage and enjoy the...benefits of our relationship. So I guess you did me a favor. At least now I don't have the slightest doubt where I stand. Misunderstandings have never been my thing."

"Are you done?"

His quiet question caught her by surprise. She thought he'd be pleased she'd reiterated his position and made it clear she knew where they stood.

"I'm done."

"Good. Now, last night wasn't the first time I've told you I'm not the marrying kind. I've even told you why. The divorce rate scares the hell out of me and it continues to climb. The fallout from a failed marriage is terrible to see. Two people who once loved each other and vowed to support each other for the rest of their lives are reduced to unrecognizable monsters filled with vile anger and hate. Kids get fought over like they're chattels without feelings or thoughts of their own. I've seen it happen time and again with friends and colleagues and even people I don't know – and it's devastated me each and every time."

He drew in a ragged breath. Morgan listened in silence. *Where was Colt going with this?* She'd heard it all before. Did she even care enough to want to find out? Much to her chagrin, her heart answered with a resounding yes.

"But despite all that," he continued, "I decided I was wrong. I want to take the chance, I want to see if we have what it takes. There's something between us, Morgan, whether you're aware of it or not. It's been there right from the beginning, from the very first moment we met.

"Back then, the timing was all wrong. We were barely adults, starting out in the world, trying to find our way. A baby wouldn't have worked for either of us and we made the only decision we could. I believe we would have become part of that statistic eventually. Our decision was right for us then and I still believe we made the right choice.

"But things are different now. We're both in such a better place. You want to know the joy of being a mother, to have a husband – a family of your own and though I didn't think I'd ever hear myself say it, I want those things, too. With you. If you'll have me."

A rush of emotion tightened Morgan's throat. She wanted to maintain her anger against him, but she could barely see through her tears. Colt wanted to have a relationship with her, perhaps even get married. It was everything she'd dreamed of and more than she ever hoped. The only thing that didn't set her heart singing was the fact he hadn't made any mention of love.

Still, she hadn't told him how she felt, either. Perhaps he was still coming around to the idea? It had taken her long enough to recognize her true feelings. She was prepared to cut him some slack. Given the fact that less than twelve hours earlier he'd told her quite plainly that he couldn't give her what she wanted, his impassioned speech of a few moments ago was nothing short of astounding.

"Morgan? Please say something. Don't leave me hanging here. Oh, hell. It's too late, isn't it? I've made a mess of it all. I've been a complete jerk, going back and forth, unable to make up my mind. I was weak and gutless. You have every right to turn me down. It's nothing less than what I deserve. I should never have expected—"

"Are you done?" she interrupted, breaking into a smile.

There was a moment of stunned silence and then, "I'm done."

"Good. Now listen, and listen well. "From the very first moment I saw you across the room at that Christmas party, I was drawn to you. It was like the music, the crowd, the room – everything disappeared." She laughed, a little embarrassed. "It sounds corny, but that's exactly how it was."

"It doesn't sound corny at all," he replied, his voice husky and low. "It was that way for me, too."

Her heart fluttered with pleasure at his announcement, but she wasn't finished yet.

"I have a lot of friends who are happily married, some for many years. I get that you see the worst of it and more than most people should, but I don't want to hear any more of your fears and insecurities on that score. Almost two-thirds of marriages last the distance. We both come from stable, happy homes. There's no reason we shouldn't be among the successful ones, but I need to know you're one hundred percent on board. I can't go into marriage or any other kind of long-term relationship without knowing you're just as certain as I am that we can make it. Do you understand?"

This time, he didn't hesitate. "Yes, I do and it gives me strength knowing you feel that way. I'm going to rely on you to keep me focused on the positive. I want to believe we can make it, I truly do. I'm determined to work on my fears and insecurities and put everything but you and me aside. We're all that matters and together, we're stronger. I need you to help me, Morgan, and in return, I'll do everything in my power to be the man you need me to be – the man I want to be."

"You want kids?" she asked and bit her lip waiting for his answer. A 'no' to kids would be a deal breaker.

"Yes, I want kids," he finally answered and she breathed a quiet sigh of relief.

"I've never had anything against children," he added. "It was what happens to them when everything falls apart that always held me back."

"We're not going to talk like that any longer, remember?" she chided gently.

"You're right."

She chuckled and was relieved when Colt followed suit. A comfortable silence fell between them. Morgan was the first to break it.

"What are you doing for dinner?" she asked. Colt quickly assured her he was free.

"Great. I'm at Dad's, with Uncle Leslie. I... I actually brought my bags over here. After last night... Anyway, he's going to make a special dinner to celebrate my birthday. He's even going to make me a cake. I told him it wasn't necessary, but he's insisting everyone deserves a cake on their birthday. I don't have the heart to tell him I can't remember the last time someone made me a birthday cake. It seems so important for him to do it, I had no choice but to agree. Will you come over and help me celebrate? I'm sure my uncle won't mind."

"I'd love to," Colt replied, his voice thick with emotion, "and I hope I can convince you to come back home with me tonight."

Morgan swallowed the lump in her throat and wondered if it would be too rude to tell her uncle she was no longer staying the night. Perhaps she'd leave that news for after dinner. After all, when he'd told her about it during their walk, he'd seemed so excited about preparing her a birthday celebration she wouldn't forget. She didn't want to take the shine off his thoughtful gesture by making him think she didn't appreciate his kindness or that she'd received a better offer.

"Great," she managed. "What time do you finish?"

"Six. I'll stop by home and shower. I could be at your place by seven."

She smiled and another wave of joy rushed through her. "That sounds fabulous. I'll let Uncle Leslie know."

"What about your dad? Is there any chance he might make it home?"

"I'm not sure. I'll have to check my emails. He was supposed to be heading home from Darwin. It's possible he might make it back tonight. That would be so amazing! It would really make my night. I can't wait to see him! Did you know, in addition to his laptop, he also forgot to take his toothbrush?"

"What do you mean, he forgot his toothbrush? Did he really do that?"

Morgan laughed. "Yes. I found it in the bathroom, where it's always kept. That gives you some idea how absent-minded he is, or at least, was while he was preparing for his trip."

"*Mm,*" Colt replied, his voice a little distant.

Morgan heard voices in the background and the sound of a ringing phone. Then Colt was speaking in muffled tones and she realized he was talking to someone else.

"I'm sorry, Morgan. Something's come up. I have to go."

"That's fine. I understand. You're at work. You're busy."

"Yes. I'd rather talk to you for the rest of the afternoon, but we have a situation that needs to be dealt with. I'll see you later tonight."

"Seven, right?"

"You betcha."

Chapter 20

Dear Diary,

It's all coming together and I can barely contain myself. Tonight is the culmination of everything I dreamed of and more. Who could imagine Leslie Lexington could one day be a wealthy man, a respected member of the community, with a house, a car and land?

It's beyond anything I could ever imagine and I still pinch myself to check that I'm awake. I feel like somehow it's all been a terrible mistake, that I'll wake up and my carefully laid plans will all come crashing down.

But no, I refuse to let my thoughts travel down that depressing path. This is karma, this is meant to be. It's only fair I take my rightful place in life and experience what my brother got for free – at my expense. It's my turn now, and that's exactly how it should be.

I was a little alarmed when she told me her detective was joining us for dinner. My initial thoughts were that it would spoil my plans and my birthday surprise would have to wait. I can hardly poison the girl in front of her boyfriend.

But then I thought about it a little more and an idea fell right into my head. It's so perfect it takes my breath away. I'll simply kill them both. An unfortunate case of severe food poisoning. I'll even come down with it myself. Perfect.

Colt ended his call to Morgan and allowed himself a tiny sigh of satisfaction and relief. She felt the same way he did and was willing to give them yet another try. Though his fears that they could make the distance hadn't been erased, the fact that she was aware of them and was willing to do whatever it took, reassured him – and the dread he always felt way down deep in his gut when he thought of marriage had eased. Turning in his chair, he faced the detective who waited to speak with him.

"Jared, what can I do for you?"

"One of the units was doing a patrol this morning on the outskirts of town. They came across a white Ford Ranger. It's been half-submerged in a dam. They've had a bit of a look around it and can't see anyone inside, but it's a bit hard with the front half filled with water."

Colt nodded. "Did they get the plates?"

"Yes, and I ran them through the system. The vehicle came back registered to Rex O'Brien."

Colt's heart skipped a beat. "From Butler Street?"

"Yes. At least, that's the address of the man the vehicle was registered to."

Colt's pulse picked up its speed. *Why the hell would a truck that belonged to Morgan's father be submerged in a dam on the edge of town?* He was meant to be in Darwin, or at the very least, on his way back home from there. Quiet dread eased into his bloodstream. Something definitely wasn't right.

"How long do the boys think it's been there?" he asked.

"Impossible to say at this stage. The patrol unit said they hadn't seen it before, but it's possible they missed it on their way around. Apparently the dam's at least fifty yards away from the road and like I said, the vehicle's partly submerged. It's easy to pass it by and not realize it's there."

"We'll need to get onto the Crash Investigation Unit. Those guys will want to take a look. We need to determine whether it's there because of an accident or if there's something more sinister involved. Are you sure there's no one inside?" Colt asked.

His colleague lifted one shoulder in a half-hearted shrug. "That's what the general duty guys said, but until we get the truck out of the water, we won't know for certain. I thought you might like to accompany me and see what we can make of it."

"Yes, of course," Colt replied and reached for his keys, his thoughts still on Rex O'Brien and the fact his vehicle apparently had never left town.

He didn't want to think about what it might mean. At least, not yet. Not until he had all the facts. Pushing away from his desk, he followed Jared out the door.

Like Jared had said, the pickup was well concealed amongst the high grasses that hid the stock dam situated at least fifty yards off the edge of the dirt road. It was easy to see why earlier patrols might have missed it, especially if they'd come past in the dark.

Pulling off his boots and socks and rolling up his pants, Colt paddled into the muddy water. The pickup had nosedived into the dam and was buried in the mud up to the chassis. The rear of the vehicle was stuck up in the air. Colt waded through the thigh-deep water and peered through the driver's window.

Wrenching the door handle, he was relieved when he managed to force it open. A small amount of water had found its way into the floor of the cab. He forced the door closed, but not before he'd had a chance to confirm the vehicle was empty.

He looked up at the sound of an approaching car and was pleased to see members of the Crash Investigation Unit making their way toward him. He'd notified them of the accident en route and had also called for a tow truck.

"What do we have?" Detective Robert Dominic called from his position on the muddy bank.

"2015 model Ford Ranger. No occupants inside," Colt replied.

"I can't see any sign of brake marks," Dominic

continued. "Perhaps there was a mechanical fault."

"The vehicle belongs to Rex O'Brien," Colt said. "I'm friendly with his daughter. He emailed her recently to say he was on his way back from Darwin. He made no mention of the car he was driving, but his pickup was missing from his garage. His daughter assumed he was in it. So unless the car was stolen and the culprit drove it straight into the dam in an effort to get rid of it, something strange is going on."

Dominic's eyebrows rose over Colt's comment, but he remained silent. Pulling out a digital camera, he began photographing the scene.

"Take a look at this," Dominic called out.

Colt moved to where the man stood. "What is it?"

"Footprints," Dominic replied.

Colt squatted and studied the baked-on shoe imprints that had been left in the muddy bank. They came from the direction of the dam and led back up toward the road.

"One set," he said. "Only one person involved."

"Yeah," Dominic replied and took a few more shots.

"We need to take some impressions," Colt said and Jared offered to go and get some plaster of paris from the car.

Although they were in a rural area with only the slight chance of onlookers passing by, Colt cordoned off the area before mixing up the plaster solution and pouring it into three of the clearest impressions. He was still waiting for it to set when the tow truck pulled up.

Colt waved the driver in, taking care to ensure the truck stayed well out of the way of the footprints and the tire marks the Ranger had made on its way into the dam. Until they'd determined whether it was a crime scene or a simple accident, it was important to preserve any evidence that might be there.

Thirty minutes later, the plaster had turned hard and Colt carefully removed the impressions and slid them into large plastic evidence bags. He'd store them until he knew what was going on and whether they'd be required.

"All right, we're done here," Colt said and the tow truck moved into position.

Slowly, the pickup was dragged up out of the mud. When it was clear of the water and unhooked from the truck, Colt strode forward and once again, opened the driver's door. A sluice of mud and water landed at his feet. It was just as well he hadn't yet pulled on his socks and boots. He leaned inside and looked around again, checking for anything that might give him a clue about how it had ended up nose down in the water.

The car smelled like the dam, muddy and dank. The pickup was a twin-cab and Colt realized the back seat hadn't gotten wet. Closing the driver's door, he opened the back door and noticed the seat was covered in hair. Coarse and pale, it looked like it belonged to a dog. A used cigarette butt had been discarded in the foot well. Two others lay on the back seat. It was fortunate only the front part of the car had been under the water or the items could have been washed away.

Digging around in the pocket of his pants, Colt produced another evidence bag. He tugged on a fresh pair of gloves and collected the cigarette butts. He didn't know if Morgan's father smoked, but someone who did had been inside the car. Though as yet there was no proof anything suspicious had occurred, the very fact Rex O'Brien's vehicle was out there at all was enough to kick Colt's instincts into high gear.

"What do you think?" Colt asked as the Crash Investigator walked near.

Dominic pursed his lips. "My preliminary thoughts are that the car was deliberately driven into the dam. There are no skid marks, torn vegetation or any other signs that the driver was speeding excessively or made any effort to avoid it. The tire tracks are indicative of a car traveling at moderate speed. Coupled with the fact there are shoe imprints heading away from the water, it's my guess this truck was stolen and dumped, or the owner did it in an effort to claim insurance."

"You're way off with the latter. Rex O'Brien's a retired lawyer. There's no way he's capable of fraud." The very idea was ludicrous. Colt compressed his lips and a fresh wave of dread stirred in his gut.

"I wonder why it didn't sink," Jared mused.

"Not enough water," Dominic replied. "It's been an unusually hot and dry summer. The dam's lower than normal. I can only guess whoever did this underestimated the depth."

Jared grinned. "Too bad for them."

Colt wished he could see the funny side. Every time he looked at the pickup, his dread increased. Without replying, he returned to the driver's side. Squatting on his haunches, he took out a flashlight and ran it slowly up and down the truck's surfaces.

It was impossible to tell if there had been any blood or other valuable evidence in the front foot wells where the water had lain, but after going over every other square inch of the vehicle, he was forced to concede there was nothing more of interest.

He turned to Jared. "I can't find any blood stains or any other signs of foul play. I guess it's possible it was stolen by kids and dumped here. The only thing that concerns me is the owner was apparently last seen in this vehicle more than a month ago, headed north. According to his brother and daughter, he's been traveling through the outback. He's due home any day."

"Well, he certainly didn't go anywhere in the Ranger," Jared commented with a slight smile.

Colt frowned. A growing sense of unease sidled through his gut. There had been a lot about Rex O'Brien's sudden decision to travel to places far away that had been unsettling to his daughter, not the least that he hadn't told her about his plans. From what Colt knew, Morgan and her father were close. His secrecy over his travels didn't make sense.

Then there were the other things – the laptop

and toothbrush left behind, the dog who'd turned up dead, the missing figurines, the long-lost identical twin brother with the criminal record who just happened on the scene and now lived in her father's home. Colt had been a detective for half a decade and he'd learned to listen to his gut. Right from the outset, something about the scenario had bugged him, but he hadn't been able to work out exactly what it was.

Now, with Rex's vehicle discovered abandoned, he couldn't help but feel something untoward had occurred and he was almost certain foul play was involved. The only logical reason Rex might try to get rid of his truck by running it into a dam was if he wanted to escape his life and not let anyone know… Or if someone else wanted it to appear that way…

But according to Morgan, her dad had been just fine with his life. There had been no mention of getting away before he took off and no reason for him to want to disappear – except, as she said, to work out all the implications of his new-found twin brother. When Colt had first suggested to Morgan that he contact the police in Tennant Creek, he'd also done a routine check of Rex's financial records to see if he could track him down that way. He'd discovered that although Rex wasn't a millionaire, he was far from struggling.

In Colt's experience, the majority of people who wanted to disappear from their normal life had debt collectors hounding them on every corner and no way of coming out on top. Rex didn't appear to be in that category and Colt was at a loss to explain why his vehicle had been found abandoned on the outskirts of Armidale when it should have been many miles from there.

He had a terrible suspicion Rex O'Brien was nowhere near Darwin. In fact, even though he had no proof other than the truck, Colt's gut told him the man had never left town and if that were so, where the hell was he? Even more troubling was the thought of telling Morgan what was circling in his mind. She was so certain her father was on his way back and might even make it home that night. Colt dreaded being the one to tell her that he didn't think it would be happening and that it was more likely she'd never see her father again.

With a heavy heart, Colt returned to the station and opened a new investigation file. He logged in the evidence he'd collected and wrote up a report. When he'd finished, he glanced at the clock and noticed his shift was over.

A surge of anticipation went through him at the thought of seeing Morgan again, but it was tinged with dread and caution. He still hadn't decided what he would tell her, if anything. First thing in the morning, he'd search the motor vehicle registry and check if Rex had purchased another car, a car Morgan had no knowledge of. Then he'd make another round of calls to the local police stations located in the towns Rex would likely have passed through. If he had in fact traveled from Armidale to Darwin in another vehicle, someone must have seen him at some stage along the way. Colt needed to locate him as a matter of urgency and set everyone's mind at ease.

With that thought in mind, Colt logged off and grabbed his jacket and keys. He'd swing by home and grab a quick shower and then head over to Butler Street and do his best to help celebrate the birthday of the woman who'd become a very important part of his life.

———————

Morgan met him at the door wearing a cherry red halter-style dress that hugged her curves. She'd applied bright red lipstick to match. His breath caught in his throat at the sight of her. She was beautiful, inside and out. How he ever imagined he could walk away from her and set her on her merry way to find some other guy to spend her life with, he didn't know, but he was glad he'd come to his senses in time – with a little help from his twin.

"Hi," she said and gave him a nervous smile.

He smiled back at her and leaned down and kissed her softly on the lips. Her mouth was warm and supple and he wanted to linger over the kiss, but they were standing in the doorway of her father's house. It wasn't the time or place. He only hoped he'd get to take her home with him that evening and they could pick up where they'd left off.

"How was your day?" he asked as he followed her into the living room. Her uncle was nowhere in sight.

"It was okay, I guess. I got an email from Dad this afternoon. He's been caught in a monsoon. It's wet season up there. He's not sure how long he'll be stuck. Some of the roads have been closed." She shrugged in disappointment. "I was really hoping he'd be back tonight. Uncle Leslie's gone to a lot of trouble to celebrate my birthday. He's been in the kitchen all afternoon."

Colt kept his expression neutral. The news that Rex wasn't on his way home, after all, was troubling. He didn't realize until that moment how much he'd hoped Rex had left in a different vehicle and was already on the outskirts of his hometown.

"When was the last time you actually spoke to your dad?" he asked, keeping his voice light.

Morgan sighed. "It's been more than a month. Probably as long as he's been gone. From what I've gathered, Uncle Leslie's unexpected arrival threw him into a bit of a spin. It seems like he wasn't himself from that moment on. I can understand how the discovery of a twin brother could turn his life upside down. It's no wonder he wasn't thinking straight and it explains why he left without calling me. I probably would have done the same. Why do you ask?"

"No reason," he said hurriedly. She looked at him with an expression that was filled with curiosity. Colt compressed his lips. *Should he tell her about the Ranger?* But this was her belated birthday celebration and after all, he wasn't sure what the abandoned vehicle meant. No blood or anything else suspicious had been found in the car. He thought about the cigarette butts and had to ask.

"Does your dad smoke?"

She blinked in surprise at his sudden change of topic. "No, but Uncle Leslie does. Why do you ask?"

Colt stared at her and his heart hammered double time. Leslie was a smoker. Leslie was a criminal with a violent past. He'd turned up out of nowhere and shortly thereafter, Rex had disappeared, along with his dog – who hadn't disappeared at all, but was buried down the back.

The thoughts rushed through Colt's head in a kaleidoscope of sound and movement. He opened his mouth to say something and then closed it again. *What good would it do to spoil Morgan's evening?* There would be time enough in the morning to bring her up to date and together, they could analyze just what it all meant.

Right now, saying anything would raise more questions than he could answer and it would surely ruin her night. No, tonight was all about Morgan. Best to wait until he had more evidence and had a better idea just what the hell was going on.

He forced a smile. "Just wondering." He put his arm around her shoulders and drew her close for a quick kiss. "Come on, enough about your dad. Let's get this party started. I brought you a bottle of wine. You like white, right?"

He handed her the bottle of Sauvignon Blanc and she smiled and thanked him. Her uncle filled the doorway that led to the kitchen.

"Oh, Detective, there you are. Morgan told me you were coming over. Welcome. I was just coming in to tell you dinner's ready."

Colt shook hands with Morgan's uncle and forced himself to smile. His mind was still spinning a mile a minute, but now wasn't the time to discuss things. He followed Morgan and her uncle into the kitchen and immediately spied a garish rug that ran across the floor between the counter and the stove. Morgan noticed the direction of his gaze.

"I'm afraid the rug's a new addition to the house."

"It's..." Colt tried to find something nice to say about it.

"Hideous, I know," she supplied, laughing. "It's so odd. Dad's always had an eye for expensive things. That rug looks like it came from a thrift shop and it matches nothing in the room. I don't understand why he bought it, or why he'd nail it down."

Colt frowned. "It's nailed to the floor?"

Morgan nodded. "Yes. Isn't that the strangest thing you ever heard?"

"I don't know about that," Leslie said, joining in the conversation. "It might have been so he didn't slip on it. I know what it's like to get older and lose mobility. My balance isn't what it used to be and I'm a little leery of loose rugs on the floor. Perhaps your dad's the same."

Morgan looked at her uncle and nodded, accepting his explanation. Colt wasn't quite so convinced. With the abandoned pickup in the forefront of his mind, he wondered how he was going to sit and share a meal with a man he suspected had done something unthinkable. Still, he forced himself to remain there.

The simple truth was, he had no evidence of foul play. It would be stupid to make accusations he couldn't yet prove and it would solve nothing. All it would do was ruin Morgan's night and she looked so pleased at the thought of celebrating her birthday with them that he didn't dare say anything that might remove her smile.

"I hope you like grilled chicken breast with hollandaise sauce, Detective."

"It sounds good, Leslie," Colt murmured.

"You're not allergic to anything are you?" Leslie pinned him with a narrowed gaze.

"No," Colt replied.

Leslie turned to his niece. "What about you Morgan? I should have asked you earlier."

"Only shellfish, Uncle."

Leslie smiled. "Then we should all be good to go. I've thrown together a salad. There's also fresh corn, hot from the oven and crusty garlic bread. To top it off, I've baked a birthday cake, just like I promised. I hope you like triple chocolate fudge." He tossed Morgan a beaming smile.

"Of course, Uncle. It sounds wonderful. You've gone to so much trouble. You shouldn't have. My birthday was more than two weeks ago."

Leslie waved away her protests. "Don't be silly, honey. I've only just found out I have a niece. There are so many birthdays I've missed out on! I'm entitled to indulge her every now and then, don't you think?"

Morgan smiled at him and pulled out a seat at the breakfast nook. "Should we eat in here?"

"No, let's eat at the dining table. It's so much more pleasant, don't you think? And after all, this is a special occasion. It deserves all the fanfare I can muster. I've already set the table. I even bought some fresh flowers. It's all waiting for you."

"Thank you, Uncle. You've been very thoughtful. Is there anything we can do to help?"

"No, but thanks for offering. Why don't the two of you go back into the dining room and make yourself comfortable."

Morgan nodded her agreement and turned to go back the way they'd come.

"I'll bring some glasses," Colt said, noticing the bottle of wine still in her hand.

"Of course. They're in the cupboard above the sink, nearest the pantry," Morgan replied.

She headed out the door toward the open concept living and dining room and Colt made his way over to the sink. Leslie fussed over the grilled chicken breasts which were arranged on a large plate. A jug of hollandaise sauce stood on the counter.

"Would you like a glass of wine, Leslie?" Colt asked.

"No thanks. I don't drink white."

Colt reached up to open the cupboard that stood to one side above the stove. A fine sheen of dark droplets stained the door. It started at the bottom and reached up halfway across the door. If Colt didn't know any better, he'd have thought it was blood.

Opening the cupboard door, he retrieved two wine glasses and held them in one hand. His gaze drifted lower and he spied another spray of dark droplets, this one lower down. It was toward the bottom of the pantry door, but looked just as suspect. Perhaps it was just because he was on edge about the discovery of Rex's pickup that the stains looked suspicious.

And then his gaze caught on a chip of wood that was missing from the side of the cupboard. The exposed wood was pale and sharp, like the damage had occurred recently. He frowned. His cop instincts hummed. He wished he could set aside his suspicions, like a normal person, and just enjoy the night. Did he have to see suspect activity every time he looked around? It was ridiculous, and yet the wary feeling in his gut increased.

Moving away, he offered to carry the salad bowl into the dining room and collected it from Leslie with his other hand. Then, determined to enjoy the night, he headed off to locate Morgan.

CHAPTER 21

Nerves rolled through Leslie's gut and he swiped sweat out of his eyes. He watched the detective depart through the kitchen door and breathed a sigh of relief. He wished like hell the man hadn't been invited over for dinner, but what was he supposed to do? Morgan had come in after her phone call, beaming from ear to ear. He could tell they'd reconciled and she was eager to be with him. The last thing Leslie needed was her disappearing back to Sydney before he could get the job done.

Having her in the same house was an opportunity he couldn't let pass by, so he'd forced a smile and had told her it was perfectly fine to have the detective share their meal. After all, there was plenty to go round.

The decision to kill them both made him nervous, but he'd thought it all out. His plan was sound and there was no reason it would fail. All he had to do was keep his wits about him and stay relaxed and calm and pretend there was nothing wrong.

With that thought in mind, he stacked a tray with the chicken, the sauce and the platter of corn. He'd return for the bread and butter and then the game would begin.

Colt bit into a piece of chicken breast and almost groaned with delight. For all of Leslie's failings, the man sure knew how to cook. The meat was tender and juicy, the sauce was just right. Colt enjoyed another bite.

"This tastes delicious, Uncle," Morgan said, swallowing a mouthful. Colt echoed the sentiment.

Leslie merely nodded and filled his mouth again. A moment later, he pushed back from his seat and murmured something about the cake. Colt stared at the man's retreating back and frowned. They'd barely started their main meal. *What was the rush?*

Taking another sip from his glass, Colt forced the dark thoughts from his mind and smiled at Morgan.

"Have I told you how beautiful you look tonight?" he murmured.

"Yes, but I'm happy to hear it again. You look pretty nice, too," she replied. "In fact, you remind me of a dashing movie star – maybe Hugh Jackman or one of those Hemsworth brothers, except for the color of your hair. Those guys are hot. So are you."

If she was shocked by the frankness of her

words, she didn't show it. Colt's blood heated and his body hardened at the promise in her eyes. Suddenly, he couldn't wait for the meal to be over so he could whisk her back home, into his bed, where she belonged.

"Here we are! The birthday cake, baked especially for my beautiful niece."

Leslie set a high, chocolate layer cake down on the table and then swiped the back of his hand across his brow. His gaze darted between Morgan and the table. *Did he really care that much what his niece thought about his efforts?* Colt couldn't help but wonder.

The cake had been iced with thick chocolate frosting and Leslie had even added candles. Colt was impressed by the man's thoughtfulness. Leslie O'Brien might have been raised without love, but he certainly had good manners.

"Wow, Uncle! This is amazing!" Morgan said, laughing. Her face was flushed with pleasure.

Colt's heart flooded with tenderness and he vowed silently to do all he could to keep that expression on her face. Leslie produced a cigarette lighter and Colt's gut momentarily tightened, but once again, he thrust the thoughts aside and sang *Happy Birthday* to Morgan.

"Make a wish!" her uncle cried and she closed her eyes for a second. Opening them again, she took a big breath and blew out the candles.

"Hurray!" Leslie cheered and began to remove the candles. Once he was done, he turned and headed toward the kitchen.

"I'll go and get some fresh plates," he called

out over his shoulder before disappearing into the other room.

Colt reached out and took Morgan's hand. It was soft and warm and felt perfect in his. He squeezed it and then brought it to his lips. He pressed a kiss against her palm, surprising himself.

He'd never been much of a romantic. In fact, he'd thought romance and all that other mushy kind of stuff was the thing of soppy romance novels and corny movies. But with Morgan, it seemed natural. He wanted to touch her as he sat there with her. And not just in a sexual way – although his body was counting down the hours – but in a loving, connected way – just wanting to feel close.

He didn't know what to make of it and he sure as hell didn't know if it was love. It was as thrilling and heady as those handful of weeks he'd spent with her a decade ago, but somehow even better. Had he been in love with her all those years earlier? Looking back, he couldn't help but wonder.

Leslie returned to the dining room, this time brandishing small plates. Setting one down in front of each of them, he returned to his place.

"How about you do the honors, Morgan and cut us each a piece?" he suggested, giving her an encouraging smile.

Morgan nodded and picked up the knife that Leslie had brought in with the cake. "How much would you like, Uncle? A big piece or small?"

"Just the tiniest piece for me, thank you, Morgan. I'm afraid I already ate too much."

"Would you like to wait for a bit?" she asked.

"We could always have it later, with a cup of tea."

"No, no, let's have some now," Colt said hurriedly, keen to see the night come to an end. He didn't want to linger over tea and cake. The sooner he got Morgan alone, the sooner he could love her with his lips and tongue and other parts of his body that were crying out for release.

Morgan cut the cake and handed the plates around. Colt took a small bite. The cake was moist and rich, with a distinctive, tangy bite to it. It was like nothing he'd ever tasted. He wasn't entirely sure he liked it.

"*Mm*, this is really good, Uncle," Morgan said around a mouthful. "Where did you learn to cook?"

Leslie grimaced and once again, wiped the sweat from his brow. "For all her faults and failings, my mother was a good cook. She forced me to spend hours in the kitchen, watching and learning. She always wanted a daughter, remember? I was meant to cook and clean and sew. She had very strict views on what was expected."

"Well, she did you a favor," Morgan assured him. "This cake is delicious. It's like nothing I've ever tasted. Sweet and rich and chocolaty, but with a bit of a bite. Is it chili powder? Is that your secret?" She laughed.

Leslie merely smiled. "A good cook never tells. My secrets will go with me to the grave."

Morgan giggled and took another bite of cake. Colt pushed his to one side. He didn't mean to be impolite, but the cake wasn't to his taste.

Leslie stared at him, a curious expression on his face. "Not eating, Detective?"

"I'm afraid I'm like you," Colt replied, patting his stomach. "Too much dinner."

Reaching over, Colt picked up his wine glass and finished the contents. He wondered how long he had to wait before thanking his host for dinner and getting the hell out of there – taking Morgan with him.

Seemingly oblivious to his impatience to get her on her own, Morgan finished the last of her cake and leaned back with a sigh.

"That was the yummiest cake I've ever eaten, Uncle, and one of the nicest things anyone's ever done. You made me a birthday cake and my birthday's already been and gone. I want you to know, that means a great deal to me."

She smiled across at him and continued. "When I first arrived and found you here, I admit, I was taken aback. I had no idea you existed and Dad wasn't here to fill in the gaps. I was confused and a little upset that he hadn't hung around and I think I was even a little resentful of you, believing that you were the reason he'd left.

"But you've been nothing but kind and generous and I couldn't ask for a better uncle. I can't wait until Dad—"

She broke off suddenly and gasped. Her face contorted with pain. Colt sat forward in concern.

"Are you all right?" he asked.

She shook her head back and forth and tears sprang to her eyes. "No. I'm sorry, I'm not feeling well. My stomach... It's burning. I think... I think I'm going to be sick."

With a cry of distress, she pushed away from the

table. Holding her belly, she made a run for the bathroom.

"Oh, dear. Poor Morgan. I wonder what's wrong," Leslie murmured. "It can't be something she ate. We all ate the same thing. I feel fine. How about you?"

Colt forced his attention back to the table and looked at Leslie. "I-I'm fine, too. I'm not sure what's disagreed with her. I'll go and check, make sure she's okay."

Colt pushed away from the table and strode off in the direction Morgan had taken. Even from halfway down the hall, he could hear her retching. He glanced to the left and passed by a bedroom. The door was open. He caught a glimpse of a double bed and then pulled up short.

A .22 rifle lay across the bed. Ordinarily, the sight of a gun might not seem so unusual. Rex O'Brien held a gun license, after all, and Morgan had told Colt her father owned a .22, the same caliber gun that had ended Rusty's life.

But there had been a lot about the goings on at this Butler Street address that was far from ordinary and seeing the rifle lying there in the open when it should have been locked away gave him pause. A sense of foreboding flooded through him, almost cementing his feet to the spot. He heard Morgan cry out in agony and his gut somersaulted with fear. He took off at a run.

———

Morgan had never been in so much pain in all her life. Her stomach burned like it was on fire and cramps twisted her insides into knots. She gasped and heaved, desperately trying to breathe through the pain. She didn't know what was going on, but she needed urgent medical treatment.

A fresh surge of hot vomit filled her mouth and erupted into the toilet bowl. Once again, she retched uncontrollably, her throat now raw. Tears streamed from her eyes. Sobs tore through her chest.

"Colt!" she cried. "Help me! Please... I need help!"

To her immense relief, he appeared in the doorway and immediately raced to her side. "Morgan! What's happening? What can I do to help?"

"Ambulance," she croaked. "Something's wrong."

Colt tugged out his phone. His lips were fixed into a grim line. Concern and something else flooded his face. "Something's wrong, all right," he muttered, "and it's more than your extreme reaction to the food."

She stared at him. Fire continued to burn through her stomach, but dread settled like concrete in her veins.

"Wh-what do you mean?" she stammered. Her heart hammered with fear. All of a sudden, she wasn't sure she wanted to know.

Colt's gaze remained on hers, his expression hard. "Think about it, Morgan. Your father's long-lost brother has appeared out of the ether, a man no one knew existed. He has a criminal record. Soon after, your father disappears. I didn't want to tell you tonight, but we found your father's vehicle abandoned outside of town. It had been driven into a stock dam. Furthermore, I just went by the main bedroom. There's a gun lying on the bed."

Colt stared at her. Morgan stared back at him, her mind flooding with shock. She wanted to put her hands up over her ears and beg him to stop talking. At the same time, she was desperate to hear what he had to say.

After all that had happened, now her father's pickup had been found outside of Armidale when he was supposed to be traveling in it way up north...

She shook her head back and forth, her gaze fixed on Colt's. "What... What are you talking about?" she gasped. "How could Dad's vehicle be here? He's up near Darwin. What's he driving? I don't understand."

"I'm sorry, Morgan, but I think your uncle's up to something," Colt said, speaking her troubled thoughts.

A fresh wave of pain ripped through her body at the thought. "Uncle Leslie...?"

"Is right here."

Like puppets who'd had their strings jerked, both Colt and Morgan swung around to face the door. Leslie stood there looking menacing, the .22 rifle in his hand.

CHAPTER 22

Morgan gasped in shock and alarm. Her hand came up to her mouth. Her heart pounded and despite the pain in her belly, her stomach clenched with fear. Her uncle stood in the doorway with a gun, a hard look on his face. Nothing about that image was good.

"Uncle Leslie? What's...going on?" she managed, relieved her fear hadn't made it to her voice.

"I'm sorry it's come to this, honey, but you leave me with no choice."

He came further into the room and she saw Colt's jaw clench, along with his fists. He moved closer to where Morgan was still hunched over the toilet. She borrowed courage from his presence.

"What are you talking about?" she asked. "You're not making any sense."

Her uncle's eyes narrowed. "Everything was going well. I had it all planned out. Your father didn't have a clue. He played right into my hands. Then you came along and everything went awry.

It's your fault it's come to this. Make no mistake, you're responsible for what happens next, including what happens to *him*."

Leslie pointed the gun in Colt's direction and Morgan cried out in fright. *Surely, her uncle couldn't intend to kill them?* The very thought was ridiculous, like something out of a B-grade movie. People didn't go around doing that kind of thing in real life. Any moment she expected someone to call "cut."

And yet, the gun in her uncle's hand was real. It was her father's gun. He normally kept it locked in a cabinet in the shed. She'd never seen it inside the house. Spying it in her uncle's hands was just as surreal as the situation they found themselves in.

"Where's Rex?"

Colt's quiet question held deadly force. Morgan's breath halted in her chest. She stared at her uncle and noticed the sudden tightening around his mouth. A pulse was visible in his neck and a strange look came into his eyes.

"Rex is in Darwin, like he said."

"Bullshit."

Morgan's hand flew to her mouth. She gasped in horror at the certainty in Colt's tone. Fear for her father, and for them, congealed in a cold, hard mass in her belly.

Undeterred by the gun in her uncle's hand, Colt took a step forward, determination in every taut line of his body.

"Where is Rex O'Brien?" he said again, biting out each word.

"Stop where you are or I'll shoot!"

Her uncle's cheeks were flushed and his chest rose and fell in a rapid staccato. Morgan's fear escalated to terror. She believed with every fiber of her being that her uncle would carry out his threat.

"Colt! Don't do anything!" she pleaded. Another agonizing pain gripped her stomach. She bent over the toilet and heaved.

"Please, Uncle. Please, Colt. I need help! Please, call me an ambulance."

"What did you give her?" Colt shouted and once again focused on his phone.

"Put the phone down! *Now!*" Leslie screamed and brandished the gun at Colt.

Colt ignored him and pressed numbers on his screen before holding the phone up to his ear.

"I need an ambulance. We're at 29 Butler Street. Yes. I think she's been poisoned. Hurry! And send the police."

The sound of the gun being cocked was the most terrifying thing Morgan had ever heard. She swung around from the toilet bowl and stared right into the barrel. Her uncle had taken a few steps forward and now stood mere feet away, the gun pointed in her direction.

"You shouldn't have done that," he growled, flicking his gaze to Colt and then back to Morgan. "I haven't come this far to have you ruin everything. You were supposed to go out quietly, or as quietly as you could with rat poison eating through your gut, but you had to spoil it." He turned to Colt, his eyes burning with accusation.

"You didn't eat your cake, Detective. How remiss of you. Now I'm forced to rely on Plan B."

Once again, the gun swung in Morgan's direction. Seconds later, the crack of the rifle filled every corner of the room. Colt dived in front of Morgan as smoke curled from the barrel. She screamed in terror. Colt's eyes widened in stunned surprise. Blood blossomed across his chest. Morgan screamed again, now almost hysterical. She lunged at her uncle, with no thought but to stop him from taking aim again.

Before she reached him, the gun went off again. Pain burned white hot in her arm. She looked down and saw the blood pouring out of her wound. The sight of it made her dizzy and the next thing she realized, she was back on the floor. The sirens in the distance were drowned out by the sound of her screaming and then she heard the distinct sound of the gun being cocked again.

———————

Leslie was filled with triumph. Both targets were on the ground. The cop was probably already dead. Another shot would ensure his niece went that way, too. She was only suffering a flesh wound, but he still had eight more bullets. Plenty enough to do the job properly.

It was too bad the poison plan hadn't worked out. It would have been far easier to explain away. He fully intended to ingest some himself – not too much, mind you. Just enough to defray suspicion while he waited for Morgan and her boyfriend to succumb.

But the cop had ruined everything. He hadn't eaten his cake. Leslie had watched him. The prick had taken only the tiniest morsel. He'd pushed the plate away and Leslie had been forced to regroup. The gun was already handy. It seemed the easiest route.

He wasn't quite sure how he was going to explain the two bodies with multiple gunshot wounds, but he'd think of something. After all, it wasn't the first time he'd killed someone and gotten away with it. But right now, he had to finish what he started and get rid of the evidence, before the police arrived. Even now, he could hear the sirens.

With renewed haste, he stepped close to where Morgan lay. Her head was bent forward, over her knees. One hand was tightened around the wound in her arm. Blood seeped between her fingers and dripped onto the floor. He was disappointed he'd missed the artery.

Anyway, it was of no consequence. He had plenty of bullets to finish the job. He moved so that the barrel was mere inches away from the back of Morgan's head and pulled the trigger.

Nothing.

"Shit!" he cursed. The gun had jammed. He should have known better than to use a rifle that looked like it was almost as old as he was. The sirens sounded louder. Stemming his panic, he did his best to clear the barrel of the jam. A loose bullet fell into his hand. A loud knocking sounded on the front door and his fear went into overdrive.

He cursed again. He didn't have time to finish her. He needed to hide them, and fast. Setting the gun down, he took hold of the cop by his ankles and dragged him out into the hall. A trail of blood followed in their wake. He'd never been so pleased for floorboards. A quick swipe of the mop and the evidence would disappear, at least to the casual eye. The cop had called in a suspected poisoning. There had been no mention of guns. Provided he could hide the bodies before the police knocked down his door, all should be well.

He dumped the cop on the floor of Morgan's bedroom and then used his boot to roll him under the bed. Racing back to the bathroom, he picked Morgan up in his arms. The bleeding in her arm had abated and her eyes flickered open and then closed. A moment later, she tensed and he realized she was more aware of her surroundings than he thought.

The knocking came louder, accompanied by a shout from outside the front door. He called back to them that he was coming and hurriedly tossed Morgan on her father's bed. Grabbing hold of the comforter, he covered her from head to toe. It wasn't ideal, but it would have to do. He just hoped the police wouldn't pay more than cursory attention to the house, if they came in at all.

Moving as quickly as he was able, he patted his hair back in place, swiped the sweat from his forehead with the back of his arm and then casually opened the front door.

"Officers, what can I do for you?" he asked, relieved that he sounded so calm.

The cop with the badge that identified him as Constable Griffith replied. "We received an emergency call. A woman with suspected poisoning?"

Leslie arranged his features in a suitable expression of concern. "Yes, you're right. My niece. She's been visiting for a while. We were having a birthday celebration dinner. She ate something that didn't agree with her. She's already gone to the hospital, but thanks for your concern."

"The ambulance hasn't arrived yet," the second officer stated, peering over Leslie's shoulder. "Who took her?"

"Ah, she went with Detective Barrington. He was here, too."

The second officer turned away and faced out into the dark. Leslie cursed under his breath. The detective's vehicle was still parked in the drive.

"Isn't that Colt's wheels?" the second officer said to his colleague.

Griffith frowned and then nodded. "Yeah. It is."

Both officers turned to face Leslie and he braced himself against their steel-eyed gazes.

"Oh, he went in my car. I was parked out on the street," he explained, trying hard to keep the nerves from his voice.

The officers narrowed their eyes at him. "Do you mind if we come in? Take a look around?"

It was Griffith who posed the question, but when the man shouldered his way through the doorway, it was obvious he didn't intend to be refused. Left with no choice, Leslie stepped back and let him in.

"Of course, Officers. Come in."

The men strolled into the living and dining room and looked around. Leslie stood back, out of the way, and did his best to appear normal. All the time, he couldn't help but think about the mess all over the bathroom floor and the gun he'd left in there. He only hoped the officers would be satisfied with a cursory inspection and leave without causing any trouble.

Morgan was suffocating. Gasping for breath, she fought against the coverings that blanketed her face. Fire coursed down her arm and she suddenly remembered where she was and what had happened.

With an effort, she got control of her panic and slowed her breathing down. Blinking in the darkness, she realized she was in bed with the covers pulled right over her head. Pushing them away, she dragged in fresh air and took a moment to get her bearings.

The room was dark with only the faintest glimmer of light from the street escaping beneath the closed curtains. Still, she recognized the shape of the darker shadows as the furniture in her dad's room. She strained to hear any noise. Was her uncle still in the house? And Colt. Where was he?

At the thought of Colt and the way he'd been right before she'd been shot, she bolted upright and jumped out of bed, unmindful of the agony in her shoulder. Her stomach still protested the poison she'd ingested and she wrapped her arms around her belly in an effort to control the cramping.

She needed to find Colt. He'd been hurt, seriously hurt. Her mind shied away from the possibility that he could already be dead. No, she refused to accept that had happened. Not now. Not when they'd just found each other again.

With the carpet silencing her footsteps, she picked her way across the room and eased open the door. The murmur of voices reached her and she strained to make out the words. At least two people and her uncle. She was sure it was him she heard. There were people in her father's house. People who might be able to help her.

With her heart in her throat, she kicked off her sandals and tiptoed quietly down the hallway. The creak of a floorboard underfoot sounded loud in the stillness. She froze, expecting the voices to stop, but the murmur of conversation continued. Breathing silently in relief, she crept forward and paused opposite her old room.

A muffled groan came from behind the door. For a second, she thought she was mistaken, but then it came again.

Colt.

It had to be him. She was flooded with relief that he was alive. She debated silently whether to continue forward and seek help or provide assistance to Colt. She stood in an agony of indecision and then Colt groaned again. Three groans in as many minutes. He was obviously still alive. If she didn't escape her uncle and get help, who knew how much longer he had. With her mind made up, she turned away and continued along the corridor.

Leslie watched the two officers prowl around the room and did his best not to let his nervousness show. Plastering a smile on his face, he stepped forward.

"So, Officers, can I get you a drink? A cup of tea, or maybe something stronger?"

Constable Griffith frowned. The other officer merely shook his head.

"W-what exactly are you looking for?" Leslie asked, tossing them another smile.

"We're not sure," Griffith replied.

The second officer eyeballed Leslie. It took all the courage he had to maintain eye contact.

"Let's just say we felt the need to look around," the second officer growled.

Leslie kept the smile plastered to his face and surreptitiously wiped away the sweat that had gathered on his brow. He wondered how much longer he was going to have to tolerate this.

"What's through there?" Griffith asked, pointing in the direction of the kitchen.

"It's the kitchen," Leslie supplied and then

panicked when he thought of the box of rat poison he'd left on the counter. He'd been so confident his plan would work, he hadn't even bothered to hide the evidence. Now he was frozen with fear at the thought of what the cops might discover. *How would he explain why there was an open box of rat poison on his kitchen counter?* Fresh sweat broke out on his brow.

"Let's take a look," the second officer murmured and Leslie's panic ratcheted up another notch.

With no reason to refuse, he turned slowly and headed for the door. With every step that took him closer, he wracked his brain for a reasonable excuse.

"Help!"

The croaky plea reached his ears and for a moment, he thought he'd misheard. He continued on toward the kitchen and then heard the noise again.

"Please! Help me! I need help."

"Holy shit!"

The sound of one of the officers cursing in surprise and alarm, had Leslie spinning on his heel and he gaped at the sight of Morgan. Stumbling barefoot into the room with blood soaking most of her sleeve, she arrested everyone's attention.

"What happened? Who are you? Griffith, call the ambulance again. Where the hell are they? They should have been here ages ago."

The second officer rushed forward and helped Morgan to a seat. Griffith pulled out his phone and turned away. Leslie watched the scene unfold as if he were in a dream. Everything he'd planned was crashing down around him, crushing every one of his dreams.

"What happened to you?" the officer asked Morgan once again.

Morgan looked straight at Leslie and his gut went cold. "It was him. My uncle. He shot me and Colt. Colt's hurt. He's in the first room down the hall. Please hurry, he needs an ambulance. Please…"

Leslie heard the words echo around him, as if they'd been shouted into a canyon. With the sound of them ricocheting off the walls, he turned tail and ran. The gun was still in the bathroom. There was no way he'd reach it in time. Instead, he headed toward the kitchen and the back door. There were more guns in the shed.

He'd barely taken three strides across the kitchen floor when he was tackled from behind. With his legs taken from underneath him, he fell heavily. Pain burst through his chest as the air was ripped from his lungs. Gasping for breath, he tried to move and found Griffith pointing a gun at his head.

"Don't fucking move! Hands out where I can see them!"

Leslie dropped his head back on the floor in defeat, anger surging through him. The sound of sirens reached his ears and he cursed loudly and bitterly. So close. He'd come so close and now the game was up.

Chapter 23

The pain was excruciating. It felt like an elephant sat on Colt's chest. He tried to breathe, but it hurt too much. He squinted against the bright light that burned into his pupils and lifted a hand to ward it off.

"He's coming round."

The words echoed in his head, but they didn't make much sense. The same voice spoke again.

"Colt, it's Beau. Squeeze my hand if you can hear me."

Beau... His brother... Beau was talking to him, asking him to squeeze his hand. Okay, he understood that one. He felt movement beside him and then Beau's hand brushed against his fingers. With a concentrated effort, Colt lifted his hand and closed it over his brother's.

"Oh, thank goodness!"

It was a female voice, breathy with unguarded relief. The voice sounded familiar... *Morgan...*

She was all right. She must be. She was close, somewhere in the room. He opened his mouth and tried to form his lips around her name. "Mor..."

A moment later, her lips pressed against his cheek and he was enveloped in her warmth and her scent.

"Oh, Colt! You're awake! Thank goodness you're all right!"

He squinted up at her. She was a blurry shape in front of him. "My head...chest....hurts."

"You took a bullet, buddy. You're lucky you're still here."

The words were spoken by his brother. He turned his head in the direction of the voice and winced. His head felt like it had been split open with an ax. In fact, he hurt everywhere. The pain pulsed through him like a live thing, hot and vibrant and aching. *Where the hell was he and why wasn't anyone giving him something for the pain?*

"Pain," he gasped.

"You're in hospital, Colt," Beau replied. "You're hooked up to a drip. You've come out of surgery. The bullets have been removed. The surgeon's happy with how it went. The pain meds will kick in soon, but you're going to be sore for quite a while. There's no doubt about that."

A soft, cool hand pressed against his cheek and he sighed in gratitude. "Your wounds will heal, Colt. We're just thankful you're alive," Morgan whispered.

Colt tried to acknowledge her words with a nod, but the movement was beyond him. With a sigh, he gave up and collapsed against the pillows. It was the last thing he remembered.

———————

Morgan watched Colt, feeling anxious and scared. Despite Beau's reassurances, she was far from confident Colt was out of the woods. He'd arrived at the hospital in the back of an ambulance, already unconscious. Despite a nurse who insisted Morgan needed help herself, she'd watched, terrified, as they'd rushed him straight into surgery. Only then did she agree to be treated.

Though she'd vomited over and over at her father's house, the doctors still pumped her stomach to make sure they'd removed all of the poison they could. They also took blood to determine the nature of the toxins, even though she told them she was almost certain it was rat poison.

She was whisked off for a scan to check for internal bleeding. Along the way, she discovered one of the active ingredients in rat poison was warfarin, an anticoagulant. The thought that she might be bleeding to death and nobody knew it frightened her almost out of her wits and she was beyond relieved when the doctor finally confirmed that it appeared the poison wouldn't cause any lasting ill effects.

They were more concerned with her bullet wound. Luckily, the bullet had passed through the fleshy part of her shoulder and had exited out the other side. After cleaning the wounds thoroughly, they were dressed with bandages. Shots for tetanus and penicillin were added for good measure.

The medical staff had wanted her to stay in hospital overnight, but Morgan insisted she needed to be with Colt and she found herself waiting outside the operating theater with Beau by her side.

She wasn't sure how he'd discovered they were there, but she guessed the police officers had told him. She didn't find out until later that Beau had arrived in Armidale only an hour earlier, intent on paying Colt a surprise visit.

Morgan winced. She'd had enough of surprise visits. She wouldn't care if she never paid a surprise visit again, though she was certainly grateful for Beau's presence.

Her uncle had been taken away in handcuffs and the memory of all that had happened still stunned her. Before the shooting, Colt had appeared convinced her uncle had something to do with the disappearance of her father. The very thought sent a flood of confusion rushing through her veins, but she couldn't deny there was a growing sense of acceptance that sat like a cold, hard lump in her belly. She was almost certain she would never see her dad again. Sadness clogged her throat. She couldn't bring herself to ask.

"Morgan O'Brien?"

She started at the sound of her name. Turning, she saw an ICU nurse waiting at the end of Colt's bed.

"Yes?"

"There's a detective waiting outside. He'd like a few words with you."

Morgan nodded. Pressing another kiss against Colt's lips, with a whispered promise to return soon, she left the room. A man who looked to be about Colt's age, with dark blond hair and a weary expression on his face stood outside the doors to the ICU. He approached her with a measured tread.

"Morgan O'Brien?" His voice was low and rough and reminded Morgan of sandpaper and whisky and late, late nights.

"Yes, I'm Morgan O'Brien," she replied. "Is there something I can do for you?"

"I'm Detective Jared Buchanan of the Northern Tablelands Local Area Command. I work in the Armidale office with Colt. I need to ask you a few questions about what happened tonight. Do you know Leslie Lexington?"

"Yes, he's my uncle, my father's identical twin brother. I believe he changed his name to Leslie O'Brien awhile ago."

"Yes." The detective looked down at the notebook in his hand and then looked at Morgan again. Her anxiety hitched up a notch.

"How well do you know your uncle?"

Once again, Morgan was filled with confusion and apprehension. "Not very well. The truth is, I didn't even know he existed until I arrived in town ten days ago. They're twins. Apparently, they were separated at birth."

The detective continued to stare at her. Morgan sighed and shook her head. "It's a long story and quite a strange one, but there's no denying the facts. Uncle Leslie looks just like my dad. Anyone who didn't know either of them well would be hard pressed to tell them apart."

"That explains the shoe imprints," the detective murmured, almost as an aside.

Morgan came to attention. "What are you talking about?"

"Your father's vehicle was found abandoned on the edge of town. We made a plaster impression of the shoe imprints left in the mud nearby. They were identical to the shoes worn by your uncle when he was arrested a few hours ago for two counts of attempted murder. He claims the shoes belong to his brother, that he's been borrowing some of his clothes."

"Yes, that's right," Morgan confirmed. "I've seen Uncle Leslie wearing some of Dad's things."

The detective's expression turned grave. "I'm afraid I have some bad news."

Fear slammed into her and all of sudden, she couldn't breathe. She wanted to put her hands up over her ears and squeeze her eyes shut, block out the rest of the world. But she couldn't do any of those things.

"W-what are you saying?" she stammered, wishing Colt was there by her side.

"We executed a search warrant on your father's house an hour ago. We found your father."

Shock and amazement barreled through her. Her mouth gaped open in hope. "You *found* him? He made it home?"

"No, I'm sorry, Ms O'Brien. We found his remains. He's no longer alive. In fact, I'd hazard a guess that he's been dead for some time. There was a rug nailed to the floor between the kitchen counter and the sink. We found blood spatter on the cupboards nearby. The rug seemed odd, fixed to the floor like that. We tore it off and found more blood staining the floorboards. Some of them were loose. We pried them up and found your dad buried underneath the house. We're waiting for the coroner to give us his formal findings on how your father died, but he had two bullet holes in his head."

A buzzing noise started in Morgan's ears and then filled every space in her head. She tried to focus on the detective, but he was nothing more than a dark, blurred shape. She thought she could see his mouth moving, but no more words reached her ears.

The shock of everything that had happened finally took its toll. With a gasp and a cry, her legs went out from under her and she crumpled to the floor.

CHAPTER 24

Three months later

As her new husband slid the satin-covered buttons of her wedding dress out of their tiny holes, Morgan felt a rush of nerves. They hadn't slept together since Colt had gotten down on one knee and proposed. At first, it had been a matter of practicality. Colt had suffered a serious gunshot wound that had torn muscles and ligaments in his chest and back. Morgan was also injured. Between the two of them, it had been all they could do to hold each other close and take comfort from the fact they'd survived a terrible ordeal.

But as they both healed, they came to a mutual decision to remain chaste until the day they married. Their coming together as a couple had taken more than a decade. They wanted to savor every moment and build the excitement and anticipation until they could finally consummate their love as husband and wife. That had been three months earlier and Morgan was now wound as tight as a guitar string. She couldn't imagine how *he* felt.

It had seemed like a good idea at the time, but after the weeks turned into months and they were desperate to touch each other, its importance to them had paled. Still, they'd managed to get by with kisses that had turned increasingly hot. Now the time had come to an end and Morgan couldn't wait.

Colt pushed the white satin confection off her shoulders and it slithered over her hips. At the same time, she reached for his dress shirt and quickly dispensed with it. She ran her hands over his naked chest, all golden and rippling with muscle. She touched the puckered scar that was still red and pronounced and sent a prayer of thanks heavenwards that he'd survived the attempt on his life. Even now, it distressed her to know that it was her uncle who'd inflicted the damage. She was grateful the man would spend at least the next two decades behind bars.

Every time she thought of what he'd done to her dad, she got angry all over again. Her father's body had been exhumed and properly buried in the cemetery next to her mom. Morgan had been heartbroken at the thought of what had happened, but for her own peace of mind and those around her, she'd let it go and was slowly accepting her dad was gone.

The only shining light amidst the tragedy was that it brought her and Colt closer than ever. Knowing how near they'd come to losing their lives had somehow strengthened the bond between them and Colt was determined to commit himself to her, put down roots, start a family. It was like he'd had an epiphany and he realized just how short life really was and was determined to make every moment count – to embrace it, challenges and all.

Morgan was more than happy to support him. She gave notice at the Sydney Harbour Hospital and packed up her house. She loved the city, but she loved Colt more and she also felt the need to remain close to her dad. Though she'd rented an apartment in Armidale, she and Colt were already on the lookout for their first home. Morgan couldn't bear the thought of returning to the house she'd grown up in and had listed it for sale. The place held so many happy memories, but it had been tarnished forevermore. She wanted somewhere new and fresh where she and Colt could make memories of their own.

"Hey, are you all right?"

The softly voiced question from her husband intruded into Morgan's thoughts. She blinked and forced them away. This was her wedding night. There was nothing and no one, but Colt.

She nodded and smiled and pressed a soft kiss against his skin. "You feel so good," she murmured.

"Three months never felt so long," he muttered, nuzzling her hair. "Whose crazy idea was that anyway?" he teased.

She laughed softly and stroked the flat planes of his belly with her fingers and lower, across the thin line of dark hair that snaked into his pants. It was like discovering him all over again. The thought filled her with equal parts excitement and shyness. It seemed like she'd known him forever and yet, she hardly knew him at all.

And now, they would finally be together – forever until they were parted in death. Their vows meant so much more to them, knowing how close they'd both come to dying.

In the dimness of the honeymoon suite in the best hotel Armidale had to offer, she gazed up at her husband and saw love and joy and amazement reflected in his eyes. As if in slow motion, she watched his head descend.

His lips touched hers, softly, sweetly and the tenderness in his kiss almost brought tears to her eyes. She returned the pressure of his mouth and her hands crept around his neck. She clung to him and kissed him with all the passion she held inside. He groaned and hot, sweet need ignited inside her.

As if reading her mind, Colt bent and lifted her in his arms. He walked to the king-sized bed and placed her on it then immediately followed her down. The lamps on the nightstand shed soft light and bathed them in a golden glow. Colt kissed her again and again until she didn't know how much longer she could stand it.

Everywhere he touched her, she burned with desire. She yearned to feel skin on skin. In silence, he reached around and unclasped her white lace bra and tossed it away and then tugged on the skirt of her dress. She lifted her hips and the dress slid lower until at last she could kick it away. She thought fleetingly of the five thousand-dollar price tag but forgot about it the moment Colt touched her again.

Naked, apart from her panties and stockings, his hand caressed her from top to bottom. Starting at her neck, his fingers slid over her skin and paused at her breasts. He teased her nipples with the pad of his thumb and sighed in appreciation when they puckered into hard little nubs. His tongue swept over them and she couldn't hold back a gasp.

The sensation of his hot, wet tongue against her nipples was something beyond exquisite. His hands moved lower, skimming her ribcage to caress the soft skin of her belly. His mouth followed the path of his hands and trailed hot kisses along her hip. He edged closer to her center and when he buried his face against the juncture of her thighs, she almost cried out in relief.

During the short time they'd been together, more than a decade ago, they hadn't engaged in oral sex. Now, as his tongue licked the soft skin of her inner lips and moved lower, she was beset by the most incredible sensations she'd ever experienced.

He unclasped her stockings and rolled them down until they gathered at her feet. Next, he slid down her panties and she helped him by kicking them off. He positioned himself between her legs and once again stroked in and out with his tongue. Up and down, round and round until she felt like she was going to explode. Over and over, his tongue made magic and all she could do was hold on. Her fingers, buried in his hair, held him in place and all the while little mewling sounds of need escaped her.

"Do you like that?" he asked, his voice low and husky with need.

"Oh, Colt. It feels...amazing. No one's ever done that to me before."

A smile of satisfaction lit up his handsome face and he returned to his task with renewed enthusiasm. The need inside her burned hotter until it was almost out of control. Her orgasm built and with it, the pressure, until she could stand it no more. Reaching the peak, she toppled over, crying out as she went free-falling over the cliff. Colt held her hips and stroked her until the very end of her orgasm.

When it was over, he lifted his head and stared up at her with eyes heavy lidded with desire. She was overwhelmed with love and the need to help him find his release.

"My turn," she whispered and moved so that he was lying flat on his back.

She undid his belt buckle and tugged the leather out of the belt loops. Next, she undid the button on his pants and slid down the zip. He wore black satin boxers and they were soft as a newborn's cheek. His erection strained against the fabric and she couldn't resist a caress.

His cock was rock hard and warm to the touch and filled her with another surge of need. She couldn't believe she wanted him again, having only just found her release. She took hold of his clothing and tugged it down and he lifted his hips to help her. A moment later, they were skin to skin from head to toe and both of them groaned with relief.

"You feel so good," he growled and tightened his hold on her.

"So do you," she whispered.

His erection pressed insistently against her belly and she slid down over his body. Her breasts skimmed over his chest, his stomach and then finally teased his cock. She bent her head and grazed the moist tip with her tongue. He offered murmured encouragement, and emboldened, she did it again.

This time, she took the whole of him all the way into her mouth. Sucking and licking, she caressed his shaft with one hand and cupped his heavy balls with the other.

"Morgan... Hell... That feels so good... Don't stop."

She renewed her efforts, pleased with his reaction and was rewarded with another groan.

"I want to come inside you," he said, his eyes shadowed with need.

She released him and moved back up to press a kiss against his mouth. He kissed her back with a ferocity that sent fire rushing once again through her veins. Desire burned. She wanted him all over again.

He moved until she lay beneath him and then positioned himself between her thighs. With his gaze locked on hers, inch by inch, he eased into her slick warmth. They groaned together at the blissful feel of the two of them finally becoming one. It was like the vows they'd said before the priest that day were echoing through the room.

"Aren't you glad you waited?" she whispered, almost overwhelmed by love and joy.

"More than glad. You feel exquisite. It feels like our very first time."

Tears filled her eyes and she smiled at him. She'd never felt so loved. He was her husband, her lover, her confidante and would be until the end of time.

"I love you, Morgan Barrington. I'll love you until the day I die."

EPILOGUE

Dear Diary,

Four gray walls surround me, two bunk beds with thin mattresses and even thinner blankets. I'm sitting in a jail cell, waiting for my day in court. My lawyer has advised me to plead guilty. The evidence against me is stacked way high, or so he says.

But I was born a fighter and I'll fight for my freedom until the very end. I refuse to lay down and die. After all, it's not the first time I've gotten away with murder...

I can still see the flames as they rushed through the rooms of the house where I used to live. Knowing my parents were trapped inside was the sweetest feeling ever. Even sweeter than the discovery I had a brother...

Things could have turned out so differently. They should have turned out differently. Morgan O'Brien ruined all my plans. I have returned to where I came from, with nothing but the clothes on my back. Even those belong to my brother – Rex O'Brien – the man who had everything.

Two parents who loved him more than they loved me.

A wife and family, a good job. A house in a nice city, people who counted him as a friend. He lived a charmed life, while I had nothing.

Everything I was entitled to he stole from me at birth. Instead of a loving family, I was tossed over to sorry-assed adoptive parents who didn't want me from the start. I was destined for trouble and that's exactly what I got. I relished acting out. As a kid, it got me the attention that I craved. It didn't matter that it was the wrong kind. Any attention's better than none, right?

Morgan O'Brien knows nothing of that. She's an only child. The much loved, much wanted daughter of my very much loved and wanted son. I was the one who was discarded like a piece of trash. I was the one who had to fight for every scrap of attention, for every morsel of love.

When I discovered I had an identical twin brother, I was beside myself with excitement. Then I did a little research on the Internet at the local library and I discovered Rex O'Brien was quite the catch. A well-respected, recently retired lawyer who lived in a respectable part of town. I found a photo of him at his farewell dinner, taken by the Armidale Express.

I couldn't believe how much we looked alike. It was like looking in the mirror. He didn't look quite as rough around the edges as me, but then, he'd had a much easier life. It was then the idea came to me and I dug around a little more. I discovered his wife had died of cancer and that he now spent his days alone. The newspaper article mentioned a daughter who lived in Sydney who visited when she could, but according to her father, she was busy with her career and often couldn't spare the time.

It all sounded so perfect. The daughter sounded like a brat. I didn't think I'd have any problem dealing with her.

I thought she'd stay in Sydney, surrounded by her comfortable life and I could go on my merry way.

I learned from Rex that he often stayed in contact with her by email. The information made me smile and I continued to make my plans. I'd email the brat of a daughter and keep her thinking the messages were coming from her dad. Over time, he'd tell her all about his long-lost twin brother, the brother he never knew he had and eventually he'd write about the trip he was taking – a trip to the outback where, sadly, he'd never return.

I intended to steal his identity, we were identical twins, after all. Identical in every way but our fingerprints, right down to our DNA. It would have been so easy. But then, Morgan O'Brien arrived in town and I was forced to come up with a better plan. And I did.

With the two of them dead, I'd be the closest surviving family member. I would inherit everything. It was perfect. Life was so sweet.

But the best laid plans can come unstuck and that's exactly what happened to me.

Morgan O'Brien. My nemesis... All I can say is this: Watch your back, brat.

Note to Readers

I do hope you have enjoyed reading Colt and Morgan's story. If you've enjoyed this book, please feel free to leave a review for The Stolen Identity at Goodreads and your favorite digital retailer. Every review is very much appreciated.

If you would like to receive news on upcoming stories, release dates, book launches and other snippets, please feel free to sign up for my newsletter. You can do this by visiting my website at www.christaylorauthor.com.au and clicking on the "Subscribe to my Newsletter" link on the right.

The Cliff Top Killer is the next book in the Sydney Harbour Hospital Series.

Here's a sneak peek:

Midwife Shelby Gianopoulos is feeling desperate. Single and alone at twenty-eight, she has spent many a family gathering fending off the increasing concern from her well-meaning relatives. Now, there's another family wedding looming and Shelby's desperate to find a date.

She can't bear the thought of being the brunt of more pitying looks and outright confrontations.

Doctor Samuel Munro is the perfect choice. Good-looking, young and single, he sets female hearts aflutter all over the Sydney Harbour Hospital. Though she barely knows him, Shelby is relieved when he agrees to accompany her to the wedding and pretend that they're in love. Little does she know they're not the only ones pretending…

Alexei Gianopolous, a senior partner at Harton & Wentworth, is living a double life. When Shelby discovers her father's secret, he stuns her even more by telling her Shelby's mother knows all about it. Toss in the fact that Shelby's brother has just come out to her and it's little wonder her mind is in a spin.

And then she discovers other peculiarities – like a dead man's baseball cap in her father's den – and she can't help but wonder what other secrets her family have hidden so well…

The Cliff Top Killer will be released on 26 December, 2016 and is available for pre-order from your favorite digital retailer.

About the Author

Chris Taylor grew up on a farm in north-west New South Wales, Australia. She always had a thirst for stories and recalls writing her first book at the ripe old age of eight. Always a lover of romance and happily-ever-afters, a career in criminal law sparked her interest in intrigue and suspense. For Chris to be able to combine romance with suspense in her books is a dream come true.

Chris is married to Linden and is the mother of five children. If not behind her computer, you can find her doing the school run, taxiing children to swimming lessons, football, ballet and cricket. In her spare time, Chris loves to read her favorite authors who include Richard North Patterson, Sandra Brown, Kathleen E Woodiwiss and Jude Devereaux.

You can find out more about Chris and sign up for her newsletter at her website:

http://www.christaylorauthor.com.au

www.ingramcontent.com/pod-product-compliance
Lightning Source LLC
Chambersburg PA
CBHW060858190726
48286CB00002B/292